I0721234

TRIDENT SECURITY
OMEGA TEAM

A DEAD MAN'S

Pulse

TS OMEGA TEAM
BOOK 1

SAMANTHA COLE

Suspenseful Seduction Publishing

A Dead Man's Pulse

Copyright ©2017 Samantha A. Cole
All Rights Reserved.
Suspenseful Seduction Publishing

A Dead Man's Pulse is a work of fiction. Names, characters, businesses, organizations, places, events, and incidents either are the product of the author's imagination or are used fictitiously. Any resemblance to actual persons, living or dead, events, or locales is entirely coincidental.

Cover designed by Samantha A. Cole
Editing by Eve Arroyo—www.evearroyo.com

AI RESTRICTION: The author expressly prohibits any entity from using any part of this publication, including text and graphics, for purposes of training artificial intelligence (AI) technologies to generate text or graphics, including without limitation technologies that are capable of generating works in the same style or genre as this publication.
The author reserves all rights to license uses of this work for generative AI training and the development of machine learning language models.

No part of this book may be reproduced, scanned or distributed in any printed or electronic form without permission. Please do not participate in or encourage piracy of copyrighted materials in violation of the author's rights. Purchase only authorized editions.

To all the members of the United States military.

For those who fought and never made it home.
*For those of you who fought and came home different than when
you left.*

*Your sacrifices mean more than words can describe and "Thank
You" will never be enough.*

Acknowledgments

To Jess, Jules, Brandie, and Kelle—I love you, gals!

To my beta readers—Allena, Ame, Angi, Cathy, Charla, Debbie, Elizabeth, Felisha, Jen, Joanne, Katie, Olivia, Susan, and Tawnya—thank you for dropping everything and speed reading this book. You helped me make my deadline in record time!

To my editor, Eve—I'm glad to have you back. *Hugs*

To my PA, Maria—thanks for taking over when I get overwhelmed!

To Judi—thanks for the kick-ass cover!

To Milynn—point it out and I'll fix it before you even finish your thought! Love ya!

To Terra & Chelle—thanks for double checking my emergency medical treatment.

To the Sexy Six-Pack's Sirens group—thanks for falling down the rabbit hole with me for every new release. Your continued support means more to me than you'll ever know!

To my readers—You humble me. Thank you.

Author's Note

The story within these pages is completely fictional but the concepts of BDSM are real. If you do choose to participate in the BDSM lifestyle, please research it carefully and take all precautions to protect yourself. Fiction is based on real life but real life is *not* based on fiction. Remember—Safe, Sane and Consensual!

Any information regarding persons or places has been used with creative literary license so there may be discrepancies between fiction and reality. The Navy SEALs missions and personal qualities within have been created to enhance the story and, again, may be exaggerated and not coincide with reality.

The author has full respect for the members of the United States military and the varied members of law enforcement and thanks them for their continuing service to making this country as safe and free as possible.

Who's Who and the History of Trident Security & The Covenant

***While not every character is in every book, these are the ones with the most mentions throughout the series. This guide will help keep readers straight about who's who.

Trident Security (TS) is a private investigative and military agency, co-owned by Ian and Devon Sawyer. With governmental and civilian contracts, the company got its start when the brothers and a few of their teammates from SEAL Team Four retired to the private sector. The original six-man team is referred to as the Sexy Six-Pack, as they were dubbed by Kristen Sawyer, née Anders, or the Alpha Team. Trident had since expanded and former members of the military and law enforcement have been added to the staff. The company is located on a guarded compound, which was a former import/export company cover for a drug trafficking operation in Tampa, Florida. Three warehouses on the property were converted into large apartments, the TS offices, gym, and bunk rooms. There is also an obstacle course, a Main Street shooting gallery, a helicopter pad, and more features necessary for training and missions.

In addition to the security business, there is a fourth warehouse that now houses an elite BDSM club, co-owned by Devon, Ian, and their cousin, Mitch Sawyer, who is the manager. A lot of time and money has gone into making The Covenant the most sought after membership in the Tampa/St. Petersburg area and beyond. Members are thoroughly vetted before being granted access to the elegant club.

There are currently over fifty Doms who have been appointed Dungeon Masters (DMs), and they rotate two or three shifts each throughout the month. At least four DMs are on duty at all times at various posts in the pit, playrooms, and the new garden, with an additional one roaming around. Their job is to ensure the safety of all the submissives in the club. They step in if a sub uses their safeword and the Dom in the scene doesn't hear or heed it, and make sure the equipment used in scenes isn't harming the subs.

The Covenant's security team takes care of everything else that isn't scene-related, and provides safety for all members and are essentially the bouncers. With the recent addition of the garden, and more private, themed rooms, the owners have expanded their self-imposed limit of 350 members. The fire marshal had approved them for 500 when the warehouse-turned-kink club first opened, but the cousins had intentionally kept that number down to maintain an elite status. Now with more room, they are increasing the membership to 500, still under the new maximum occupancy of 720.

Between Trident Security and The Covenant there's plenty of romance, suspense, and steamy encounters. Come meet the Sexy Six-Pack, their friends, family, and teammates.

The Sexy Six-Pack (Alpha Team)

and Their Significant Others

- Ian "Boss-man" Sawyer: Devon and Nick's brother; retired Navy SEAL; co-owner of Trident Security and The Covenant; husband/Dom of Angelina (Angel).
- Devon "Devil Dog" Sawyer: Ian and Nick's brother; retired Navy SEAL; co-owner of Trident Security and The Covenant; husband/Dom of Kristen; father of John Devon "JD."
- Ben "Boomer" Michaelson: retired Navy SEAL; explosives and ordnance specialist; husband/Dom of Katerina; son of Rick and Eileen.
- Jake "Reverend" Donovan: retired Navy SEAL; temporarily assigned to run the West Coast team; sniper; fiancé/Dom of Nick; brother of Mike; Whip Master at The Covenant.
- Brody "Egghead" Evans: retired Navy SEAL; computer specialist; husband/Dom of Fancy.
- Marco "Polo" DeAngelis: retired Navy SEAL; communications specialist and back up helicopter pilot; husband/Dom of Harper; father to Mara.
- Nick "Junior" Sawyer: Ian and Devon's brother; current Navy SEAL; fiancé/submissive of Jake.
- Kristen "Ninja-girl" Sawyer: author of romance/suspense novels; wife/submissive of Devon; mother of "JD."
- Angelina "Angie/Angel" Sawyer: graphic artist; wife/submissive of Ian.
- Katerina "Kat" Michaelson: dog trainer for law enforcement and private agencies; wife/submissive of Boomer.
- Millicent "Harper" DeAngelis: lawyer; wife/submissive of Marco; mother of Mara.

- Francine "Fancy" Maguire: baker; fiancée/submissive of Brody.

Extended Family, Friends, and Associates of the Sexy Six-Pack

- Mitch Sawyer: Cousin of Ian, Devon, and Nick; co-owner/manager of The Covenant, Dom to Tyler and Tori.
- T. Carter: US spy and assassin; works for covert agency Deimos; Dom of Jordyn.
- Jordyn Alvarez: US spy and assassin; member of covert agency Deimos; submissive of Carter.
- Tyler Ellis: Stockbroker; lifestyle switch—Dom to Tori; submissive to Mitch.
- Tori Freyja: K9 trainer for veterans in need of assistance/service dogs; submissive to Mitch and Tyler.
- Parker Christiansen: owner of New Horizons Construction; husband/Dom of Shelby; adoptive father of Franco and Victor.
- Shelby Christiansen: stay-at-home mom; two-time cancer survivor; wife/submissive of Parker; adoptive mother of Franco and Victor.
- Curt Bannerman: retired Navy SEAL; owner of Halo Customs, a motorcycle repair and detail shop; husband of Dana; stepfather of Ryan, Taylor, Justin, and Amanda. Lives in Iowa.
- Dana Prichard-Bannerman: teacher; widow of retired SEAL Eric Prichard; wife of Curt; mother of Ryan, Taylor, Justin, and Amanda. Lives in Iowa.
- Jenn "Baby-girl" Mullins: college student; goddaughter of Ian; "niece" of Devon, Brody,

Jake, Boomer, and Marco; father was a Navy SEAL; parents murdered.

- Mike Donovan: owner of the Irish pub, Donovan's; brother of Jake.
- Charlotte "Mistress China" Roth: Parole officer; Domme and Whip Master at The Covenant.
- Travis "Tiny" Daultry: former professional football player; head of security at The Covenant and Trident compound; occasional bodyguard for TS.
- Doug "Bullseye" Henderson: retired Marine; head of the Personal Protection Division of TS.
- Rick and Eileen Michaelson: Boomer's parents; guardians of Alyssa. Rick is a retired Navy SEAL.
- Charles "Chuck" and Marie Sawyer: Ian, Devon, and Nick's parents. Charles is a self-made real estate billionaire. Marie is a plastic surgeon involved with Operation Smile.
- Will Anders: Assistant Curator of the Tampa Museum of Art Kristen Anders's cousin.
- Dr. Roxanne London: pediatrician; Domme/wife (Mistress Roxy) of Kayla; Whip Master at Covenant.
- Kayla London: social worker; submissive/wife of Roxanne.
- Grayson and Remington Mann: twins; owners of Black Diamond Records; Doms/fiancés of Abigail; members of The Covenant.
- Abigail Turner: personal assistant at Black Diamond Records; submissive/fiancée of Gray and Remi.
- Chase Dixon: retired Marine Raider; owner of Blackhawk Security; associate of TS.

- Reggie Helm: lawyer for TS and The Covenant; Dom/husband of Colleen.
- Alyssa Wagner: teenager saved by Jake from an abusive father; lives with Rick and Eileen Michaelson.
- Dr. Trudy Dunbar: Psychologist.
- Carl Talbot: college professor; Dom and Whip Master at The Covenant.

The Omega Team and Their Significant Others

- Cain "Shades" Foster: retired Secret Service agent.
- Tristan "Duracell" McCabe: retired Army Special Forces
- Valentino "Romeo" Mancini: retired Army Special Forces; former FBI Hostage Rescue Team (HRT) member.
- Darius "Batman" Knight: retired Navy SEAL.
- Kip "Skipper" Morrison: retired Army; former LAPD SWAT sniper.
- Lindsey "Costello" Abbott: retired Marine; sniper.

Trident Support Staff

- Colleen McKinley-Helm: office manager of TS; wife/submissive of Reggie.
- Tempest "Babs" Van Buren: retired Air Force helicopter pilot; TS mechanic.
- Russell Adams: retired Navy; assistant TS mechanic.
- Nathan Cook: former computer specialist with the National Security Agency (NSA).

Members of Law Enforcement

- Larry Keon: Assistant Director of the FBI.
- Frank Stonewall: Special Agent in Charge of the Tampa FBI.
- Calvin Watts: Leader of the FBI HRT in Tampa.
- Colt Parrish: Major Case Specialist, Behavioral Analysis Unit.

The K9s of Trident

- Beau: An orphaned Lab/Pit mix, rescued by Ian. Now a trained K9 who has more than earned his spot on the Alpha Team.
- Spanky: A rescued Bullmastiff with a heart of gold, owned by Parker and Shelby.
- Jagger: A rescued Rottweiler trained as an assistance/service animal for Russell.
- FUBAR: A Belgian Malinois who failed aggressive guard dog training. Adopted by Babs.
- BDSM: Bravo, Delta, Sierra, and Mike, two Belgian Malinoises and two German shepherds, the new guard dogs at the Trident compound that Ian named using the military communication's alphabet.

Part One

OMEGA TEAM
TRIDENT SECURITY

One

First Sergeant Logan "Cowboy" Reese slammed his eyes shut so he didn't have to see his friend's face . . . his dead friend's face. Danny "Clutch" Coleman had been bullwhipped for over two hours by the fuckers holding Logan's team hostage, but it'd seemed longer. Much longer. An eternity.

Coleman's screams of unimaginable pain had been impossible to evade in the adobe building the two remaining teammates were imprisoned in. When the cries eventually died down and were replaced by celebratory gunfire and shouts of praise and worship to Allah, Logan had known what would be coming next. It was the same thing that had happened after the other members of his MARSOC (United States Marine Corps Special Operations Command) Raider team had been tortured—they were beheaded. Then one of those fucking murdering bastards would bring in the dead man's head and taunt the remaining prisoners with it.

Out of the original seven Marines who'd survived an ISIS ambush, which had them out-numbered about nine to one, and left five teammates dead, Logan and Joe "Stash" Moretti were the last two left alive. One of them would probably be inhumanely brutalized and slaughtered sometime tomorrow, and the last man would likely be dead within forty-eight hours —unless a miracle happened. But Logan had stopped believing in miracles two or three days ago.

The tango was yelling something at them, and although the words were in a local dialect he wasn't familiar with, Logan was pretty sure the bastard called them fucking pussies. Well, if being human enough to mourn the loss of his friends made him a fucking pussy, then so be it. At least he had a conscience and a soul, something he doubted the men partying it up outside had ever heard of.

When the wooden door slammed shut again, Logan dared to raise his eyelids. He blinked away the tears in his eyes and heaved a sigh of relief. This time, they hadn't left the decapitated head sitting on a shelf for him to stare at. But the metallic smell and taste of blood still hung in the air. It mingled with the stench of urine and feces. Each cell had a hole in the ground that would make even the worst porta-potty seem like it was in a five-star hotel. There was just enough slack in the shackles and chains for him to use it. The one-hundred-plus heat of the day was making every smell and sensation ten times worse than it probably was.

Clutch's screams and the crack of the whip as it sliced the air and human flesh still resonated in Logan's mind. His buddy had screamed and cursed the bastards who'd tortured him, but he had never begged for death like they'd wanted him to. Logan hoped when it was his turn, he'd be able to draw on his teammate's courage and grit.

Part of their training to become Raiders had been how to withstand torture and resist giving the enemy anything beyond your name, rank, service number, and date of birth. But until one experienced the worst an enemy could do to them, no one could fully comprehend what their breaking point was. Although there had been many questions asked about the US military, what their plans were, and where their troops currently were, the main objective had been to inflict as much pain as possible before killing them.

Shifting on the dirt floor, he swallowed hard and glanced between the steel bars at Moretti in the cell next to him. The Marine was unconscious, having succumbed to the effects of the fever he'd been running the past thirty-six hours or so. His skin was still flushed and covered with a sheen of perspiration —he had to be burning up. Logan had no idea what had caused it, but in this hellhole, it could have been from anything—an infection from a wound, a virus, or a reaction to the swill and foul water they'd been given for sustenance. Maybe it would be better if Moretti never woke up. At least then, he wouldn't suffer as the others had.

At first, they'd refused to eat anything that had been thrown at them, but their Gunnery Sergeant had ordered them to ingest what they could, no matter how nasty it was. They would need to be hydrated and strong enough to escape if the opportunity arose. Unfortunately, Brent "Gunny" Sherwood hadn't made it past the second day. He'd managed to yank his restraints from the wall and then jimmied the lock on his cell door with one of the crooked nails that had fallen loose. He'd just gotten out of the cell when two tangos came in and peppered his legs with bullets from an assault rifle, ripping them to shreds. Sherwood was then dragged outside, tortured, and killed the same way Kevin "Moonshine" Mooney had been the day before.

The day after Gunny was murdered, Gavin "Flipper" Pruitt was the next to be slaughtered like no other animal on earth should be, followed by Phillip "Kandy" Kane. Five good men—good Marines—had died at the hands of these psychotic terrorists, and although their families would be told they'd been killed in action, no other details would be given.

While it might sound cruel to leave them guessing, in this case, they were better off not knowing. Logan didn't want his parents or sister to ever know how he'd met his maker if this was where he died.

Logan pulled on the chain that connected the shackles on his wrists to the wall behind him. After Sherwood had gotten free, the tangos had added several more spikes through the chain links into the adobe, ensuring no one else could get loose. Maybe Logan should have fought the assholes when they'd come into his cell despite the threat of the three guns pointed at him. A death caused by a hail of bullets would have been preferable over what awaited him on the other side of that door when his time came. But a part of him had held onto a sliver of hope that a rescue would come. Now as each hour passed, that sliver got smaller and smaller. Even if a rescue came, he was a dead man. He would never recover from this nightmare, maybe physically, since he hadn't really been injured up to that point, but definitely not mentally or emotionally. Each time one of his buddies' heads had been brought in, another part of his heart and soul had died.

Letting his head fall back against the wall, he tried to remember how his life had been a few years ago or even a few weeks ago. He'd been happy. Everything had been going exactly as he'd dreamed it would as a kid. His grandfather and father were retired Marines. Logan had known by age five he wanted to follow in their footsteps, and everything he'd done from that point until he'd enlisted on his eighteenth birthday had been with the goal of becoming a Marine in mind. He'd kept up his grades, gone out for team sports almost every season, and had even been in the Junior ROTC program during high school.

Once he'd finished boot camp, he'd been assigned to Marine Corps Base Camp Lejeune in Jacksonville, North Carolina. After his first three years as a Marine and two long tours overseas, he'd applied for and been accepted into MARSOC training. His father had been so proud the day he'd called home and told his family he would be one of the elite Spec Ops Raiders. Not only did the title demand respect and awe, as did the Navy SEALs, it was also a chick magnet. If it was a tossup between fucking a Marine or a Marine Raider, the latter usually won the girl, nine times out of ten.

Upon completing his ITC—Individual Training Course—the intense, seven-month program all candidates had to go through, he'd been an official MARSOC Critical Skills Operator (CSO). The training wasn't for the faint of heart or the weak-minded. It was physically and mentally demanding, and most candidates dropped out long before graduation neared. Upon completing the course, he'd been assigned to the 2nd Marine Raider Battalion, also located in Camp Lejeune, and had been there ever since. He'd been twenty-two when he'd earned his CSO status, and nine years later, he was left wondering if it had all been worth it, knowing how the end of his life was going to play out.

Of course it's been worth it, asshole. He could hear Clutch's voice in his mind—the stupid jerk was probably giving him the finger from the great beyond. *Think of all the lives we've saved. Hell, think of all the women we've fucked . . . that's more fun. Hold out as long as you can, brother. Make it back for both of us. And the first woman you screw when you get back there, tell her you're me, so there'll be one more woman screaming my name in ecstasy.*

The door swung open again, and two other terrorists strode in, tossing plates of rancid rice through the steel bars onto the floor of the two occupied cells. Logan just ignored them, making no attempt to retrieve the food. One of the men yelled and gestured from him to the plate—from the few words Logan understood, he was being ordered to eat. Well, that wasn't happening. Just looking at it made him want to throw up, so he closed his eyes again as the yelling continued. Maybe a little competition would shut the asshole up. "Ninety-nine bottles of beer on the wall, ninety-nine bottles of beer! Take one down, pass it around, ninety-eight bottles of beer on the wall! Ninety-eight bottles of beer on the wall, ninety-eight bottles of beer! Take one down, pass it around, ninety-seven bottles of beer on the wall!"

Logan kept singing as the Afghanis stared at him in confusion. His raspy voice was getting stronger with each word and so was his heart. They hated all things American, and what was more American than "Ninety-Nine Bottles of Beer on the Wall"? The only things he could think of were apple pie, a freckle-faced girl next door, and baseball. "Ninety-three bottles of beer on the wall, ninety-three bottles of beer! Take one down, pass it around, ninety-two bottles of beer on the wall!"

The men must have thought he'd finally cracked under the pressure because they left without saying another word. Logan got all the way to sixty-three bottles of beer on that damn wall before exhaustion began to overtake him. Who knew singing that ridiculous but catchy tune could be so tiring?

Logan had no idea how long he'd slept, but he was jolted awake when an explosion rocked the compound. His eyes flew open just as a second, and then third, blast sounded, followed by automatic rifle fire, and deafened the world around him. Struggling to stand on his weakened legs and bare feet, he tried to see through the thin spaces between the wooden slats of the door at the front of the building and the tiny, glassless windows at the sides and rear to figure out what was happening. At some point during his sleep, the sun had set and the moon had risen. A lit oil lantern sat on a shelf next to the door and illuminated the makeshift prison, but it prevented him from being able to see anything in the darkness outside. It was too soon to know if this was a rescue staged by the US military, but a seed of hope bloomed in his gut.

"Stash!" His tone was filled with urgency. "Stash, wake the fuck up, man!" Logan yanked on his restraints, even though they hadn't loosened all the other times he'd tried to free himself. "Stash!"

More explosions went off as the battle raged on outside. If this was a war between ISIS and anyone other than the US or its allies, Logan and Moretti would be dead sooner than expected. But since they'd be dead in another day or two anyway, maybe this was a better way to go.

Shouts filtered in over the commotion. Some were in Arabic, others in English. And not just the heavily accented English spoken in Afghanistan, but—thank you, Jesus—that of those who could have only been born and bred in the good ol' US of A.

"Hey!" Logan shouted. "In here! We're in here! Hey! Americans! In here!"

The door burst open, and to Logan's horror, an insurgent rushed in, his assault rifle up and ready to blow the prisoners to smithereens. Without conscious thought, Logan dropped to the ground, trying to make himself the smallest target possible as the trigger was pulled.

But nothing happened. The gun had jammed.

The bastard shook the rifle as if that would get it working again just as two dark figures in camo and war paint skirted around the door frame and fired their own weapons. The tango danced unnaturally as his body was riddled with bullets. The gunfire ended when he fell to the ground, his dead eyes staring at the ceiling, seeing nothing.

One of the two men let his rifle hang from the strap around his neck and back while the other kept watch for danger at the door. Occasionally he set off a burst of bullets at someone or something outside Logan couldn't see from that angle.

The first man retrieved the keys from the dead guy's body

and worked quickly on the metal lock on Logan's cell. At least he didn't need to blow it with C4. As the steel door was pushed open, the man finally looked at him. "Lieutenant KC Malone. US Navy SEALs are here to save your sorry fucking Marine ass."

Never had Logan heard more beautiful words in his entire life. A turbulence of emotions rolled through him. "First Sergeant Logan Reese, and I think I love you."

"Just don't fucking kiss me, 'cause I don't swing that way." Malone hurried over and, after finding the key to the shackles wasn't with the other ones on the chain, dropped them and pulled out a lock-pick set. As he worked to free Logan, he cocked his head toward the next occupied cell. "Are you the only two left?"

Logan had to swallow the lump in his throat. "Yeah, but Stash has been out of it for over a day with a fever. The others . . ." He couldn't finish the statement.

Malone got one of his wrists free and started on the other. Sympathy filled his eyes and voice. "We know. We found them, and we'll be bringing them home with us."

It took a moment for Logan to realize the gunfire had died almost completely. There were a few scattered bursts here and there, but for the most part, there was silence from the automatic weapons. As more US troops entered the building, Malone paused his lock picking, stepped on the heavy keyring, and with a flick of his foot, slid it toward the open door behind him. "Peanut, here's the key to the cell door."

The shortest of the men, presumably "Peanut," grabbed it from the dirt floor and then quickly unlocked the other cell. Hurrying to the unconscious Marine, he glanced at Logan as the second shackle fell from his wrist. "Is he injured?"

"He was saying he thought a few ribs were broken, and he's got bruising on his back. Other than that, I don't think so." Logan touched his abused wrists, which had been rubbed raw, and winced. "But he's had a temp for almost two days now and been out of it since around noon yesterday."

While he hadn't had a watch or clock to tell time, the sun's location in the sky had helped him keep track.

As the SEAL assessed Moretti's condition and began treatment, another man stepped into Logan's cell. "Reese? You okay?"

Even with his face covered in black camo paint, the familiar voice told Logan exactly who the man was, and the empathy he heard almost ripped him to shreds. Apparently, the rescue had been a joint mission between the SEALs and Raiders. Captain Louis "Bear" Bradshaw was Logan's team leader. "As good as I can be, Cap."

There no longer appeared to be an urgency in the other men's movements and tasks, so it was safe to assume the ISIS members had all been killed or captured. Bradshaw stepped forward and pulled Logan into a manly but gentle embrace, clearly not caring that his charge was covered in dirt, grime, and sweat. If his superior hadn't been holding him up, Logan would have dropped to his knees as the relief at being rescued, combined with the grief for his lost teammates, hit him hard. He wasn't ashamed of the tears that spilled forth and rolled down his cheeks. He was alive. He was going home. And he'd never be the same person he'd been before.

OMEGA TEAM
TRIDENT SECURITY

Two

Slamming her locker door shut, Dakota Swift grabbed her duffel and headed for the door. Her 3:00-11:00 p.m. shift on patrol for the Tampa Police Department hadn't been over fast enough for her tonight. It had taken everything in her not to stomp into her captain's office to raise hell. Thankfully, she'd resisted since it wouldn't have helped her case any and probably would have resulted in a charge of insubordination.

Seven years. Seven fucking years. Seven . . . fucking . . . long . . . years. She slapped her hand on the heavy, wooden door leading out to the hallway and sent it banging against the concrete wall. A few officers, some in uniform, others in plain-clothes, were in the corridor, coming and going from the shift change, and most startled at the sound, then sent her a range of looks from annoyed to sympathetic.

So, word was already getting around. She ignored them all, striding down the hall to the exit for the parking lot behind the station where her vehicle was parked.

"Hey, Dakota! Wait up!"

The shout came from behind her at the other end of the

hall, and she almost didn't slow down, but Officer Ricardo Hernandez was one of her best friends—and had been since they'd gone through the academy together. When she reached the double doors, she paused long enough for him to catch up. He was four inches taller than her own five foot five and outweighed her by at least eighty pounds, yet she could still take him down on the sparring mat. In fact, she could take down most of her fellow male officers, something she knew grated on many of them.

Sighing, Dakota tried to sound like she was just tired and everything was fine when it wasn't. "What?"

"Outside." Gesturing for her to lead the way to the parking lot, he followed her out to her SUV. After making sure no one was within earshot, he crossed his arms over his chest and shook his blond-haired head. "I'm sorry. I heard they shit-canned your transfer request again, the fucking pricks."

Swallowing hard, she willed herself not to cry. In front of Ric was one thing, but if anyone else saw her, they'd use it as proof she couldn't handle the promotion to the Special Ops Division. She'd been trying to get into undercover work for four years now, and every time a position opened, she got passed over. Several times, it had been for someone with less time on the job than her. She didn't know what problem the higher-ups had with her—she was a damn good cop, with several commendations and no black marks in her file. Her immediate supervisors had written glowing letters of recommendation too. Yet, once again, they'd given the position to someone else. She couldn't even claim it was sexual discrimination since another female officer had gotten the go-ahead the last time a spot was open.

To top everything off, as soon as her father heard about it, he'd be siding with the brass, as he had been for years. You'd think her old man would be thrilled his daughter followed in his footsteps onto Tampa PD, but he wasn't. He'd wanted her brother to be the one to fill his big shoes, but Gerry Swift had gone into engineering instead.

"Yeah, well, I don't know why I'm surprised." She snorted. "I wouldn't put it past my father to have been the one to blackball me. God forbid his daughter advances to a position he'd never held while he was working here."

Ric rolled his eyes. "No one is blackballing you. If they were, you'd have the worst shift in the worst corner of the city for the rest of your career instead of working next to yours truly.

"C'mon. Let's head over to Chasers for a beer." When she opened her mouth to turn him down, he held up a hand to stop her. "C'mon, one beer won't kill you. Besides, I need you as my wingman. Some chick from a fender-bender report I took earlier might be stopping by, and you need to tell her about all my wonderful attributes, so I can get laid."

This time, it was Dakota rolling her eyes. "You're such a man-whore."

"Yup. And it wouldn't hurt you any to pick out some stud for a roll in the hay every once in a while. I mean, seriously, when was the last time you got laid?"

Obviously far too long ago since she honestly couldn't remember off the top of her head, so she bypassed the question. "One beer. The minute you've got the green light and two tickets to paradise, I'm out of there."

Less than five minutes later, they pulled into the parking lot of the tavern that was a known cop hangout. Turning off the ignition, Dakota made sure she had her keys, phone, wallet, and money. Before exiting the vehicle, she removed her concealed, holstered firearm from the back waistband of her jeans and locked it in the glove compartment. Guns and alcohol didn't mix.

Ric was waiting for her at the establishment's entrance, and as she approached, he pulled on the handle, holding the door open for her. The man had manners, charm, and looks, and not for the first time, she regretted there was nothing between them. But hooking up with Ric would be like hooking up with her brother.

Loud music and conversation filled the bar, along with cops, badge groupies, and plain ol' civilians out for a good time. It was a popular place—the food was good, prices were reasonable, and the bartenders gave the occasional buy-backs—a free beer or drink after every third or fourth one. The bar's owner was a retired TPD sergeant who made sure his patrons were well taken care of.

After running a hand through his short hair, Ric waved at a few people and pushed his way through the crowd with Dakota on his heels. She tended to be overlooked in situations like this when most of the people around her stood over six feet tall, and more than once, she'd been stepped on in crowds, so she usually let her friend lead the way.

Toward the back, the mass of bodies opened up a bit as Ric found a group of cops who'd just gotten off shift with them. Dakota greeted them as well and then waited for one of them to flag down the bartender for drinks for the newcomers. Taking her usual beer, she thanked him before glancing around the bar. There was the usual college clique, badge bunnies looking to hook up with a cop, one girls' night out for a bachelorette, and plenty of others. Her gaze passed over a table full of men and then shot back with interest to a handsome, dark-haired hunk in a dress shirt and slacks. His sleeves were rolled up, showcasing his muscular arms, the top button of his shirt was undone, and his tie was loose around his neck.

Well, well, well. At least something is going my way today. Only took twenty-three hours and fifteen minutes for it to happen.

Shane Littleton was a Dom she knew from Pandora's Box and, at twenty-seven, was two years younger than her. They'd played together a few times, enjoying the fact neither wanted a relationship outside the club.

But what's he doing here when he lives an hour away?

When a set of teal green eyes met her brown ones, her gaze immediately and involuntarily dropped to the floor, in silent respect for his title, before rising again. He winked at her and then, using the hand resting on his thigh under the table, gave her a crook of his finger, inviting her over. Giving him a subtle shake of her head, she pulled out her cell phone and located his name in her contacts. The only reason she had the Kissimmee fireman's number was because they'd made plans in advance to play one night a few weeks ago, and she'd needed a way to let him know if she got held up at work.

Using her forearm to hold her beer bottle against her side, Dakota typed out a quick text to Shane.

> Sorry, Sir. Not here. With my coworkers.
> Just got off shift.

She turned away to acknowledge a question one of her fellow cops asked her as the Dom grabbed his cell from the tabletop in front of him when it lit up and read the text. Moments later, her phone vibrated in her hand.

> SHANE L.
>
> No worries. Does "not here" mean we can meet somewhere else, or will my favorite sub have to disappoint me tonight?

The corners of Dakota's mouth ticked upward as she typed in a response. She had no illusions he didn't have a small harem of favorite subs. Nor was he unaware she enjoyed several Doms at the club.

> If you can wait a bit. It would look funny if I
> left five minutes after walking in.

Seconds passed.

SHANE L.

> I'd wait for you all night, my little subbie.
> BTW you look hot. Makes me wonder what
> you're wearing under those tight jeans.
> Hopefully nothing.

One beer and forty minutes of relatively boring conversations later, Dakota said good night to Ric and the other cops and caught Master Shane's gaze across the still crowded bar. She knew she didn't have to worry about whether or not he'd had too much to drink to scene with her or drive because alcohol was something he avoided, preferring tonic and lime. He'd told her one night while administering her aftercare following a scene that alcoholism ran in his family, and he never wanted to fall into the same trap, having seen what it did to his parents and grandfather.

When he stood and evidently told his buddies he was leaving, she headed for the door. After a quick negotiation in the parking lot, they got into their respective vehicles, and she followed him to a BDSM club about twenty minutes east of Tampa and forty minutes west of the Kissimmee suburb he lived in. She'd heard of the Pleasure Dome but had never been to it. Shane had told her that even though it was open to the public, it was one of the better non-exclusive clubs in the area. He was friends with the owner and, on the drive there, would be able to arrange a private playroom for them. While she trusted the Dom in more ways than one, having him back at her place was a hard limit for Dakota. She insisted on keeping her sexual lifestyle and her personal and professional lives as far apart as possible.

Mixing them could be disastrous, and it wasn't a risk she was willing to take.

Pulling into the club lot, Dakota parked her SUV next to his truck, and before she had a chance to open her door, he'd done it for her. Holding out his hand, he helped her from the vehicle, and delicious chills went down her spine. This was the only time in her busy life she let a man take over and treat her as a submissive. All other times she spent proving to her co-workers, father, and everyone else that she was alpha enough to hold her own.

Instead of using the front entrance, Shane led her to a side door and knocked. Dakota glanced up and noticed a security camera. The Dom at her side saw where she was looking and said, "No worries. Master Robert is very trustworthy. The cameras are for safety only, and as long as nothing is reported that would make a review necessary, the videos are erased after a week."

The door swung open, and a huge bouncer held out a hand to Shane. "Hey, man. Been a while."

The two men shook. "Yeah, it has. I called Rob on the way over. Said he'd hold a room for us."

"Yup. Room six is all yours."

"Thanks." Without further conversation, Shane led Dakota down a dimly lit hallway. Loud club music filled the air, making the floor and walls vibrate around them. Opening a door labeled Room #6, he gestured for her to precede him into the dungeon-like space. Royal blue, black, and gold were the colors of the décor which was a mix of elegance and medieval—at least it appeared very tidy and hygienic. The familiar, citrus-scented cleaner used by many clubs tickled her nose. For some reason, it complimented the smell of sex.

When the door closed behind her again, the music's volume dropped dramatically, although they could still feel the bass thumping off the carpeted floor. "Strip and present, pet."

"Yes, Sir." It didn't take long for Dakota to shed her sneakers, jeans, shirt, bra, and panties, placing them on a chair next to the door. She then sank to her knees in the middle of the room, placed her upturned hands on her thighs, and bowed her head in submission as Shane took off his tie, shirt, shoes, and socks, leaving his dress pants on. When they'd been negotiating the scene earlier, he'd mentioned he and his buddies had been at a christening that afternoon for his college roommate's son. It'd been the first time she'd ever seen him out of the leathers he wore at Pandora's Box.

After placing the duffel bag he'd brought in with them on the bed, he began to rifle through it. She knew it was filled with various adult toys for play, and she felt more aroused as the sensual atmosphere took over her body and mind. And speaking of a *body*, Shane Littleton had it in spades. With a face and physique that stopped traffic, he'd been featured twice in his department's annual beefcake calendar, which raised funds for the widows and children of fallen firemen.

After gathering what he wanted from the bag, Shane placed the items on a small table and left the duffel underneath it. Since she was close to the table, Dakota could see what he'd chosen without lifting her head more than a scant inch. The items sent a shiver of anticipation down her spine, and her pussy wept. It had been about six or seven weeks since she'd been at Pandora's Box, the last time she'd played with Shane. Rarely did she go that long without scening with a Dom. But she'd taken a lot of overtime shifts lately, on top of packing and moving from her old apartment to the condo she'd bought last month. She was finally a homeowner—one more thing that fueled her independence in the world.

"Stand and get on the spanking bench. I've been itching to get at that sweet ass since I saw you walk into Chasers tonight."

And she was itching to have his dominant hands on her

ass. Dakota didn't know why she was so drawn to the lifestyle she'd discovered with a friend about five years ago and had no interest in analyzing things to figure it out. When Brenna had first mentioned she wanted to check out a munch, Dakota thought she was kidding. A munch was a gathering where those interested in discovering more about BDSM could speak to experienced subs and Doms to help decide if they wanted to try it. Surprisingly, she'd been intrigued enough to investigate the lifestyle further. Brenna had also continued to explore her sexual submissiveness and recently moved in with the Dom she'd been collared by last year. Dakota knew an engagement ring was secretly being made for when he popped the question.

Settling on the red leather padding on the spanking bench, Dakota tried to relax and push everything out of her mind except what Shane was about to do. His hands trailed up her legs and then over her ass and lower back, rubbing and squeezing her flesh to bring the blood to the surface. "So, pet, what's going on in that head of yours? You have a small tell when something's bothering you and don't want to talk about it—you nibble on your bottom lip."

She'd never realized she did that, but now that it had been pointed out to her, she'd probably notice it from now on. Knowing the only way she could get out of answering the question, now that they were in D/s mode, was to say her safe-word, she sighed. "I got passed over for Special Ops again, Sir."

Since Shane was a fireman, she'd found it comfortable to talk about "on-the-job" stuff with him. Firemen, cops, paramedics, EMTs, and ER nurses understood what each other dealt with on a regular basis. Even though there was usually a healthy rivalry between the police and fire departments, there was also a strong camaraderie.

His right hand left her skin and a split second later made contact again with a hard slap on her right ass cheek, eliciting a gasp and moan from her as the sting made her wetter. "That sucks. Did they give you a reason why?"

"They never do, Sir."

Smack. That one landed on the left side of her ass. "You'd be good at it." *Smack.* "What about the detective bureau or taking the supervisor's test?" *Smack.*

Goose bumps popped all over her body. This was what she'd needed . . . what she craved. A way to deal with the disappointment, the anger, and all the other negative emotions that came with her job. She couldn't cry in front of her fellow officers unless it was because of the death of one of their own because it showed a weakness that could be used against her. The same went for her father—crying was for sissies, even coming from the female sex.

Gavin "Iron Guts" Swift had been a highly decorated police officer who'd made it to the rank of sergeant before a back injury had ended his career fourteen months before he got his twenty years in. At least it had been an on-the-job car accident, so all his medical expenses were paid for by workman's compensation, and he received a disability pension which was roughly seventy-five percent of his active-duty salary.

Shane continued to pepper her ass and upper thighs with slaps that she felt deep in her core until she was ready to beg him to fuck her senseless, escaping the outside world for a little while. Tomorrow, she would think about her future. Tonight, there was no room for her thoughts—all she had to do was feel.

Three

Thirteen Months Later . . .

S itting on the edge of a large planter filled with flowers, Ian Sawyer waited for his target to exit the building in front of him on the outskirts of Washington, D.C. Logan Reese had been ignoring his phone calls and emails for the better part of two months, but Ian wasn't one to give up easily. However, if today's face-to-face meeting was a failure, it would be time to move on and choose someone else.

Some people might call him and his brother Devon crazy for wanting to hire a former POW for the new spec-ops team for their business, Trident Security, but they could spot an intelligent and competent warrior a mile away. Considering they were both retired Navy SEALs, it was easy to recognize someone with the same training and mental capacity. Just prior to his capture in Afghanistan, Reese's name had been thrown into the hat for consideration for the job by his uncle, a good friend and business associate of Ian's. However, most would have tossed the man's file in the garbage after what he'd gone through. But Ian was interested in seeing if the talent

Reese had possessed before his ordeal still existed. If it did, and he was willing to agree to Ian's terms, the job would be his on a trial basis.

Another five minutes passed, but Ian didn't mind—it was a beautiful, sunny day, something he didn't get to sit and enjoy often enough. Although, lately, he'd been taking more time off work just to enjoy days like this with his fiancée, Angie. The sixty-seven-degree weather in D.C. in February was a bit of an anomaly and would be disappearing again soon. Once more, he was glad they'd decided on Tampa for their home base. The average temperature down there now was between in the mid-seventies, and it would start climbing into the eighties in a few short weeks.

A light breeze brought the aroma of "dirty dogs" past his nose—his teammate, Marco DeAngelis, was from Staten Island and always referred to street vendors' frankfurters that way because of the water they were sitting in on the carts. It was a New York City thing. Yet, despite the disgusting moniker, they were the best-tasting dogs around.

There was a stand half a block away, and the smell made him hungry, but he didn't want to miss Reese walking out of the building. He knew the man was still inside, attending one of his bi-weekly sessions with a psychologist who specialized in veterans with PTSD. If his classified military file wasn't ficti-tious—which it wasn't—then Reese was worth the wait. Having a high military and federal security clearance, Ian had been able to read about many of the missions Reese and his teammates had been on, and the retired SEAL had been impressed with what he'd been privy to. It was the main reason Reese was still in the running for the new team. He was the only one of the six chosen who hadn't signed on yet.

Putting together the new team was taking longer than Ian had hoped, but to get the best possible candidates, he had to wait for a few of them to cycle out of their final military tours or resign from their law enforcement commitments. There had also been other delays due to Trident's own missions and obligations. So far, only two of the recruits had reported for their new jobs—the others would be joining them over the next six months.

Tristan McCabe was retired from the Army Special Forces, and Cain Foster had come to Tampa from the Secret Service. Both men excelled in their training, and their leadership abilities shined through. Devon and Ian were going to have a hard time choosing one of the two men to lead the Omega Team. That was the name Ben "Boomer" Michaelson had dubbed the new squad before deciding the original one was the Alpha Team. Since those six men were all dominants in the BDSM lifestyle, the names had stuck.

The glass door of the main entrance swung open, and a six-foot-one man, whose nickname in the Marines had been "Cowboy," strode out, slamming his sunglasses over his brown eyes. But not before Ian had seen him assess every person within his sight. At thirty-two, a few years younger than Ian, he was still in excellent shape, moving like a panther, despite the weight he'd lost since Afghanistan. The way the tan cargo pants and red T-shirt he was wearing fit told Ian the man had at least maintained some sort of workout regimen—it was probably therapeutic for him. His dirty-blond hair was longer than required in the military, but spec-ops teams had a lot of leeway with it and their facial hair, needing to blend in for a mission.

Standing, Ian stepped into Reese's path with a non-threatening expression on his face. "First Sergeant Logan Reese."

The man stopped short. His hands clenched into fists as he glanced around to see if Ian had anyone else with him. There was no way he could miss the military demeanor and probably assumed there were others around—which there weren't. His jaw ticked under the whiskers that were probably a few weeks old. "Who wants to know?"

"Lieutenant Ian Sawyer—retired Navy. You're a hard man to get ahold of."

Through his shades, Reese glared at him. "There's a reason for that. Mainly, I didn't need you to tell me in person that I was no longer on the list of candidates for your new team."

Ian crossed his arms over his chest and stepped to the left when Reese tried to walk around him. "Who says you're no longer on the list? I'm here to discuss your coming to Tampa to see how you mesh with the other team members."

"Mesh? Are you fucking kidding me? I'll tell you how I'll mesh. I'll be there half a day before you'll be telling me to pack my shit. Look, just because you're friends with Larry doesn't mean you have to go through the motions. Let's just say we both agreed I'm not cut out for your company and leave it at that. You're off the hook."

Reese moved to the right, and Ian followed, again blocking his path and pissing him off further. "This has got nothing to do with Larry. If I didn't think you were a good candidate, you could've been my own brother and I wouldn't have offered you the tryout." Larry Keon was Reese's aunt's ex-husband. He was also the number two man at the FBI. As Assistant Deputy Director, Keon was Trident Security's main contact at the agency and the person who sent many of the private ops details their way, having dealt with SEAL Team Four on many occasions.

"Back off, Sawyer. I don't need your fucking pity." He was gritting his teeth, the veins in his neck bulging with his restraint, and Ian had to give him credit for not taking a swing at him.

"Good, because I don't do pity. It's a useless piss-poor emotion. No one wants to be on the receiving end of it, so it's a waste of fucking energy." He glanced around, his sharp eyes taking in their surroundings. What he was about to say would be a bit of a bomb. "Look, between you, me, and the squirrel over there playing with his nuts, I've read the reports on your mission—the unredacted reports." Reese removed his sunglasses, his eyes flaring in shock, and Ian shrugged a nonchalant shoulder. "It pays to have a high clearance, and before you say it, I didn't get them from Larry. I saw them on a visit to the Pentagon." Pain filled Reese's eyes as the memories haunting him bubbled to the surface, probably not for the first time today. "You survived, Marine, when your teammates didn't. Had the situation been reversed, and you were dead while one of them came home, would you want them sulking on your grave, or would you tell them to man the fuck up? There's so much good you could be doing on my team. But if having your own pity party for the rest of your life is what you want to do, so be it."

It was time to give Reese some space, and Ian stepped backward. "Think about it. I'll be at the Blarney Stone until fourteen-hundred hours, having lunch. It's a pub, two blocks that way." He hitched a thumb over his shoulder. "If you're not there by fourteen-oh-one, I'll throw your file in a dumpster and be done with you."

Without waiting for an answer, Ian turned on his heel and walked away, hoping the kid made the right decision for his own sake.

Repeatedly clenching and releasing his fists, Logan glared at Sawyer's retreating back and then glanced around to see if anyone was watching him. He wouldn't put it past the retired SEAL to have someone observing from nearby. The man may not be a living legend, but he was damn, fucking close. He'd been highly respected in the spec-ops community, and that had rolled over to the security business he owned with his brother. Several former teammates of SEAL Team Four had faithfully followed him into the private sector and now worked for him.

He has the best of the best—so what the fuck does he want with a broken-down has-been?

Taking one more inventory of the surrounding area, Logan strode toward his truck that was parked at the curb. Climbing in, he started the engine but didn't put it in drive—he just stared out the window at nothing in particular. Today's session with his shrink hadn't gone well—he was almost ready to give up on the therapy—and he'd already been stressed out when Sawyer had walked up and introduced himself. Logan was sure his former uncle, Larry, had called in a favor and asked for Sawyer to take on the poor, useless retired Marine. But then again, Sawyer's words came back to him.

"You survived, Marine, when your teammates didn't. Had the situation been reversed, and you were dead, while one of them came home, would you want them sulking on your grave, or would you tell them to man the fuck up? There's so much good you could be doing on my team. But if having your own fucking pity party for the rest of your life is what you want to do, so be it."

Logan's jaw tightened as his anger level rose again. *Who the fuck does Sawyer think he is?*

Yanking the gearshift, he threw the truck into drive, and with barely a glance over his shoulder to check the traffic, he peeled out of the spot with no idea where he was heading. Rolling the windows down, he breathed in the fresh air—well, as fresh as Washington, D.C. air could be.

He drove aimlessly for about twenty minutes, not wanting to go home to his empty, undecorated apartment. After staying with his folks in Virginia for six months after his release from the military hospital in Germany, he'd finally insisted it was best if he moved out. He hadn't been able to return to the condo he'd shared with Danny Coleman—there were too many memories of his best friend there. Besides, Clutch had owned it, and his family had decided to sell the unit. It'd taken Logan an entire day to pack up the shit from his room, and after he'd stored everything in his parents' garage, he'd gone out and gotten rip-roaring drunk.

When he'd sobered up again, the pain he saw in his parents' eyes had registered. They'd been afraid—not of him, but of what he was doing to himself. His life had become a cycle of restless sleep, eating out of necessity, attending his therapy sessions, running four miles a day, and getting shit-faced two or three times a week. While he hadn't died in that shack in Afghanistan, he might as well have. Inside, he was just as dead as his buddies—only his heart hadn't stopped beating yet.

While his parents had told him it was fine for him to stay with them, he knew it was hard having him in the house. They had to walk on eggshells, worrying something they would do or say would trigger a negative response from him—especially when he was asleep. They'd taken to using an old cowbell to announce themselves if they needed to awaken him since he usually came to swinging. Thankfully, he hadn't hit either of them, although he'd attacked a male nurse during his stay in the hospital when he'd stirred from a medicated sleep to see the dark-haired man standing over him. It had taken two orderlies to pull him off the nurse who Logan had almost strangled to death. Thank God, the poor guy had survived, but Logan had ended up being afraid to fall asleep until he'd been released and flown back to the US. Even now, he was worried he'd hurt someone without realizing what he was doing.

A honking horn startled Logan, and he moved his foot from the brake to the accelerator, sending the vehicle lurching forward before he gained control again. It took him a few moments to realize where he was. Somehow, almost on autopilot, his truck had steered itself to the entrance of Arlington National Cemetery. Passing through the gates, he drove into the visitor's parking garage. Throngs of tourists, young and old, were heading toward the Tomb of the Unknown Soldier for the dramatic changing of the guards, but Logan didn't follow the crowd. Instead, he headed in the other direction. The rows of white on a sea of green spread over 624 acres, where more than 400,000 individuals were interred or inurned. Each one had either served their country, many dying while doing so, or they'd been married to someone who'd served in the military, dating as far back as the American Revolution all the way through to today. In fact, far up on a hillside to Logan's right, another hero was being brought home to the hallowed ground while their family mourned.

Three volleys of seven rifles being fired for a twenty-one-gun salute had his muscles tensing and heart rate speeding up before the somber bugle notes of "Taps" floated through the air. Logan swallowed the lump in his throat, grateful his watery eyes were concealed by his sunglasses as he passed two middle-aged women tending to a young soldier's grave site. *Jesus.* The tombstone said the poor guy had only been twenty years old when he'd died five years ago—not even old enough to drink legally, yet old enough to give up the ghost for his country. According to the information under his name and dates of birth and death, he'd been awarded the Purple Heart and the Silver Star, so it was likely he'd been killed in action, and the medals had been given to his family.

With his gut churning, Logan continued his three-quarter-mile hike to the section where his teammates were interred—at least most of them were. Seth Granger, one of the guys killed during the initial ambush, and Kevin Mooney, the first one slaughtered at the insurgents' camp, had both been buried in other veteran cemeteries closer to their families in Oregon and New Mexico, respectively. The only other teammates from that fateful mission who weren't buried here were Logan and Joe Moretti. The latter had recovered from the bacterial infection he'd developed in that hell hole but was suffering from a severe case of PTSD—worse than Logan's. The two men had only spoken a few times by phone since returning to the US, and Logan was afraid someday he'd receive a call that Stash had committed suicide in his hometown in Maine. The man was seriously fucked up in the head, and half the shit he'd said in their brief conversations hadn't made any sense. He was on some heavy-duty psychotic meds and had been in and out of the hospital over the past year with PTSD-induced episodes that had scared the shit out of his family.

As he neared his buddies' grave sites, Logan slowed and shortened his stride. The last time he'd been here was about two months ago, and instead of getting easier, each visit was harder than the last. The first tombstone he came to was Gunny's. A few feet to the left were Clutch's and Flipper's. And buried in the row directly behind those three were Kandy and their four other friends who'd been killed in the initial attack. All had been awarded the Purple Heart and several other medals posthumously.

Logan squatted in front of Clutch's grave and stared at the white inscribed stone, waiting for his grief to overtake him as it did every time he came here. His eyes closed as the painful memories assaulted him. These men had died protecting what this country had been built on. They'd joined the hundreds of thousands of men and women who'd made the ultimate sacrifice for people they'd never met—people who would never know their names or truly understand why they'd died. No sacrifice on earth was greater than laying down your own life so others could live and be free. And in this day and age, so many were too self-absorbed to comprehend that fact. The disrespect some young people showed to veterans nowadays was similar to what those who'd served in Vietnam had experienced upon returning to the States. To see your flag trampled, pissed on, or set on fire by the very people who lived under it was disgusting. If they only knew how oppressed and terrifying their lives would be without that flag, the Constitution, and the men and women who defended them with their dying breath, maybe they'd understand and give the rightfully earned respect.

"Is he a hero?"

Opening his eyes, Logan found the source of the tiny voice. A little boy, about six years old, dressed in blue jeans and a sweatshirt with the US flag on it, was staring at him with a curious expression. Glancing around, Logan saw a woman, who was probably the boy's mother, since she had the same blonde hair and blue eyes, hurrying toward them from a few rows away.

"Charlie! Don't run off like that and scare Mommy. Leave the gentleman alone." She stopped behind her son, placing her hands on his shoulders, and gave Logan an apologetic gaze. "I'm so sorry he bothered you. We were just visiting his grandfather's grave."

Still squatting, Logan shook his head. "No need to apologize, ma'am." He smiled at the boy. "Hi, Charlie. My name's Logan, and yes, my friend Danny was a hero." Pointing to the stones bearing the names of the rest of his buddies, he added, "They're all heroes. That's Phillip, Gavin, Brent, Dwayne, Javier, Stuart, and Brandon. They were my teammates."

Little Charlie's eyes grew wide. "So, does that mean you're a hero too?"

Oh, fuck. How did he explain to a kid so young that the last thing he would call himself was a hero? Yeah, he had a bunch of medals in a box in his apartment, which only came out when he had to wear his dress whites or blues. But many times over the last year, he'd felt like a fake, pinning them to his uniform. He hadn't died like these men in order to get those medals. He hadn't made the ultimate sacrifice like they had.

Logan let out a sigh and removed his sunglasses. "What do you think a hero is, Charlie?"

He'd expected to hear something like Superman or Spiderman flying through the air, but damn if the kid didn't surprise him. Charlie gently patted Danny's white marker. "A hero is someone who fights the bad guys, so I can sleep at night and go to school and watch TV and play outside. Heroes keep Mommy and me safe. My grandpa was a hero—he died in-in-in . . ." He glanced up at his mother. "Where did Grandpa die, Mommy?"

"Lebanon, sweetie." The woman's gaze met Logan's, her pain still evident in her pretty, blue eyes. "My dad was a Marine killed during the Beirut bombings in 1983. I was only two then, but my mother kept his memory alive for me."

Logan knew all about the bombing of the US barracks in Lebanon that had killed 220 Marines, eighteen sailors, and three soldiers. It had been the deadliest day for the US Armed Forces since Vietnam and the deadliest single terrorist attack on American citizens prior to 9/11.

"He died in Lebanon," Charlie said, continuing his explanation to Logan. "My daddy's a hero too. He's a police officer. He fights bad people too."

Sometimes it took the words of a child to make things clearer in your mind. This right here . . . this little, six-year-old boy and his mother were exactly why Logan and his teammates had signed their lives over to Uncle Sam, put on those uniforms, and picked up their weapons. They'd sacrificed their own lives, liberties, and pursuits of happiness so this little kid and millions like him felt safe enough to sleep at night and smile and laugh during the day.

Logan still had demons he'd have to face, but sweet, freckle-faced Charlie had reminded him why he'd enlisted in the first place all those years ago. His buddies were gone, but he had the opportunity to continue the fight in their honor. He imagined they would be telling him to man the fuck up, just as Sawyer had, instead of rolling over and waiting for the day he would take his last breath. Until now, he'd just been a dead man with a pulse, and it was time to change that. There was so much more he could do before he joined his buddies here on this hallowed ground, and it was time to find out if he could be a part of a team again. A team that put the lives and freedoms of others before their own.

Instead of answering the boy's earlier question, Logan stood tall and peered down at him. "Do you know how to salute, Charlie?"

"Yes, sir!"

"I always salute my teammates before I leave. Will you salute them with me?"

Beaming, Charlie moved to stand beside him, facing Clutch's grave. He watched and waited for Logan to lift his right arm and then followed suit, his little hand stiff at his temple. His father must have taught him how to do it right.

Together, they slowly brought their arms back to their sides, and Logan pivoted to face him. After giving the boy's mother a smile, which she returned, he said, "It was very nice meeting you and your mom, Charlie. I hope I can live up to your expectations of what a hero is someday because I'm really going to try."

Four

"So, is he going to take the job?"

As Angie's lyrical voice drifted through his cell phone, Ian flagged down the waitress for the bill. "Doesn't look like it. He's got five more minutes before I walk out of here."

If Reese didn't show, Ian would have to go back to the five other files he had sitting on his desk and make a decision with Devon on who to offer the position to. But he really wished the guy would show up—not only because Ian thought he'd be a perfect fit for the new team, but because the retired Marine needed a reason to get up every morning. Otherwise, he'd just waste away—another dead soul among the living.

"Will you be in the mood to go to the club tonight, Sir?"

Despite his disappointment over Reese, a grin spread across Ian's face. That single word "Sir" out of his submissive's pretty mouth always got his dick twitching, no matter what was going on at the moment. The club she was referring to was Ian and Devon's other business, which they co-owned with their cousin, Mitch Sawyer. The Covenant was a private, elite BDSM establishment in the Trident Security compound that the Alpha team all belonged to, having been in the life-style during their military years.

When Ian first met Angie, she hadn't been in the kink community but had a healthy curiosity about it. He'd introduced her to his world, and she'd come to love and need it as much as he had.

"When am I not in the mood to go play, Angel?" The waitress slid a thin leather folder with his bill in it onto the table and then stepped away again.

A feminine snort came over the phone. "Okay, that was a stupid question. But if your answer had been 'no,' I was prepared to bring out the big guns."

"Which would be?" His woman had definitely caught his attention with her flirtatious tone.

"Oh, just that I got a delivery today from someone's favorite lingerie catalog."

And, damn, now he was hard as a rock. He had a huge lingerie fetish, loving how a woman looked and felt in silk and lace, and Angie enjoyed indulging him in it. His fiancée rocked sexy undergarments like no other woman he knew—the more see-through, the better. When she and Ian had first started dating, Angie had found out she'd been harboring an inner exhibitionist up to that point in her life.

"The red, fishnet body stocking?"

"Mmm-hmm," she responded in a husky, sultry tone. "The crotchless one. I think you'll want me to wear the red stilettos with it too."

"Are you trying it on right now, standing in front of the full-length mirror?"

"Mmm-hmm."

Fuck, she was killing him. He winced as his pants tight-ened in his crotch, as he shifted to retrieve his wallet from his back pocket. He was about to tell her to get her green vibrator —or JGG for jolly-green-giant—for some phone sex, but across the dining room, the front door to the pub swung open, and in walked Reese. His sharp eyes scanned the patrons, and when he spotted Ian, he marched over, sheer determination on his face. Without acknowledging or noticing the fact Ian was on the phone, he said, "I'm in."

After staring at the man for a moment, Ian nodded and then pointed to the opposite seat in the booth. The phone sex would have to wait until he was on Trident's private jet later. At least, then, he'd be able to get himself off at the same time she did. "I have to go, Angel. My appointment just showed up."

"Oh, good. Love you, Sir. Call me from the plane."

"Love you, too, Angel. And I will—have JGG primed and ready to go." A few months ago, he would've been embarrassed saying "I love you" to her over the phone in someone else's presence, but now, he didn't care who knew how much he loved his woman. She was the reason he lived each day with a lighter heart than he'd ever known, and now he had the chance to offer someone else a different reason to get up every morning.

Disconnecting the call, he set the phone on the dark wooden table as Reese took a seat. Ian flagged the waitress back over and handed her the bill with his credit card. "Sorry, we'll be here longer than I thought. Keep the tab open for now, and please bring me another Bud Light. Reese, you want anything?"

The man glanced at the woman. "I'll have the same, please."

"Sure thing," she responded before heading over to the bar.

Ian studied his potential new employee—it wasn't a done deal yet. There were several mandatory requirements Reese had to accept. "You got in just under the wire. You sure you want to do this?"

The man's eyes narrowed. "What? Did you finally come to the conclusion hiring me was a bad idea sometime in the past two hours?"

Shaking his head, Ian pushed his phone aside and crossed his arms on the table. "Not at all. Just making sure you're a hundred percent positive before I expend any more energy on you." He paused. "How was your session with the shrink?"

"Confidential."

Ian snorted at the annoyed tone of voice for that one word. "Not if you're on my team it isn't. Rule number one for me hiring you—you'll continue to see a shrink in Tampa whenever you're in town. Two or three times a week, depending on what the doc says. I've got three of them from the government-approved list, who are experienced with veterans with PTSD, for you to choose from. You don't like any of those, then we'll look until we find one we both agree on."

Reese's jaw had tightened, but when Ian raised an eyebrow at him, he nodded. "Okay. Rule number one I can live with." With a little snark, he added, "I assume there's at least a rule number two."

"Smart man, although you know what they say about assuming anything. Rule number two is you're one hundred percent open and honest with me. I can work around any missions you're uncomfortable with, but you've got to open your mouth and tell me. I'm not going to show you the door if you do, but you can be damn sure I'll kick your ass out if you fucking lie to me or withhold the fact you can't deal with something."

After a brief pause, that demand garnered a slightly better response. "Understood. Anything else?"

"Those first two are not negotiable, and neither is rule number three." Ian steeled himself for the hissy fit that might follow his next words. "After you get some training time with your new team, we'll all sit down, and you'll tell them what happened in Afghanistan. Everything that's not classified."

This time, the man's jaw dropped. Fury flared in his eyes, and Ian waited for the "fuck you, asshole" followed by the table being flipped over . . . or something to that effect. Reese leaned forward, glaring at him, but kept his voice low. "Are you fucking kidding me? Who the hell is going to want to work with me after hearing what I've been through? Fuck! I can't even tell the damn shrink what happened."

Ian knew he wasn't referring to the classified shit, which he couldn't tell anyone—not even a government-approved psychologist. He meant he hadn't told the doctor how he'd listened to his teammates being tortured, one by one, and then had to see their decapitated heads. Ian also knew this was Reese's third or fourth shrink he'd tried to open up to. "What have you told him so far? Have you told him you have survivor's guilt? How you breathed a sigh of relief when you weren't the next one dragged out of the cell? And how guilty you felt seconds after that relief disappeared as you listened to your buddies being tortured? Cowboy, man, all that's normal. Well, as normal as shit can get after what you've been through. And if none of your shrinks have gotten that out of you after all this time, then you're seeing the wrong fucking ones." He paused as a thought occurred to him. "Hang on a second."

The waitress returned with their beers and then left again. As Reese continued to stew silently, Ian grabbed his phone, found the number he was looking for in his contacts, pressed Send, and waited for the call to be answered.

"Hello, Ian. You've got three minutes before my next client walks in." Dr. Trudy Dunbar was a psychologist he'd known for the past few years. Although she wasn't in the lifestyle herself, she'd done her dissertation on BDSM, so they referred members of The Covenant to her when a Dom or sub needed professional treatment. It wasn't uncommon for an individual's personal problems to interfere with their playtime or reasons for being in the lifestyle, which could result in someone getting hurt. Trudy had helped several members of the club. She was also on the government's approved list to work with veterans who were privy to sensitive or classified information and knew how to skirt around the subjects that couldn't be talked about.

"Hey, Doc. I need a military referral up in D.C. One of my new employees has been seeing someone, but I don't think it's working for him. Survivor's guilt from things associated with SERE, among other stuff." The acronym stood for Survival, Evasion, Resistance, and Escape in the world of spec ops, with "resistance" referring to torture. He didn't want to say that over the phone in the busy restaurant, but the doc would easily figure it out. "He'll need three to six months up here before he moves to Tampa, and then I'll hook him up with you or one of your approved colleagues."

"D.C., huh? Who's he seeing now?"

Not needing to ask, he responded, "David Preston."

Surprised at hearing the name of his shrink, Reese's eyebrows almost hit his hairline, yet he didn't say anything. Trudy's fingernails clacking on a keyboard came over the phone, so Ian held it away from his mouth. "How do you think I found you today? I wouldn't have a successful business if I couldn't track your ass down in less than five minutes. Well, technically, my geek extraordinaire, Brody Evans, found you, but I refuse to let him know he deserves the credit. His fucking ego is already too big when it comes to shit like that."

"Ian?"

"I'm still here, Trudy. Whada ya got for me?"

"Sara Tennyson is in Georgetown. I met her at a conference last year and was very impressed with her lecture on PTSD in POWs. She's worked with a few that had been captured and rescued in Iraq and Afghanistan. Did he try a session with her yet?"

He eyed Reese. "Have you tried Dr. Sara Tennyson?" The man shook his head. "No, he hasn't. Can you send me the info?"

Before he could finish the question, his phone chimed with an incoming text. "Done. I have to run. If you need anything else, call me after four p.m."

"Thanks, Doc. I owe you." He disconnected the call and retrieved a pen and business card from the side pocket of his cargo pants. After copying the information Trudy had sent him, he slid the card over to Reese. "Give her a call. Like I said to the doc, you've got six months—max—to get your head on straight and get down to Tampa. That's when the last of the new team cycles out of their respective tours and report for duty. In the meantime, hit the gym, firing range, and sparring mat, and get your ass back in fighting condition. When you're ready to move, we've got bunks at the compound—you're welcome to stay there until you decide to look for your own place. As for telling the rest of the Omega Team what you went through, it's their right to know who's covering their six. I don't want to hit them with it right away, though. I want you working as a team first, so they can see how good you are before they have to make a decision on whether or not they want to work with you."

Reese appeared to mull everything over. His anger had dialed down and morphed into understanding. "And if they decide I'm not good enough, or they don't want to work with me because they don't think they can trust me, then what?"

Leaning forward, Ian pinned him with an unwavering stare. "Then I'll put you on my team. That is, as long as you don't give me any reason to regret it and force me to fire your ass. I'm willing to give you a chance if you're willing to take it, Marine. No promises that everything will be a fucking fairy tale with pink unicorns and Snow-fucking-White—that's not the world we live in—but if you give me one hundred percent, I'll give it back to you in return. So . . . is this a done deal, or do we have to sit here and negotiate some more?"

He held out his hand and waited. Seconds ticked by before Reese nodded and extended his own, and they shook on it. "Done."

"Welcome aboard."

THE DOM SAT BACK in the comfortable, wingback chair and watched the female sub get worked over with a whip during the evening's demonstration. His cock got harder with each crack of the leather, then a sharp cry of pain, followed by a moan of pleasure. Actually, he could do without that last part. It was the first two things that turned him on. In his mind, he was the one wielding the whip, and instead of the pink welts up and down the woman's back, they were deep and bleeding. She would be begging—not for more, as she was now, but for him to stop. For him to end her suffering in the only way possible . . . with death.

Why that was his fantasy, he didn't know, but lately, that was what he needed to conjure up in his mind in order to ejaculate, whether in some sub's mouth, pussy, or ass, or his own hand. But it was a fantasy he couldn't indulge in—at least, not here in the club. One of the main requirements for using a whip in the respected BDSM clubs in the area was that the Doms had to prove they were proficient enough that they never broke the skin with the repeated strikes. It took months, even years of training and practicing to become good enough —he knew because he'd gone through it and was approved for the impact play at several clubs. Practice and testing were done with thin pieces of paper taped against the wall. If the Dom could hit the paper, over and over, without ripping it, then they were allowed to whip a sub on the play floor.

Shifting in the chair, he tried to give his hard-on some room in his leathers. He'd found the lifestyle a few years ago, pretty much by accident, but it hadn't taken him long to realize it was what he'd been missing in his life. The sights, smells, and sounds that filled the air during play called to him. The first night he'd been surrounded by it all, he knew it was where he belonged, and he'd immediately signed up to train as a Dom. Yet, lately, he was getting the feeling that something was missing again. What would it be like if he didn't have to hold himself back? If he could push a sub past her yellow limits and beyond her red limits? If he didn't have to honor a safeword? It would be up to him, not the sub, to say when enough was enough. He couldn't do that here, but maybe he could find a place where he was the ultimate rule maker and only his word mattered. It was something to think about.

He reached out and stroked the blonde hair of the sub who had agreed to play with him later. In a snug, black, strapless bodice and a short, leather skirt that barely covered her ass cheeks, she was kneeling on a pillow on the floor next to him. Her pale, porcelain skin coincided with her Irish heritage, and he wondered what it would look like covered in stripes from his whip—not pink, but red. Deep, dark, crimson red.

With the macabre image in his mind, he leaned down and whispered in her ear, "Come, my pet, it's time to go play."

TRIDENT SECURITY
OMEGA TEAM

Eleven Months Later . . .

Pushing the heavy glass and metal door open, Dakota left the station, still confused about her conversation with her sergeant. For the first time in a very long while, she held onto a glimmer of hope. He'd told her a Captain Al Bowman had requested a meeting with her at the Special Ops Division. Her confusion was because she'd finally given up on applying for an undercover position six months ago. She'd scored high on the supervisor exam and was also on the detective's list, but in her heart, she'd still been disappointed at being consistently passed over for UC work.

Opening the passenger door to the patrol car, she climbed in. Some days, she rode solo, but today she was partnered with Ric, who was staring at her expectantly. "Well? What did Sarge want?"

Dakota opened and closed her mouth several times before the words finally came. "Captain Bowman in SOD wants me in his office ASAP. Any idea who he is? I've never heard of him." With nearly 1000 officers on Tampa PD and over 350 civilians in support positions scattered between fifteen police stations, it was impossible to know everyone.

Putting the vehicle in drive, Ric pulled out of the parking lot and headed across town to where the Special Ops Division was located. "No idea. Maybe newly promoted?"

"Could be." Her mind raced as she tried to tell herself not to get too excited. It would suck to get all psyched up, only to find out the meeting had nothing to do with a UC assignment.

"Think you're in?"

"How? I didn't put an app in the last time a position opened." But her previous applications would still be on file. "Anyway, I don't want to get my hopes up, so let's talk about something else until I find out what's going on."

Ric knew her well enough to change the subject to the date he'd gone on the night before. By the time he pulled into the station that housed the SOD, Dakota had her nerves under control again. Leaving him in the car, she headed inside and found her way to the captain's office. After she introduced herself to his secretary, the woman picked up the phone and notified Bowman that the officer he was expecting was there. Dakota was then told to have a seat, as the captain would be a few more minutes.

Thankfully, the chairs in the sitting area were wide enough to accommodate the duty belt resting on Dakota's hips. A holstered .40 caliber handgun, extra ammo clips, two pairs of handcuffs, keys, pepper spray, and a PR24 baton were all attached to the belt. Add a backup pistol in a holster above her ankle, a Taser strapped to her left thigh, and her bullet-proof vest, and she was carrying twenty extra pounds of equipment on her frame.

While waiting, she pulled out her cell phone and scrolled through some emails and Facebook notifications that had popped up over the last few hours. There was nothing big or overly interesting, but it kept her mind busy and the butterflies in her stomach in check.

Suddenly, the door to the captain's office swung open, and a familiar-looking man, wearing a navy-blue polo shirt with the TPD SOD logo and khakis, waved her inside. His crew cut was sandy-blond, and his kind, green eyes welcomed her into his office. Standing, Dakota racked her brains, trying to remember where she knew him from but couldn't place him—*must have been at some police function.*

Entering the spacious office, she was surprised to see two other men in civilian clothes sitting at a small conference table. And, holy hell, were they good-looking. One was in his late thirties, with black hair. He had on a blue polo shirt that matched his incredible eyes. The other was about ten or fifteen years older, with eyes the color of hot cocoa and salt-and-pepper hair—giving new meaning to the words "silver fox." Their intense stares in her direction had her legs quivering, and she had to fight the urge to drop her gaze to the floor, followed by the rest of her to her knees.

Stop it. You're at work, not the club.

The man who'd waved her inside held out his hand. "Officer Swift, I'm Captain Al Bowman." After she shook his hand, he gestured to an empty chair at the table. "Have a seat. Let me introduce you to Special Agent Colt Parrish of the FBI and Ian Sawyer from Trident Security."

Neither man said anything, but both acknowledged her with a nod of the head. Dakota swallowed hard as she took her seat. Bowman sat next to her, and silence filled the room. All three men were studying her, and she fought the need to squirm under their scrutiny or glance down at her uniform to see if something was out of place. Unable to take the silence, she cleared her throat and directed her gaze toward her superior. "Was there a reason you wanted to see me, sir?"

The man glanced at Sawyer and Parrish. The former's

mouth ticked up at the corners but never fully formed a smile, while the other man remained stoic. When both gave another curt nod, Bowman leaned forward and rested his arms on the table. "I've called you in for a special reason, Swift. There's an assignment I think you'd be perfect for—and not just because of your stellar career and the high praise you've received from your superiors—although those are major pluses. What I'm about to say has only been shared with these two men—no one else in the department is aware of this, to my knowledge. If you turn down the assignment, the information goes no further than this room, and you have nothing to worry about. It's obvious you don't recognize me, but we have been introduced before, about six months ago . . . at Pandora's Box."

Dakota's confusion gave way to shock as her jaw dropped along with her stomach. *Oh shit*. "I'm sorry, sir, I-I don't recall . . ."

He held up a hand. "That's okay. It was only a brief introduction, and don't worry—I didn't ask to negotiate with you, nor did you turn me down." A grin spread across his face. "One of the owners told me you were on the force—she didn't want either of us running into an issue. I've made it a point to avoid you since then, so I'm not offended you don't recognize me."

Now Dakota remembered him, and being part of the same police department wasn't the only reason he hadn't tried to negotiate with her months ago. The other was that Captain Bowman was gay. She recalled he was a Dom with a long-term male submissive. Clearly, he had no problem announcing the fact he was in the lifestyle, but he still kept a few facts to himself.

Shit. That was why she'd joined a club in Kissimmee, an hour's drive from her condo. She hadn't wanted to run into anyone from the department. She had a hard enough time being a female officer in a man's world and didn't need any of those men to know she was a sexual submissive. Pandora's Box was a members-only BDSM club that thoroughly vetted all applicants. It was the only reason the owners of the club, Mistress Raven and Madame Lola—who preferred the rarer title to honor her French heritage—knew Dakota was a police officer in the first place.

"Sorry I didn't remember you right away, Captain, but now, I do recall meeting you."

"Good. Now, I wouldn't normally out you like this, but Master Ian, Master Colt, and I need your help. I'm sure you've heard about the Kink Killer."

Holy shit. She should have known the two other men were Doms from their intense stares alone. And they needed *her* help? The press had dubbed the sadistic psycho, who was whipping his victims to death, the Kink Killer—*how fucking original*. Five women had been kidnapped and murdered so far that they were aware of. Several other missing women might be victims, but their bodies hadn't been found, so they couldn't be officially added to the count. "Who hasn't? It's been all over the news and the department."

Parrish picked up a pen and twirled it through his fingers while he spoke. "Well, we've managed to keep a few things away from the press. Have you had breakfast yet?"

His fast change of topic confused her. "Um . . . no, not yet."

The fed slid a manila folder toward her. "Good, because the photos are quite gruesome."

Swallowing the saliva that had gathered in her mouth, Dakota opened the file. As she stared at the first picture, she understood his concern. Her stomach roiled at the sight, and she was grateful it was empty. Any seasoned veteran of law enforcement would have reacted the same way as long as they had an ounce of sympathy. Whoever the woman had been, she was now a mass of abused flesh. Her body, from her neck to her feet, was covered in deep lacerations. There was barely a quarter of an inch between them.

Dakota glanced at Parrish in revulsion. "He cut them all like this? With what?"

"A bullwhip."

Her jaw clenched as her gaze returned to the photo. There were almost no marks on the victim's face, so they'd probably been able to identify her easily, but the rest of her body looked like something one would see in a slaughterhouse.

The next few photos were of different women who had been tortured to death in the same manner. "Jesus Christ."

"He can't help them now," Sawyer deadpanned, although it was clear he wasn't trying to be funny.

Parrish dropped the pen on the table and leaned forward. "Here's where you come in, Officer Swift. We've put together a task force to catch this bastard. In order to do that, we need to send officers and agents to the clubs in and around Tampa —undercover. Obviously, we can't just send anyone in—they need to have knowledge of the lifestyle and be able to pass as either a submissive or a Dom—especially in the private clubs. If you accept the assignment, you'll be under Captain Bowman's and my command for the duration of the case."

"I'm in." There was no hesitation on Dakota's part, and none of the men appeared surprised at her quick response. This was what she'd been striving for all these years—a chance to prove she was good enough to be transferred to SOD. There was no way she'd decline the assignment. "What's next?"

"You take the rest of the morning off and report to the FBI headquarters at three p.m.—plain clothes. And I'm sorry in advance for the fed you'll be partnered with, but I have no choice." Parrish grimaced. "We don't have enough Doms and subs on the force and local federal agencies, whose attachment to law enforcement is unknown, to cover all the clubs—public and private. We're pairing up some of the local agents with an experienced member of the lifestyle. You'll be the lead inside whatever club you're assigned to, even though you'll go in as a sub. Your partner will be told that, and if he gives you any trouble, I want to know about it."

Oh, great. She was probably going to get stuck with a high-and-mighty asshole. "Understood."

"Unfortunately, the local SAC, Stonewall, is a prick, asshole, twatwaffle, and douchebag all rolled into one," Sawyer said before grinning at her. "Can't you tell I just love the guy?"

She smiled back, liking the man even more as he was treating her as an equal and not a peon. "Absolutely, sir. If you don't mind me asking, what does Trident have to do with this?"

Dakota had heard about the private security company located in Tampa. It was comprised of retired members of the military, mostly Navy SEALs, and was well respected among the law enforcement agencies in the area.

"Not as much as I'd like." He gave an annoyed side glance in Parrish's direction. "Since I own The Covenant with my brother and cousin, we've been brought in as consultants, nothing more."

Wow! Not only was the hottie a retired SEAL and a Dom, but he owned *the* most elite BDSM club on the Gulf Coast of Florida.

The FBI agent raised an eyebrow at Sawyer. "We've been through this before. Dickhead . . . I mean, Stonewall is in charge of Tampa, and I'm here just for this case. He has the final say on personnel at the moment. It doesn't work in your favor that you continue to piss him off every chance you get."

"I can't help it—it's my charming personality." Sawyer's droll tone of voice had Dakota chuckling. She wondered what he was like when he was in full-Dom mode—probably terrifying and panty-dropping simultaneously.

Parrish rolled his eyes and stood. "Officer Swift, welcome

aboard. We'll see you at three at the FBI office. I'll leave your name at the front desk. After you check in, head up to the fourth floor and ask anyone where the task force is meeting."

"Thank you, sir," Dakota responded as she stood with the other two men. "I'm looking forward to it."

She shook hands with Sawyer and Parrish, but when she turned to Bowman, he indicated for her to sit back down. "I'd like a few more minutes with you, Swift."

As the others left, she sat again. Bowman strode across the room to his desk, retrieved a folder, and returned to his seat. When he opened the file, she was surprised that the first page was an application to join SOD with her signature at the bottom. It was one of five she'd submitted before finally giving up hope of being transferred into the coveted division.

Bowman leaned against the chair back, and his gaze met hers. "Why didn't you submit an application two months ago when another position opened?"

Seriously? Her jaw tightened. "It was obvious after five attempts I wasn't going to get the transfer, so I set my sights on the detective bureau and the supervisor's test."

The man nodded in understanding. "I assume you've wondered why you were repeatedly passed over."

"I did." She wasn't sure where he was going with this, and there was no way she would make it easy on him.

"For the record, I just took over the division three months ago after a promotion when Captain Fallon retired. I've been impressed with your record for several years now, and every time a position opened, I pushed for you to be given the spot. Each time, Fallon tossed your file aside without even looking at it. It had nothing to do with you and everything to do with the fact that Fallon hated your father. The two of them had gone to the academy together and, I guess, rubbed each other the wrong way."

Dakota gaped at the supervisor. All this time, she'd figured someone had a hard-on for her and that was why she'd been passed over. The thought never occurred to her that it was due to a dispute between her father and the head of the division.

"I've got two positions opening in the next few months. One UC is retiring, and another recently got engaged and decided to return to patrol. If you're still interested, I'd like to see your name on the application list again. Prove yourself on this case, and I can almost guarantee one of the positions is yours." He grinned. "Since I'm the one who makes those decisions now."

"Th-thank you, Captain. I'm honored."

"You're welcome, Swift. Just don't screw up between now and then and make me regret this conversation."

There was no way she was going to screw up. Her heart was pounding in her chest, and she fought the urge to throw a fist in the air in celebration.

When the captain stood, she followed and shook his outstretched hand. "Thank you again, sir. Will you be at the meeting later?"

He nodded. "I'll see you then. Head on back to your station. I'll call your lieutenant now and tell him you're assigned to me until we catch this bastard."

Dakota almost ran out of the building. After she jumped into the passenger seat of the patrol car, she slammed the door shut, looked at Ric, and then yelled at the top of her lungs, "Yes!"

TRIDENT SECURITY
OMEGA TEAM

Six

Logan glanced around Ian's Oasis, the backyard setup that had been built between the third and fourth warehouses in the compound housing Trident Security and the Sawyers' other business, The Covenant. After finding out about the BDSM club during a weekend trip to Tampa, shortly after accepting Ian's job offer, he'd done a little research on the lifestyle. The Sawyer brothers had been adamant about their new employees signing non-disclosure agreements specifically for the club, in addition to ones for the cases Trident was involved in. They'd also warned that any negativity expressed toward gays, the opposite gender, or lifestyle members would result in immediate termination. Logan's cousin was a lesbian, and since he was close to her, he'd accepted the whole LGBT community without prejudice while he was still in high school.

Due to the intense scrutiny they'd been subjected to in order to be hired, all members of the Omega Team were allowed in the club, even though Cain Foster and Tristan McCabe, the co-team leaders, were the only two who participated in the lifestyle. If any of the others wanted to participate, they had to go through training, biannual physicals, and blood work. In the five months Logan had been working for Trident, he'd been in the club a few times but never during open hours.

After accepting Ian's job offer, Logan spent the next six months throwing all his time and energy into making sure when he got to Tampa, he was in fighting shape again—mentally and physically. Between his sessions with Dr. Tennyson and hitting the gym, firing range, and sparring mats, as ordered by his new boss, he'd made a large leap back into the land of the living. He'd forced himself to meet up with old friends and fellow Marines for some fun and had gotten involved with the local American Legion post. He had even been attending group therapy with other veterans who'd gone through their own personal hell and somehow survived. Dr. T. had recommended it to remind him life still went on and, despite what he'd been through, it was okay to smile and laugh again. It was his tribute to his fallen buddies—to try and enjoy life for them instead of mourning the fact they couldn't do it themselves.

Before he left Washington D.C. en route to Tampa, he'd gone to Arlington National Cemetery one more time. His twice-weekly visits had become a habit. He'd sit and update Clutch and the others with what was going on in his life and the lives of the other members of the 2nd Marine Raider Battalion—he'd only wished the one-sided talks gave him the peace he was searching for.

He hadn't seen little Charlie and his mother, Dawn Roberts, again until his final trip to the grave sites. Whether it was irony or fate, he'd been glad to run into them. Charlie had grown an inch or two during those six months, but he was still the wide-eyed kid who believed in real-life heroes. Logan had told them a little about his new job in Tampa, and when they wished him luck, he'd given Dawn his email address in case Charlie wanted to write to him. His new pen pal had sent him an email that night, and Logan still heard from the boy every Sunday.

Why Ian and Devon Sawyer were willing to take a chance on him, Logan would probably never know, but he was grateful they had. As a member of the Trident Security Omega Team, he now had something to look forward to—a reason to put those nightmares and the failed mission behind him. He just hoped he didn't fuck it up. His team would be counting on him, and he didn't want to disappoint them. To do so might be fatal—for him or them.

After arriving in Tampa to start his new career, he'd spent the first night in a bunk room at the Trident compound while waiting for a moving van to arrive with his shit. One of his new teammates, Valentino Mancini, had passed on the information through the company's secretary, Colleen, about an apartment for rent in the complex where he was living. Logan had contacted the leasing company and, based on the pictures they'd emailed him and Mancini's recommendation, had signed a rental agreement before leaving D.C. He'd wanted his own space where he could get some time alone if needed— something that wasn't entirely possible at the compound since sometimes the two teams hung out in the great room near the bunks. There was a TV with a gaming system, a small kitchenette, a pool table, a foosball table, and a dart board for everyone to enjoy.

When he'd gotten settled, he'd met with Dr. Dunbar and found he liked her as much as he did Dr. T. With Logan's approval, the latter had sent his new psychologist the notes she'd made on him over the six months he'd been seeing her, so Dr. Dunbar could easily pick up where they'd left off. Between the two psychologists, it had gotten easier to talk about what he'd gone through—however, not every session was a cakewalk. But now, instead of wallowing in self-pity and guilt and attempting to drown himself in alcohol, he turned to exercise and meditation—and two beers were now his maximum in a twenty-four-hour period.

The other demand his new boss had made had been completed yesterday. Logan had sat down with Ian, Devon, and his new team and told them what he could about what had happened in Afghanistan. While his stomach had clenched at the thought of spilling his guts to them and possibly having them refuse to work with him, he understood why it had to be done. None of the Omega Team had ever worked with each other before, and trust between them was something that needed to be built up and earned for the team to be successful. Logan was grateful that the whole "Hi, my name is Logan, and I'm a former POW who was hours away from being tortured to death before I was rescued . . ." announcement was over with, and he was still part of Omega. The other members had voted unanimously for him to remain on the team with the condition that he'd tell them if he couldn't handle an assignment or his PTSD reared its ugly head.

"Hey, Cowboy, you doing okay?"

Lindsey "Costello" Abbott's voice brought Logan back to the present, and he smiled at the female sniper who was splitting her time on assignments with both the Alpha and Omega teams. "Doing just fine. Better than I have in a very long time."

"Good to hear," Kip "Skipper" Morrison said as he slapped Logan on the back. In addition to being retired from the Army, the man had come to Trident from LAPD's SWAT team, returning to the state he'd grown up in. "Just remember that feeling when the bosses dump us in the Rockies next month."

Yeah, none of them were looking forward to leaving the warmth of Florida for the snow-covered Colorado Rocky Mountains in a few weeks. It would be their final training mission before the Sawyers released the Omega Team out on their own assignments without being paired with an Alpha Team member. They'd be dropped into the wilderness by helicopter with two days to make it back to civilization, with minimal supplies and relying on each other to get there. A satellite phone would be on hand for emergencies, but only life-threatening injuries were included in that category.

Clearly having overheard the conversation, Darius "Batman" Knight joined the trio as he swallowed a mouthful of beer. "Definitely remember that. I'm sure Ian's got some surprises in store for us." Retired from the Navy, the man had served on SEAL Team Four with all six members of the Alpha Team and knew them well. And as Logan had gotten to know his new bosses, he was inclined to agree with Knight. "The son of a bitch knows how to throw the fucking proverbial curve ball, so you better learn to duck."

The small group's laughter drew a few glances from the larger crowd who'd gathered to celebrate Ian and Angie's pregnancy announcement. Both teams, family members, and friends of the couple were present while Nick Sawyer and Jake Donovan, Ian's brother and teammate, respectively, checked in via Skype from their condo in San Diego. The two men were a couple and would be moving back to Tampa in a few short months after Nick finished his last commitment with the Navy on SEAL Team Three. Donovan had been in California the past eighteen months or so setting up the Trident Security West Coast team, which would be doing their own final training mission in the Rockies two weeks after Omega.

Other Trident employees in attendance included office manager Colleen Helm, with her husband/Dom Reggie, who was a lawyer for the Sawyer brothers' businesses, and Nathan Cook, a computer guru who'd previously worked for the National Security Agency (NSA). Tempest "Babs" Van Buren, a kick-ass helicopter pilot and mechanic, and her assistant Russell Adams, who was retired from the Navy, were also enjoying the party. The latter had his PTSD service dog, a Rottweiler named Jagger, almost glued to his leg. From what Logan had learned, the dog's presence had made a dramatic, positive change in the former homeless man's life.

"What? Who?" Everyone's attention was drawn to Ian as his shocked questions were barked into his cell phone. His eyes went wide. "Are you fu—" He stopped short when he noticed his adult goddaughter Jenn was nearby with little Mara, the daughter of Alpha Team member Marco "Polo" DeAngelis. The toddler's ears picked up everything lately, which she would then try to repeat. "Are you kidding me? That's insane!"

The last of murmuring conversations halted among the guests as Ian's voice grew louder and angrier. "All right. I'll be there in twenty. Don't start the interrogation until I get there . . . Parrish, you can wait twenty frigging minutes! I—"

Ripping the phone from his ear, he glared at it. "Bastard hung up on me." He looked up to find everyone staring at him. His gaze searched and found Reggie Helm and then Calvin Watts, who Logan knew was on the local FBI's Hostage Negotiation Team. "Need you both to come with me. Parrish said they made an arrest in the serial killings, and you'll never freaking believe who it is because I sure as hell don't."

Oh crap. While everyone wanted the bastard, who'd been torturing and killing submissives in the BDSM lifestyle in and around Tampa, caught, it was clear Boss-man wasn't happy about the suspect that'd been arrested. When the name Carl Talbot was spat out of Ian's mouth, there were stunned gasps followed by cries of disbelief. Unfortunately, Logan had no idea who the man was.

Foster and McCabe stepped over to their teammates as Ian, Helm, and Watts ran to the latter's vehicle with a promise they'd update everyone as soon as they could. Foster shook his head. "It can't be. I've known the guy for about a year now, and while he's a sadist in the kink community and a Whip Master here at the club, I can't see him being good for this."

Logan eyed the team leader. He didn't understand the lifestyle, and Foster's statement confused him even more. "Maybe because I'm out of the loop, but a sadist, who whips people for fun, sounds like a viable suspect to me."

"That's because you don't get BDSM—most people who aren't in the lifestyle don't. While some people do it for 'fun,' as you said, most Doms and submissives need different aspects of BDSM like the air they breathe. Some people need a particular kink to get through life. In Talbot's case, he needs to be needed by the submissives—and what some submissives need is to be whipped. He trained long and hard to become a respected Whip Master like Donovan and Mistress China." Foster subtly pointed at an angry, petite, Asian-American woman talking animatedly with DeAngelis and Brody "Egghead" Evans, another member of the Alpha Team. Logan was stunned that the gorgeous, dark-haired woman named Charlotte Roth, who he'd been introduced to earlier, wielded a whip in the club. "A trained Whip Master never breaks the skin and knows exactly when to stop. I've watched Talbot many nights at the club and never once saw anything that would make me think he's the sick bastard who killed those women."

"Isn't that what people usually say after some guy blows away his entire family?" Lindsey asked. "They never thought he could do that."

McCabe nodded his head. "True. But I'm with Cain. Even though I'm still a Dom-in-training, I can't see Talbot being the killer." He shrugged. "All we can do now, though, is wait to hear what Boss-man learns."

The mood of the party had changed dramatically. Several women involved in the BDSM community wiped tears from their eyes, while others vehemently defended Master Carl. Logan still didn't quite get it. Maybe when he had some downtime, he'd research the lifestyle his teammates and coworkers were into some more. For now, he strode over to one of the coolers filled with beer and grabbed his second and final one of the day.

⚔

Ian stormed into the Tampa FBI office on the heels of Calvin Watts, with Reggie Helm right behind him. The only reason Ian wasn't leading the way was that they were heading toward an interrogation room and needed Watts's key card to get into the secure area.

Still in shock from the phone call he'd gotten about twenty minutes ago, Ian hoped like hell the Dom they'd brought in for questioning concerning the homicides wasn't guilty. Master Carl Talbot was a long-time member and Whip Master of The Covenant. The sadist's title and proclivity were probably why he'd ended up on Special Agent Colt Parrish's radar. Technically, he hadn't been arrested yet, but from what Parrish had told Ian over the phone, it might only be a matter of time.

Parrish was one of the agency's top investigators regarding serial killers, and he'd come from Quantico, Virginia, when the body count started to climb and the press got wind of the story. While Ian wasn't a huge fan of the man, dealing with him was far better than going head-to-head with SAC Stonewall. At least Ian and Parrish both agreed the FBI supervisor was a prick.

Watts waved his wallet in front of a scanner next to a door leading to the secure area, and when the light on the device turned green, he grabbed the handle and pulled. There were four interrogation rooms off the hallway, with an observation room between the two on the left and another between the two on the right. A light above one of the doors on the left was lit, signaling an interrogation was in progress. Ian followed Watts into the attached observatory as Helm barged his way into the room where Parrish was peppering Talbot with questions. Both men startled at the intrusion.

Ignoring the other men and one woman who'd been in the observatory following the interrogation, Ian watched through the one-way glass as Helm cut off whatever the Special Agent had been about to say with a slash of his hand through the air. "I'm Mister Talbot's lawyer, Reginald Helm, and this interrogation is over. Either charge him, or we're leaving."

Parrish wasn't happy with that announcement if his frown and furrowed brow were any indications. Ian realized with relief that they didn't have enough evidence to formally arrest Talbot. Hopefully, that also meant Parrish was completely wrong about his analysis and had hauled in the wrong man.

As Parrish stood and gestured to the door, Helm snatched the bottle of water sitting on the table in front of Talbot, who had obviously taken a drink from it. "You want DNA, you get a court order," Helm snapped at the fed before facing the one-way mirror. "Ian, we'll wait for you in the parking lot."

When Talbot stood, Ian studied the man he considered a friend. There was no way the fifty-four-year-old was the killer, even though his tall, thin build, pointed nose, narrow eyes, and dark hair, which was graying at the temples, often gave him the look of a vampire when he was dressed in his club leathers. Today, the college professor was dressed comfortably in khakis and a green polo shirt.

Moments after the three men left the interrogation room, the door to the observatory swung open, and Parrish stepped in. In addition to Ian and Watts, also present were TPD Detective Isaac Webb, Dr. Suki Ralston, an FBI Behavioral Analyst, commonly known as a profiler, and two other special agents who'd been assigned to the case. Biting his tongue, Ian waited for Parrish to speak since he was very close to blowing his top.

The case's lead agent propped himself against the wall with his shoulder and crossed his arms. He glared at Ian. "You had to bring the fucking lawyer with you, didn't you?"

"Damn right," he growled, "because you've got the wrong fucking guy. If I thought Carl had a minute chance of being the killer, I would've dragged his ass in here myself."

"He doesn't have an alibi, or one he's willing to share, for any of the kidnappings. As for the murders, we know the suspect is keeping them for anywhere between twenty-four to seventy-two hours, so he could have made the necessary appearances to throw everyone off his scent."

Ian glanced at the petite, dark-haired beauty at his side. Despite it being the weekend, she was dressed in a business suit with a skirt and four-inch heels that showed off her shapely legs. If Ian wasn't married and madly in love with his wife, he might have made a play for the woman—although he doubted she was a submissive. "What about you, Doc? What's your opinion?"

This was Dr. Ralston's third trip down to Tampa from Quantico to update the profile on the UNSUB, or unknown suspect. She preferred to see the crime scenes herself, but since she was working on several cases, it wasn't always possible for her to be there. From what Ian had heard, she was one of the best, holding a Ph.D. in Criminal Psychology. He'd been impressed with her initial and follow-up analysis of their killer, even if it hadn't helped them catch the bastard yet.

Ralston's gaze flashed to Parrish and then back to Ian. "I actually agree with you. I don't believe Carl Talbot is our UNSUB. Not only is he older than I suspect the killer is, but his occupation and background also don't match my profile. However, that being said, behavioral analysis is not absolute.

It's a tool, and I've been wrong before." A small smile formed on her attractive, exotic-looking face, and her brown eyes twinkled. "Not often, mind you, but it has happened once or twice. Anyway, I will agree with Agent Parrish that any potential suspect, no matter how slight a chance of being our UNSUB, needs to be eliminated."

Ian nodded his head and then glanced at Parrish. "Okay. I don't like it, but I understand. However, I hope you're still looking for other suspects because there's no way I'll believe Talbot is our killer."

"That's because you like to beat on women as much as he does."

Ian roared and lunged at the arrogant man who'd stepped through the open door, but Webb, Watts, and Parrish quickly got between them and held the retired SEAL back, preventing him from killing SAC Stonewall. The prick never knew when to keep his damn trap shut. Ian fought against the hands restraining him while glaring at the smirking agent. "You fucking bastard! You know nothing about me or the fucking lifestyle! Nothing happens in my club that's not safe, sane, and consensual!" It was the mantra of the BDSM community, and Ian made sure it was followed to the letter in The Covenant.

With a hand on Ian's chest, Parrish shoved him back. "Easy, Sawyer. Calm the fuck down. I can't have you hitting a federal agent." He then turned around and punched Stonewall in the jaw, sending the balding, overweight man flying back onto his ass. Glaring at the local SAC, the pissed-off Dom opened and closed what had to be an aching fist, which now had two split knuckles from the impact. "I, however, have no trouble putting the ignorant asshole in his place since, technically, he doesn't outrank me."

Sputtering and holding his sore jaw, Stonewall struggled to get to his feet. "You're out of here, Parrish! I don't care what I fucking have to do—you're out of my jurisdiction today! And I'm filing assault charges!"

The special agent rolled his eyes and waved the other man off. "Yeah, yeah, yeah. Tell it to the director. He hates your guts as much as I do."

Stonewall's red face was probably the result of a combination of pain, embarrassment, and high blood pressure as he stormed down the hallway. When Parrish faced the others in the room, the three other agents failed at hiding their grins— Stonewall was their direct supervisor, and no love was lost between the agents and their superior.

Ian snorted and crossed his arms over his massive chest. "Damn. Even though I'm still pissed at you, that made my day —hell, probably my week, but don't tell my pregnant wife that. And while I still want to deck the asshole myself, I don't feel like doing five years in the slammer."

Ten minutes later, Ian and Watts left the building and met the other two men in the parking lot. Ian eyed Carl. "You okay?"

"Never better." The man's eye roll belied his response.

"Want to tell me who your alibi is? You know, the one you don't want to expose?" Ian wasn't stupid. If Carl had someone who could provide him with an alibi, but he wouldn't divulge who it was, that meant the person was a closeted submissive with a very public persona. The last thing the Dom would do was out someone in the lifestyle unless it was necessary.

Crossing his arms, Carl shook his head. "No, I don't. And don't ask me again, Ian. I hope that dickhead agent is looking at someone else besides me for killing those women because I sure as hell didn't do it."

Before anyone could respond, Watts's agency pager went off, and he glanced at the text message. "Shit." Pulling his keys out of his pocket, he handed them to Ian. "Got a reported hostage situation at the federal courthouse. Take the truck back to your place, and I'll pick it up when I can."

As the HRT negotiator ran back into the building to get his gear, Ian pushed the door unlock button on the key fob. "Let's get the fuck out of here. You coming back with us for the barbecue, or do you want me to drop you off at your place?" he asked Carl. "I assume they didn't let you drive here."

"No, they didn't." He arched an eyebrow, which only further enhanced his vampire look. Give him fangs, pale his skin a few shades, and put him in his club leathers, and he'd give Bela Lugosi a run for his money. "Sure you want a serial killer suspect at the party?"

Ian slapped the man on the back. "No, but I do want my friend there."

SMILING, the Dom carefully cut out another newspaper article about his latest masterpiece. To announce he was the artist killing submissives would be the end of his work. No. That couldn't be allowed. There were too many more women who deserved to be turned into pieces of art. But after he left this world, they would discover all the evidence he was leaving behind, and then everyone would know his name. He would be famous. For generations, they'd hear all about how he held this city in his hands, sending waves of fear throughout the submissives who were always looking over their shoulders, wondering who he was and if they would be his next victim.

Not every submissive was lucky enough to be chosen, to be added to the list of women who had begged him for death. Initially, he hadn't been choosy—he'd admit that now. But over time, he realized the stronger ones—those who put up a fight—were the most satisfying when he finally broke them.

After Masterpiece #4, Naomi Nguyen, he'd started video-taping his time with them, savoring every crack of the whip, every scream of pain, every plea for him to end their suffering. Little did they know, in his world, they didn't have a safeword. Nothing they could say would make him stop until *he* decided it was time. *He* made the rules.

Carefully placing the article in a photo album next to the others, he adjusted his headphones as he listened to the play-back of Masterpiece #6 cursing his soul. Unfortunately for her, his soul had been cursed long before he'd ever met her. Closing the album, he set it on the shelf in his living room and then studied the photographs on the coffee table. Each one was of a submissive who'd caught his eye. It was amazing how much information about themselves people put on social media.

Hmm. Which lucky submissive would become Master-piece #10?

PART TWO

TRIDENT SECURITY
OMEGA TEAM

Seven

Standing in line to order his caffeine fix, a petite brunette in front of Logan caught his attention when she glanced over her shoulder at him with assessing brown eyes as if sensing someone larger loomed behind her. She studied him for a moment before facing forward again. He hadn't intended to get in her personal space, but it was crowded in the small shop, and if he moved back, he'd step on one of the two little kids standing behind him with their mother.

In her late twenties, he guessed, the brunette was about six inches shorter than him, with a curvy but toned frame and brown hair that stopped just below her shoulders. A snug, pale blue T-shirt stretched across her back, and his gaze shifted lower to her scrumptious, denim-covered backside. The jeans were faded in all the right places and fit her like a glove. When she approached the counter, he loved how the globes of her ass swayed with the movement and wished he had the right to run his hands over them.

Damn! He shifted his own hips and forced himself to look away. At least he didn't have to worry anymore about the temporary impotence, which the doctors had said resulted from his PTSD. That had lasted about six months, and he'd almost taken out a billboard ad to celebrate his first hard-on after returning to the States. Unfortunately, he hadn't used it or any of the ones that'd followed—at least not with a woman. He was afraid of things not working right if he got involved with someone, even though he had no trouble jacking off. He was also terrified of what might happen after having sex with a woman. His sleep usually resulted in a lot of swinging of fists and kicking of feet when the nightmares plagued him. There had actually been a few times he'd fallen off the bed onto the floor fighting an invisible enemy.

"Excuse me, sir? You're next."

Shaking his head to clear it, Logan stepped toward the counter, where the barista was waiting for him, and realized, with a hint of disappointment, the woman he'd been fantasizing about was already on her way out the door. *Oh, well*. It didn't matter since he wasn't the horn-dog he'd been years before, and hitting on her was out of the question. At least it was for now . . . he had more important things on his mind than getting laid. There was a mandatory meeting at the office this morning, and the main topic was going to be the teams' assignments, including the Kink Killer case. Maybe when things calmed down a little, he'd consider hooking up with a woman. Not anything long-term, just the occasional roll in the sack with no strings attached.

Logan placed and paid for his order of a plain black coffee and then stepped to the other end of the counter to wait for it. When a pretty blonde handed the brew to him with a huge, inviting smile, he thanked her and then headed for the door. Compared to the woman who'd caught his eye a few minutes earlier, the coed behind the counter was barely out of her teens, which was far too young for him.

Checking his watch as he exited the shop, he noted he had

fifteen minutes to make the five-minute drive to the TS compound.

When he stepped outside, the morning sun had risen further, and he lifted his face, enjoying the heat momentarily. It'd been two days since his team had returned from their final training mission in the Rockies, and Logan finally felt warm again. After the freezing temperatures they'd endured, in addition to everything else they'd gone through, he didn't want to see another snowflake for at least a year.

Striding to his car, he slowed when he saw three punks in their early twenties surrounding the woman from the coffee line, and she didn't look happy about it. They had the typical thug-life look to them: baggy clothes, with the waistband of their jeans hanging three-quarters of the way down their asses, white wife-beaters on their thin torsos, and $150 Jordan sneakers on their feet.

Logan placed his coffee on the hood of his truck and stepped closer to the group.

"Come on, sweet thing," one of them tried to cajole her. "Me and the boys'll show you a good time. A few lines, and you'll be begging for it, baby."

Yeah, that was fucking original, asshole. Unimaginative flattery like that will get you nowhere.

Before the woman could answer, Logan growled and moved in front of her, pushing the thugs back with just his mere size. After all his workouts, his muscles were back to where they'd been before his capture, and his shoulders were broader than the three dickheads' put together. He also stood at least three inches above the tallest. "It doesn't look like the lady is interested in you, your lines, or your good time, so take a hike."

At least one of them was too stupid to take Logan's advice and pulled out a switchblade. When the retired Marine heard the *snick,* he went on the offensive. His hand snapped out, snatched the idiot's wrist, and twisted until the open blade fell harmlessly to the pavement, and a scream of pain filled the air. One of the other punks abandoned his buddies and took off running, but the third asshole lunged forward to help his friend, who was now kneeling on the asphalt, begging to be released. Keeping a firm grip on the wrist he was inches away from breaking, Logan sidestepped the second attack and kicked the guy in the knee, dropping him to the ground next to his buddy. Another howl of agony joined the first.

With an eye on the now-disabled assailants, Logan glanced at the woman to ensure she was okay. What he hadn't expected to see was her arms crossed over her chest, her right hip cocked to the side and the pissed-off glare on her face that wasn't directed at either of the men who'd been harassing her. Instead, her anger was aimed at him. *What the fuck?*

"If you're okay, can you call the cops?" Logan asked, unsure what her problem was.

Lifting the hem of her shirt about two inches, she flashed a silver shield clipped to her belt. "I *am* a cop, and I didn't need your help, *thank you.*" The last two words were said in a sarcastic tone, which he could have let slide, but then she had to add, "Now, unless you want to end up in a cell next to them, I suggest you leave."

Logan couldn't have been more stunned if she'd hit him with a two-by-four.

Well, fuck this shit.

Letting go of dirtbag number one, he stepped back and brushed his hands together. "Sorry I came to your defense like my parents taught me to. Next time, I'll ask if a woman is a cop or if she needs help first before I jump in with my Superman routine. Have a nice day." Yeah, his sarcastic tone matched hers, but he didn't care.

Striding back to his truck without a backward glance, Logan grabbed his coffee off the hood, climbed in, and started the engine. Once he put it in drive, he finally looked over at the woman, who had told the punks to get lost as Logan had walked away. She glared at him as he pulled out of the parking space before giving her a snappy salute on his way to the exit.

DAKOTA STARED at the back of the blue pickup truck as it drove past her. Why did every freaking alpha male think every woman needed to be saved? She'd been about to put those punks in their place when the good-looking Lone Ranger had ridden in to save all of humanity. Well, at least this little corner of it. Then he'd fucking saluted her.

Maybe if you'd been a little less sarcastic, he wouldn't have been so insulted. Shit. Oh well, too late to fix it now.

In a way, she felt bad about how she'd gone off on him, but her morning had already sucked and was possibly going to go downhill from there. The federal agent she'd been partnered with for the past few months had been a nice enough guy, but he sucked at being a Dom. Cameron Davis couldn't cut it, and it was obvious to the members of the club they'd been assigned to that the man didn't belong in the lifestyle. She'd been torn between keeping her mouth shut and not rocking the boat and reporting it to SAC Parrish. The two hadn't played in public and had used the private playrooms for appearances only. The only things that had occurred behind closed doors had been a comparison of notes, conversations about the weather, and reading books they'd both stuck in Davis's *alleged* toy bag. Before returning to the crowd, they messed up their hair and clothes, then did some pushups to get sweaty and give a freshly-fucked flush to their faces.

Each night, after leaving the club, Davis had driven her "home" to the condo she was sharing with another female FBI agent, Gina Harvey. Again, it was for appearances. Parrish hadn't wanted any of the UCs to return to their private residences in case the Kink Killer had targeted them. But so far, neither woman had been approached by anyone after being dropped off in the parking lot.

Yesterday, Davis had finally admitted to himself and her that his inability to blend in with those in the lifestyle was a deterrent to their investigation. He'd gone to Parrish and suggested he be reassigned to a perimeter post. The dominant SAC had agreed and arranged for Dakota to partner with an agent from Trident Security. Ian Sawyer had told her to meet him at the company compound at 0900 to be introduced to Logan Reese, and she hoped he was a better UC than Davis. Two more victims had been tortured, killed, and dumped in the Tampa area since Dakota had joined the task force. It grated on all involved in the case that they still had no leads on who the sadistic bastard was.

Climbing in her SUV, she had an hour to kill before her meeting, so she drove to Oaklawn Cemetery, where her mother was buried. Tina Marie Swift had been an OR nurse at Tampa General Hospital, but her life had been cut short by a heart attack at the young age of forty-one when Dakota had been a freshman in high school. Tina's family and friends had been devastated by the loss of the vibrant woman who always had a smile on her face.

Stopping the vehicle near the section where her mother's grave was located, Dakota climbed out and walked the rest of the way. It had been a few weeks since she'd last been there, but her father must have visited in the last day or so because the roses he always brought sat on the top of the granite marker. While Gavin Swift had been hard on his children, pushing them to be the best of the best, he'd been madly in love with his wife of nineteen years. Yes, they'd had their ups and downs, like every other married couple, but Gavin had worshiped the ground Tina walked on and vice versa.

"Hey, Mom," Dakota said as she squatted beside the grave. Since she had a meeting soon, she didn't want to kneel and get grass stains on her jeans. One of the things she loved about working undercover was that she got to choose what to wear each day instead of the mandatory polyester uniform.

She continued to talk to her mother as she pulled a few weeds out from around the base of the gravestone. After fifteen years, she still sought advice from the woman who'd given birth to her, even though Tina could no longer pass on her words of wisdom. Dakota would talk about both her professional and personal life and believed her mother would have been proud of what she'd achieved in both. She just wished her father could be proud of her too.

Standing, she brushed her hands together to rid them of the dirt and blades of grass. She kept a bottle of hand sanitizer in her work duffel bag, which was sitting in the trunk of her vehicle. After cleaning up, she said goodbye one more time to her mother and then left the cemetery, feeling a little better about her day. Now, it was time to head to Trident and meet Mr. Logan Reese—her new partner and pretend Dom.

God help me.

TRIDENT SECURITY
OMEGA TEAM

Eight

"All right, everyone here?" Ian asked as he set his coffee at the head of the conference table in the Trident Security office and then took his seat.

Pushing the brunette from where she'd been hovering in his mind, Logan glanced around at the others in the room. Most of the Alpha Team, sans Boomer and Brody, and all of Omega were there. Jake Donovan was also sitting in on the meeting while in town for a few days. He'd been in San Diego for the last eighteen months but would return to Tampa to rejoin the Alpha team in about eight weeks. The remaining two attendees were Travis "Tiny" Daultry, head of The Covenant security, and Doug "Bullseye" Henderson, recently hired by the Sawyer brothers to run the Private Protection Division. He'd received the nickname after taking a bullet protecting Ian's goddaughter. Judging by the number of folders sitting in front of Boss-man, they would all be busy with assignments over the next few weeks.

Across the table, Knight cleared his throat. "Before you get started, Mallory sent me an email last night, and once again, she wanted to thank everyone."

The young coed had been kidnapped by four bank robbers while taking nature photographs in the Rockies. The men had nothing to lose since they'd murdered a guard and a cop during their escape and had been hiding out in the mountains where the Omega Team had been doing their trek back to civilization. The team had managed to rescue her. Three of the criminals hadn't survived, and the fourth was handed over to the local law enforcement. During the hike out of the wilderness, Mallory and Knight had developed a sibling-like bond, and he'd given her his email and cell number in case she ever needed anything.

Ian smiled. "Angie was wondering how she was doing."

"Other than being sore, she's doing okay, apparently. She's a strong girl and will probably recover well. In fact, she said she's thinking of enlisting and is going to talk to the local recruiters." When several people opened their mouths, Knight held up his hand with a chuckle. "And no, she hasn't decided which branch. But I may have pushed the Navy a bit in my reply."

Everyone laughed when Lindsey threw a pen at him, which he caught. "That's wishful thinking on your part, Batman. Cowboy and I impressed her more than any of you slackers did, and I'll bet you a hundred dollars she'll join the Corps."

"You're on!"

DeAngelis rolled his eyes. "Jeez, Ian, the Omega Team sucks at betting. They've gotta come up with stuff that's original."

"Uh-uh," Ian responded with a smirk. "It's bad enough Egghead keeps losing to you then upping the ante for the next time. I'm starting to think he enjoys losing. I could've really done without his performance the other night. It'll take years to bleach that out of my mind. I have no idea how Fancy puts up with him."

Devon, DeAngelis, McCabe, and Foster roared with laughter. The rest of Omega and Donovan had missed the show Brody had to give after losing another bet to his best friend. Logan wasn't sure if he was glad or disappointed over the fact. The Dom had to wear a pair of leather short-shorts and a headband with two bouncing penises on it while singing karaoke on the center stage at The Covenant. Apparently, his version of "Honky Tonk Badonkadonk" was what nightmares are made of, and most of the crowd had almost needed oxygen masks from laughing so hard.

A comfortable but insulting banter started up among the different military branches over what the bet should be before Ian rapped his knuckles on the table. "All right, enough. Sling the mud later. We've got a lot on today's agenda."

When the room quieted, he continued, "First things first, Tiny has received a promotion and other duties. In addition to the club, he's now in charge of the compound as well. Any issues that pop up with the guards or security measures, he's your man." A few smiles and words of congratulations came from around the table, and the big man thanked them.

"Next up, Bullseye, a few things have changed on your agenda. Princess Tahira will *not* be coming to Tampa at the end of next month. Instead, she's going on a cruise with her cousins and a few friends. According to Amar, the royal guard will take the trip with her, so you're off the hook."

Her Royal Highness was from the small, North African nation of Timasur and often visited one of the royal family's vacation homes located in Clearwater. When monarchy members were in Florida, TS coordinated with their head of security, Mousaf Amar, and assisted in guarding them.

"I also received a call from Abigail over at Black Diamond Records. Summer Hayes closed on an estate last week in Indian Shores, and the security system is outdated. Head over there either today or tomorrow and evaluate what needs to be done for a full upgrade, then send the proposal to Abigail, and she'll get it approved. Summer will be touring Canada over the next four weeks, so that's your time frame for the completed job."

While most of the people in the conference room hadn't noticed Mancini's eyebrows raise at the mention of the country singer, Logan had. It seemed the pretty blonde had caught his interest when they'd met a few months back at a barbecue here at the compound, but she'd given him the brushoff—polite as it had been.

Ian slid three folders down the table to Knight, Abbott, and Mancini. "You three are heading to South America—Argentina, to be exact. The FBI has another lead on the white slavery case, and until they figure out if there's a leak in their house, you'll be going undercover. Whenever they've tried to get close to Emmanuel Diaz, the operation closes shop and moves. Batman, since you're probably the most familiar with Diaz from the missions with Team Four, your assignment is to work your way into his cartel. Your cover will be a buyer for a few overseas contacts with very specific tastes and requests. Costello and Romeo, you'll be his backup. You're a couple and will be down there as missionaries."

Mancini arched an eyebrow. "Missionaries? Doing what?"

"The missionary position," Devon cracked with a grin as little JD slept on his shoulder, eliciting another round of laughter and a few eye rolls.

Chuckling also came from the doorway as two more people entered the room. Logan and the rest of Omega had all been introduced at one time or another to T. Carter and Jordyn Alvarez. Not only were the couple spies for a covert agency for the United States, but they were also friends of the Alpha Team and members of The Covenant. Carter held out a chair for Jordyn before taking a seat next to her. "Devil Dog beat me to the pun," he said, "but since his kid's adorable, and that's the only way he can beat me at anything, I'll let it slide."

"Fuck you, jackass."

"Swear jar!" a few people were quick to call out. Between JD, Marco's daughter, Mara, and Ian and Angie expecting, they were trying to cut down on the amount of foul language at the compound, which was going to be a major feat, hence the $5 per curse "swear jar." The money collected was going to Healing Heroes, a non-profit that had trained their assistant mechanic's service dog, Jagger.

Taking JD from his father, Jordyn settled into her chair as the baby briefly opened his eyes, yawned, then went back to sleep on her shoulder. "You'll be at Sister Patrice's orphanage under the guise of improving the well system, which is currently in the works anyway. Your cover is already in place as environmentalists."

"An orphanage?" Lindsey asked. "We're not putting any kids in the line of fire, are we?"

Carter shook his head. "No. We wouldn't do that. Sister Patrice has developed her own network of mercenaries, I guess you can call them, for lack of a better term. They'll guard the orphanage, but we don't foresee any issues. You'll only be sleeping there for appearances. Just watch your backs coming and going from the area. It's about ten miles from Diaz's current setup—close enough for your cover to work."

"Sister Patrice is a friend of mine," Jordyn added. "It won't be the first time the orphanage was used for a mission. She's tough as nails and can take care of her kids."

"Amen to that." Ian's gaze went back to the three agents going on the assignment. "CC will be flying you down to Argentina tomorrow. Polo is putting together everything you'll need—IDs, communications, weapons, et cetera—while Nathan is fine-tuning an ironclad persona for you, Batman.

It's one that Deimos has been cultivating for years, in case the need ever arose." Deimos was the agency Carter and Jordyn worked for, and up until a few months ago, none of the others in the room had known it existed. "Everything you need to know about 'Glen Hamilton' is in your file. The jet will be loaded and ready for an oh-eight-hundred flight. In the meantime, I put everything we've got on Diaz and his current right-hand man, Felix Secada, on your desks. You three can hit that now. Jordyn will fill you in on the details of Sister Patrice's place in a few. Let me know if you have any questions."

Dismissed, the trio stood and left the room to dive into what was probably a mountain of intelligence as Ian addressed the rest of them. "Moving on. Boomer and Egghead will be out of town for at least the next seven to ten days on an intel assignment. Devon is also heading out for a few days with Carter and Jordyn on another detail. Now, as you all know, the FBI is finally, *finally*, going to use us for the Kink Killer investigation instead of leaving us sitting on the sidelines looking pretty. It only took how many months? Whatever. Anyway, the higher-ups fucked Stonewall hard and dry for not utilizing all available resources. While he's trying to get the plug out of his ass without using his hands, Parrish is in charge. I'll put $10 in the swear jar later."

Ian pointed to the remaining members of the Omega Team. "You four will be paired up with LEOs from Tampa PD and the FBI." LEO was short for a law enforcement officer on either the local, state, or federal level. "Foster and McCabe, your partners have minimal training as submissives for this assignment, while Morrison and Reese, yours have been in the lifestyle for at least a few years. You'll meet them later today, and then tonight, you'll start basic Dom training in The Covenant with Polo. Foster and McCabe, I want you and your partners there too, so you all can get to know each other well enough to pass as D/s couples."

Stunned, Logan managed to keep his outward appearance composed. *Dom training? Partnered with a submissive woman who was also an FBI agent or TPD officer? He can't be serious. Scratch that—he is serious.*

As if he'd sensed his agent's shock, Ian added, "The reason I'm not using the Alpha Team on this is that they're too well-known in the lifestyle community. Foster and McCabe have only played in The Covenant, and you two haven't played at all, so no one in the other clubs should recognize you. As for our club, there will be an Alpha Team member present during open club hours. With the security measures we've put in place over the past few months, I'm hoping we've given this bastard enough deterrents to avoid targeting one of our subs. Reese, your partner had issues with her last one from the FBI—which I'll discuss with you later—so we're switching the club she was assigned to. While it's not unusual for subs and Doms to show up with a new one shortly after ending a contract with another, I don't want to take chances the UNSUB would question her walking in with someone new. The first few shifts you'll be doing will be on perimeter watch outside one of the clubs until Polo thinks you won't be a dumb-dumb Dom. Same goes for you, Morrison. You'll need to know how to act in there so you don't draw any scrutiny—it'll defeat the purpose of being there. Experienced Doms and subs can pick out a newbie like a shark zeroing in on a bucket of chum."

He paused to check a text message when his cell phone chirped. "All right, that's it for now. Reese, grab a fresh coffee and have a seat in my office—your partner should be here in a few minutes. Morrison, you'll be introduced to yours tonight at the club. In the meantime, follow up on that embezzlement case you're working on. McCabe. Foster. You two head over to the FBI office—Parrish will introduce you to your partners."

Ian stood, signaling the end of the meeting. "Reverend, I need you for a minute."

As Jake Donovan followed their boss out into the hallway, the others stood and began to disperse. When Devon offered to take JD back from Jordyn, the petite woman shook her head, cuddling the baby closer. "Nope. I'll keep him while I run over to chat with Angie and Kristen for a bit before we head to the airport. I don't get to hold him often enough."

When she left the room, Devon looked at Carter and laughed. "Do I hear a biological clock ticking?"

The spy shrugged as they headed for the door. "I asked, but she wants to wait at least another year or two while we work out the logistics, so we can both continue to take assignments. I just need you guys to continue with the procreations, so she can get her baby fix every now and then."

Logan was the last one out the door. Taking Boss-man's advice, he turned left and walked into the small employee kitchen to refill his coffee before ambling back down the long hallway in the other direction to Ian's office. He'd just sat in one of the guest chairs when Ian strolled in, shutting the door behind him.

"How are things with Doc Dunbar?" his boss asked, taking his seat behind the large, dark wood desk.

Logan had expected this—it had been a while since Ian had asked how the therapy sessions were going. "Good. No problems have popped up lately. But I'm sure she's already told you that. I like her—she's as good as Dr. Tennyson."

"Glad to hear it. I've known Trudy for a few years, and she's helped us with some situations and cases in the past. The doc is also one of the psychologists we refer club members to."

Logan's eyebrow shot up in surprise. "She's into the . . . um . . . lifestyle?"

"No, she's not, and I wouldn't have outed her like that

without her consent if she were. Members of the BDSM community like their privacy. It's one of the reasons for the non-disclosure contract you all had to sign."

The team had also been told if they saw anyone who they knew was a member of The Covenant out in public, they were to act like they didn't know them or as if they knew them from somewhere else. Ian sat back in his chair. "Look, I know you're about to get pushed out of your comfort zone, but I think you might benefit from it in addition to dealing with the case. But if you've got a problem with it, now is the time to tell me."

Before Logan could respond, the intercom on the desk buzzed, and Colleen's voice came through the speaker. "Ian, Officer Swift is here."

The boss stabbed a red button on the device. "Send her in." Ian stood and pinned Logan with a stare. "Give it a shot. You'll have a week or two before you'll be going into one of the clubs. If you find you can't do it, let me know—we'll move people around and leave you on a perimeter detail."

Unsure of what Ian had meant when he'd said Logan would benefit from learning to be a Dom, Logan figured the assignment wouldn't have been given to him if it was expected he would fail. Taking a deep breath, he let it out and nodded. "Okay. I'll give it a try."

The door behind him swung open, and he glanced over his shoulder to get his first look at the woman he'd be seeing a lot of very soon—literally. A brunette walked in, and not just any brunette, but the hot little number from the coffee shop, who'd basically told him to mind his own fucking business. The woman he'd been thinking about since he'd pulled out of the shopping center and driven to the compound. While her attitude had pissed him off at first, the more he thought about how she'd stood up to him, the more it turned him on. If they'd been in Hollywood, it would have made for a great meet-cute—the scene in a movie when a romantic couple meets for the first time.

Logan grinned as he stood. *The day is about to get a lot more interesting.*

Nine

Pulling up to the guard shack and gate in the fence surrounding the Trident Security property, Dakota handed her license and department ID to the man on duty. It was her first time here, and she wasn't surprised the company with high government clearance had more than adequate security measures. The physically fit guard had to be former military or law enforcement by the way he carried himself. Dressed in tan cargo pants and a navy-blue polo shirt, his eyes were sharp and assessing, even though his demeanor was friendly. Strapped to his hip was a holstered Smith & Wesson .40 caliber handgun. Dakota imagined he could easily handle any problems that may arise on his shift.

After confirming her identity, he opened the gate and waved her through. She drove further up the long driveway until the trees on either side revealed the compound. Sawyer had told her to drive through the second gate on the interior fence that separated The Covenant from the other buildings. If she hadn't been told what to expect, she'd never have believed the über private kink club was behind the metal and concrete walls of a warehouse.

The second gate slid open as she approached. Glancing around, Dakota spotted several security cameras. Someone had known her vehicle was there and had granted her access to the inner sanctum. She parked next to the first building on that side of the fence as the text message with directions to the compound she'd received had instructed. The place was huge, with two other warehouses further down. In between the buildings, she'd spotted an obstacle course and a helicopter pad with—*holy shit*.

If Dakota wasn't mistaken, that bird was an MH-X Silent Hawk. *They have a fucking stealth chopper! That is so freaking cool!*

Ric was an amateur helicopter pilot who always showed her books, magazines, and internet articles about the latest aircrafts with all the bells and whistles. Her friend and co-worker would be salivating right then if he was there.

Barking and voices caught her attention as she opened the driver's door and climbed out. To the south of the parking lot was what looked like a Hogan's Alley, similar to what the FBI and other agencies used for training. It was set up like any Main Street, USA, with storefronts propped up by angled beams behind them. Metal targets could pop up or swing out from various alleys, windows, and doors for shooting practice. Next to that was a four-story concrete building that was missing the glass from its windows. It was similar to what they had at the police academy, where officers would do searches for the bad guys and practice responding to different scenarios. The buildings usually had interior walls which could be moved around to change the setup, so no one got complacent with the same routine.

Between the parking lot and the Hogan's Alley stood a group of six men and women, each with a K9 practically glued to their left leg. A woman with brown hair pulled up in a ponytail was demonstrating the "stay" command using hand signals with a lab mix. The other five dogs were either Belgian Malinois or German shepherds, both excellent breeds for law enforcement, military, or private security K9s. Dakota chuckled as the Malinois at the far-left end apparently got bored. He laid down and rolled over onto his back as if asking for a belly rub. Instead of being annoyed at the dog's inability to focus, the instructor smiled and shook her head like it was a regular occurrence with him.

Dakota glanced around the compound again before heading to the door leading to the Trident Security offices. Inside, she introduced herself to the receptionist, who then picked up the landline phone on her desk and stabbed one of the preprogrammed buttons on it. "Ian, Officer Swift is here."

After receiving a response and hanging up, the young woman pointed to a closed door behind her. "He's waiting for you. Go right in."

"Thanks." It had been about two weeks since she'd last seen the co-owner of the private company at a task force meeting. The more she interacted with the man, the more her respect and admiration for him grew. While he could be one of the most sarcastic people she'd ever meet, it was evident he was a good leader as well as an excellent Dom. From the bits and pieces of conversations she'd had with him or overheard these past few months, she got the impression his wife was a bratty submissive who kept him on his toes—he'd probably accept nothing less.

Turning the knob, Dakota pushed the door open and stepped into an office that clearly belonged to a man. The decor was mostly wood and leather, with earth tones giving a warm feel to the room. Sawyer was standing behind his desk and pointed to an empty chair in front of it. "Swift, have a seat. Thanks for coming. This is your new partner, Logan Reese, otherwise known as Cowboy. Logan, Officer Dakota Swift from TPD."

As she approached, her gaze finally shifted to the other man in the room, who'd peered at her over his shoulder before standing with a huge grin on his face. *Oh shit.* It was the Lone Ranger from the coffee shop parking lot—how hadn't she noticed how good-looking he was? *Because you were too busy being a bitch to him.*

A deep, annoying chuckle emanated from his throat as he gestured toward the iced coffee in her hand. "We sort of met already, Boss-man, but it's nice to put a name to the face. It's a pleasure to meet you, *Officer* Swift."

It was impossible to mistake the sarcasm in his voice, and Dakota rolled her eyes. The tone of her response matched his. "Why doesn't it surprise me that your nickname is 'Cowboy'?"

"Problem?" Ian frowned while glancing back and forth between them.

"No," they replied simultaneously. Dakota wished she could wipe the amused smirk off Reese's face—his handsome face with those smoldering eyes and lush bottom lip that was ripe enough for a nibble. *Damn.*

"Good. Keep it that way. Take a seat, and let's get started."

Sitting again, Ian leaned back and settled into the soft, black leather as Dakota and Reese sat in the guest chairs opposite him. "Swift, as I told you on the phone, Reese is a former Marine with no Dom training. That changes tonight. We have a few UC couples meeting at The Covenant this afternoon at sixteen-hundred hours. The newbies will be getting a crash course on how to pass themselves off as Doms or subs. In the meantime, the two of you will spend your duty shifts for the next two weeks monitoring the perimeter of Heat—see if anyone looks suspicious or appears to follow a sub out of the area. Remember, this bastard is doing a damn good job of blending in, so it could be anyone."

His gaze flitted to Reese, and Dakota's automatically

followed. She tried to ignore the scent of her new partner's cologne as it wafted in her direction every now and then. She didn't know what brand it was, but damn, whatever it was, he wore it well.

Giving herself a mental shake, she tried to concentrate on what Sawyer was saying. "Cowboy, Dakota's been on this detail for a few months now and is up to date on everything we have. Pick her brain whenever you can. When you've finally cleared for the club scene, and something is said or done that you're not sure about, ask her—she's been in the lifestyle for a few years, and there shouldn't be much she hasn't encountered before."

Picking up a business card that had been sitting on the desk, Ian handed it to Reese. "Hit that place today or tomorrow. It's got a larger selection of fet-wear for men than we have in the club's boutique—Dakota can help you out if necessary. Pick up a few pairs of leather pants and a vest or two and give the receipts to Colleen for reimbursement. Motorcycle or western boots are preferred by most Doms. At the training later today, Polo will get you set up with a personal play bag for you to bring into the clubs. The standard items will be in it for appearances, but it also has a secret compartment for a few toys we don't want anyone to know you're carrying. Polo will go over all that with you. Dakota, dress in appropriate fet-wear for all training sessions. I want you to be completely comfortable with each other before we turn you loose. Since The Covenant, Heat, and most of the other clubs are closed on Mondays, I suggest you two go out for a drink and something to eat after training and get to know each other better. It's imperative that you look like a D/s couple at all times."

Reese cleared his throat, clearly uncomfortable with what he was about to say or ask. "Does that mean we need to . . . um . . . play at the clubs?"

Before Ian could answer, Dakota shook her head, making

sure she looked and sounded like the professional she was. "Not exactly. With my last partner, we did the basics for appearances—I'll kneel at your feet when you're sitting and appear as a submissive in every way. Davis and I made it known we weren't into exhibitionism, so we disappeared into one of the playrooms for about an hour, then made it look like we'd had an intense scene before joining the crowd again. In your toy bag, there will be a tablet that's patched into the club's surveillance system, so we can monitor what's going on out in the public areas while we're supposedly scening."

"After talking it over with Parrish, we're updating that," Ian said before Reese could respond, and Dakota's jaw nearly dropped to the floor. "A majority of the victims were known to be brattier than the others. We're instructing all the UC subs to step up their game. With any luck, our killer will target one of you. So, that means, yes, you might be doing some scenes in the public areas. Obviously, we're not asking you to have sex or anything close to it, but a few punishments here and there may get the attention of our UNSUB. Again, Marco will be going over all this with you later." He glanced at his watch. "I've got another meeting I need to get to, so unless there are any immediate questions or concerns . . ." Reese shook his head, and Dakota forced herself to do the same. Ian stood. "Then you're on duty at sixteen-hundred hours."

"Thanks, Boss-man," Reese said, getting to his feet. When Dakota stood, he swept his hand to the door. "After you."

She cleared her throat. "Thanks, Ian."

As Dakota strode toward the door, her mind in a whirlwind, she felt rather than heard her new partner on her heels. When she reached the main reception area, a hand wrapped around her elbow, stopping her short. Reese turned her to face him. "Look, we obviously got off on the wrong foot earlier. Can we start fresh?"

She arched an eyebrow at him and was surprised when he

held out his hand. "Hi, I'm Logan Reese. Retired Marine, hopeless gentleman, and all-around good egg. And you?"

Unable to stop the grin that spread across her face, she glanced at his hand a moment longer before shaking it. "Dakota Swift. Tampa PD, grouchy bitch, and a bit scrambled."

If she'd thought he was good-looking when he smirked, he was devastating when he full-out smiled. "That wasn't so hard now, was it? Care to join me on my shopping excursion? I honestly have no idea what's in when it comes to leather."

A part of her wanted to take him up on that, curious to see how he looked in snug, black leather pants, but his charm was getting to her, and no way was she getting involved with someone she worked with. Not while her undercover career was at stake. "Um . . . I think I'll pass. I have a few things I need to take care of before coming back here later. I'm sure you'll do just fine. Ask for Linda. She'll be more than happy to help you. It's what she does best."

Of course, she didn't add that Mistress Linda was a sadist. Let him find out for himself. *Hmm.* Her inner brat was already making an appearance. "Gotta run. See you later."

Before she could change her mind, she turned on her heel and made a beeline for the door.

OMEGA TEAM
TRIDENT SECURITY

TEN

Following his new partner to the reception area, Logan watched as she marched out the door and headed to her car. Damn, he thought with a grin—Officer Dakota Swift is a real firecracker. Not only was she hot as hell, but she also had a temper and a chip on her shoulder to boot —a chip Logan was looking forward to knocking off. Maybe this detail wouldn't be so bad—at least he was attracted to her. Too bad that attraction was one-sided.

"Darn it!"

Logan turned his attention to Trident's office manager as Colleen slammed the phone down on its cradle. Currently, they were the only two people in the outer reception area.

"Something wrong?" he asked when she stood from her desk in a huff.

"Yeah. Jake's over in the club with Roxy and has his cell turned off. Roxy does too. They must be downstairs in the pit because they're not picking up the landline, and Tap Corrigan at TS West needs to talk to him ASAP—as if I didn't have enough to do today." She waved her hand over the files and correspondence stacked in neat but high piles on her desk.

It was unlike the woman to be stressed out—she ran the office with model efficiency. "I'll run over and get him for you," he offered since he didn't have anything pressing to take care of at the moment.

"Really? Oh, that would be awesome, Logan." Her desk phone rang, and she thanked him profusely before sitting again and picking up the handset. "Trident Security, how can I help you?"

Pushing the door to the parking lot open, Logan didn't notice any vehicles that hadn't been there when he arrived earlier, so that meant Officer Swift had already hightailed it out of there. On the far south side of the lot, Kat Michaelson, Boomer's wife, was working with the new hires for Trident's Personal Protection Division and the existing compound guards to train five K9s. Her aggressive and passive K9 training services were under contract with the Florida State Police and Tampa PD, and she was also hired to train dogs for professional and private use. Since the compound's BDSM club, The Covenant, had become fodder for the paparazzi recently, thanks to a bitch with a vendetta, changes to the security measures had been made. The eastern fence line had been extended out a quarter of a mile, and a new guardhouse and entry gate had been added. The wooded area between the compound and the main road helped keep prying eyes or cameras away from the club's entrance.

Two of the dogs would be on duty with the guards, while Beau, Trident's original K9, a lab/pit mix, would protect the inner compound, which was fenced off from the club's building and parking lot. Beau was currently lying at Kat's feet, so she'd probably been using him for demonstration purposes. The parking lots had cool surface treatments over concrete, which reflected sunlight instead of absorbing it, keeping it comfortable for the dogs' paws in the hot summer.

Logan slowed his pace as he observed Kat putting the

humans and their four-legged counterparts through their paces. Four out of the five dogs had been named Bravo, Delta, Sierra, and Mike. Only Ian Sawyer, a retired Navy SEAL and lifestyle Dominant, would use the military alphabet to spell out BDSM for the canines' names. The fifth dog had started out being called Glock, but the goofy Belgian Malinois had quickly gone through a moniker change. He was now officially known as FUBAR—fucked up beyond all recognition.

From what Boomer had mentioned earlier, FUBAR would probably be a training fail. Still, Kat would give the dog with the ridiculously extra-large ears a few more days to hopefully turn around. If he didn't, they'd find him a good home. If that happened, Logan would love to keep the dog, or any other one, having grown up with several, but he never knew when an assignment would keep him away. At least when he was here, he'd sometimes play fetch with Beau.

Passing through the pedestrian gate in the fence, he strode toward the warehouse that was home to The Covenant. The main entrance was up a flight of stairs on the second floor. It still amazed him that the metal-sided building was completely different inside. Reaching the top step, he found the place locked, as it usually was during off hours. A quick scan of his handprint on the device beside the door unlocked it for him. The system was used throughout the compound, including the residences on the far side.

Entering the Victorian-themed lobby, he crossed the plush burgundy carpet to the ornate wooden double doors with iron pulls. They looked like they came from a vintage castle somewhere. A lot of thought and money had gone into decorating this place.

Grabbing the left one, he opened the door and walked through.

The upper level was shaped like a horseshoe, overlooking the play floor below, which had been dubbed "the pit." A beautiful mahogany bar was to Logan's left, at the bottom of the "U," while sitting areas lined the balcony on both sides. At the far end was a small store, which sold fet-wear and adult toys, the office and supply room, and a hallway that lead to the new "garden." Logan had seen it once, and it was pretty cool, carpeted with soft, fake grass and filled with palm trees, tropical plants, and flowers. Of course, between all that were stations with spanking benches, St. Andrew's crosses, and other BDSM equipment. Overhead was a clear, retractable roof to let the light from the moon and stars come in at night. To keep out the bugs and any cameras attached to drones, helicopters, or satellites when the roof was open, there was a thin netting that those underneath could see through. However, from above, it reflected light off it, preventing anyone from seeing in.

Hearing murmured voices, Logan didn't see anyone and was about to head to the grand staircase that led to the pit, but a *crack* split the air, freezing him in place. Suddenly, he wasn't in Tampa anymore—hell, he wasn't in the United States anymore—he was back in that hellhole in Afghanistan. His eyes glazed over as his legs began to shake and his stomach clenched.

"Clutch," he whispered seconds before another *crack* echoed around him. When his best friend's nickname passed his lips a second time, it came out as a blood-curdling scream.

Jake "Reverend" Donovan descended the grand staircase as a bullwhip cracked from the center of the pit. Dr. Roxanne London, aka Mistress Roxy, was practicing her technique on the elevated stage. Instead of a submissive being restrained to the large, leather-covered St. Andrew's cross, there was an 11" x 14" piece of paper that was the Whip Master's current target.

He'd been in the Trident office when she'd called to let Ian know she would be in the club since neither Mitch nor any employees were around. Ian had then asked Jake to come over and check on the red-headed Domme. Apparently, she came to "practice" when she was having a bad day, refusing to take it out on her submissive wife, Kayla, or anyone else.

Plopping into a chair in the seating area to the right of the stage, Jake watched her in silence, knowing she was aware of his presence. She was a beautiful, tall woman, who drew lust-filled stares from men and women wherever she went, and if he weren't gay, he'd probably be lusting after her too.

When Jake had fallen in love with Ian and Devon's younger brother, they'd offered him a position establishing the Trident Security West Coast Team while Nick was finishing his last eighteen months on SEAL Team Four in San Diego. It'd worked out perfectly for everyone. Now that Nick only had eight weeks left before his retirement from the Navy was official, Jake had been packing up their condo in stages so that they could move after a much-deserved vacation to Hawaii.

After a meeting in Washington D.C. with the director and assistant director of the FBI, Jake had made a pit stop in Tampa for a few days before heading west again. While he was there, he'd run around getting the paperwork needed to transfer his and Nick's driver's licenses, vehicle registration, insurance, bank accounts, etc., back to Florida. At least they already had a furnished place to stay.

Ian and Devon had two other large apartments built behind theirs in the residential warehouse. One was Nick and Jake's, while the other belonged to Jenn, who the Alpha Team considered to be their niece, having served with her father on SEAL Team Four. She'd moved to Tampa from Virginia after her parents had been murdered a few years ago.

Dressed in jeans, white sneakers, and a green tank top, Roxy paused in her repeated strikes to the paper, which didn't have a slash on it due to her precise marksmanship. Picking up a bottle of water that had been sitting on the floor next to a white blouse she must have removed and her oversized, brown purse, she opened it and drank half of the clear liquid. A sheen of perspiration on her face, neck, and arms did nothing to compromise her beauty. If she hadn't been a pediatrician, she could have been a very successful model.

"Having a bad day?" Jake asked, remaining in his seat, his arms crossed over his chest, and his long, jean-clad legs stretched out before him.

Closing her eyes for a brief moment, she nodded her head. "Very. Lost a patient this morning. Eight years old. She never once cried during an appointment in all the years she was my patient, not even when getting a shot."

"What happened?'

"Cerebral hemorrhage. No warning. One minute she was alive, sitting in her classroom at school. The next, she was dead." Roxy's hazel eyes watered, but she held back her tears. "The ER contacted me when she was rushed in, but there was nothing anyone could do."

Taking a deep breath, she let it out and then placed the water bottle back on the floor before picking up the bullwhip again. "So, I'm spending my lunch hour assaulting an innocent piece of paper."

"The bratty eleven by fourteen probably deserves it."

A small smile appeared on Roxy's face. "Thanks, Jake, I needed that."

"Anytime."

When the sound of the large, wooden lobby doors opening sounded throughout the silent club, they both glanced up the stairs but didn't see anyone. It was probably Mitch or one of the employees coming in to do a stock inventory of the bar or store.

Turning back to the large cross, Roxy positioned herself,

reared back, and with a flick of her wrist, let the whip slice through the air. *Crack.*

Again, the paper moved when struck, but she still hadn't ripped it.

Crack.

"Cluuuuutcccchhhhh!"

What the fuck! Jake leaped from the chair as the terror-filled scream pierced the silence, and he ran for the stairs.

Behind him, Roxy dropped the whip to the stage floor. "My God, who is that?"

Jake didn't know what was going on or who had screamed, but he prepared himself for anything. Reaching the top step, he found Reese frozen, his eyes seeing something that wasn't there—something horrific that had taken him far away from where he stood.

Fuck a duck!

Familiar with veterans who suffered from PTSD and with the retired Marine's history, Jake approached cautiously. "Reese." No verbal answer, but the man's gaze flickered in his direction, so Jake tried again. "Cowboy, it's Jake. You okay?"

"Nooooooooo!" Reese roared and then swung his fist.

Thankfully, Jake was fast on his feet and had been ready for it. He brought his arm up, blocking the punch. "Reese!"

But the other man's traumatic experience still had him gripped in its talons. He lunged at Jake, tackling him to the floor. Jake struggled to get the upper hand and fend off the attack, all the while trying not to hurt Reese unless it became necessary. As they rolled around on the carpeted floor, knocking over a few chairs and pub tables, Jake saw Roxy breach the top stairs. "Stay back! PTS—*oomph.*" Reese had gotten a good shot to his opponent's left kidney.

Rolling to the right, Jake took Reese with him and then used a wrestling move to flip the man over so that he could restrain him in a tight hold. Jake's arms went under Reese's before clasping his hands behind the man's neck. He then wrapped his long legs around Reese's, pinning him in place. The struggling continued, but Jake had the controlling advantage. "Roxy! Get back! He's having a flashback!"

The pediatrician ignored his order and knelt next to the two men. It took Jake a moment to realize she had a wet bar towel in her hand and was running it over the exposed skin of Reese's arms, neck, and face.

"Easy," she cooed softly. "Come back to Tampa . . . you're safe here. What's his name, again? I only met him once."

Jake felt Reese's struggling wane a bit, but his lungs heaved for oxygen. "Logan Reese. Or use his nickname, 'Cowboy.' Just be careful."

"Logan . . . you're safe . . . you're with friends . . . it's okay . . . come back, Cowboy." As the good doctor talked the man down, the tightness of his muscles eased marginally. "That's it . . . you're safe, Cowboy. You're not in that bad place anymore. You're in Tampa, among friends."

Reese finally stilled, and then Jake's heart clenched as a sob broke loose from the man's chest. With caution, Jake relaxed his grip. When it appeared the worst was over, he released Reese, who was still taking in gulps of air with his eyes closed, and rolled to a sitting position, trying to catch his own breath. Roxy continued to run the towel over heated skin, all the while murmuring that everything was okay.

Seconds ticked by. When Reese opened his eyes, Roxy's gaze met his, and she smiled radiantly. "Hi, Logan. Remember me? My name's Roxanne, and I'm a physician. Are you okay now?"

Swallowing hard, Reese stared at her a moment, then at Jake. Horror and embarrassment flared in his eyes, and his face was coated in sweat and flushed with exertion. "That depends. Did I hurt anybody?"

Jake snorted as he got to his feet, trying to hide how sore

his left side was—Reese didn't need guilt topping off all his other emotions right now. "Like I'd ever let a jarhead get the best of me." Holding out a hand, he helped Roxy up first and then extended it to Reese, who paused before accepting it. "What happened?"

Well, it was clear he'd had a post-traumatic episode, but what had brought it on, only he knew.

Running his hands down his face, Reese inhaled deeply. "I-I'm not sure. I . . . um . . . came here to get you for Colleen." He gestured toward the double doors. "I came in . . . and . . ." A flash of confusion crossed his face, then his eyes lit up. "A-a crack . . . like a whip . . ."

Roxy cursed under her breath. Jake knew it wasn't her fault—neither of them had any way of knowing Reese would walk in and have the reaction he did. But Jake also knew why the sound of the whip had set the former POW off. "That's exactly what you heard. We were practicing. Has that happened before?"

"Not in a few months," Reese said while shaking his head. "And usually, it's when I'm asleep and have a nightmare. I've heard things that have sounded similar to—to a whip, but I never went completely out like that. It's also not a common thing to hear most of the time."

Striding behind the bar, Jake grabbed three bottles of water from the cooler. After handing one each to Roxy and Reese, he cracked open the last one and guzzled half of it. His mind played back the past few minutes, and an idea came to him. However, there was one thing he had to say before anything else. "Cowboy, first off, you know you have to let Ian, Dev, and your team leaders know what just happened."

If Reese didn't, Jake would. He hated being a snitch, but if it happened again, it could put the man's teammates at risk.

Reese didn't look happy about that, but after a moment's

hesitation, he nodded, his gaze dropping to the floor in defeat. "I know."

"Good. And don't worry—I think Ian's surprised you haven't had a moment like this since you joined the team." He paused. "I may have an idea that might help you, but first, we have to talk to Trudy." Jake knew Reese had been seeing Dr. Dunbar, who was a long-time friend of his. He wanted to run the potential plan by the psychologist before suggesting it to Reese. It might be risky, but it also might just work.

Eleven

"Are you fucking kidding me?" Logan gaped at Donovan, who was leaning against the edge of Dr. Dunbar's desk with his arms crossed over his chest. Unfortunately, the retired SEAL wasn't smiling or laughing, which meant what he'd just suggested wasn't a joke. From the couch in the office's sitting area, Logan turned his attention to the psychologist, who was perched on the wingback chair where she normally sat for their sessions. "Okay, he's not kidding, so my next questions have to be, is he fucking insane, and do you have the number for the local loony bin on your phone?"

The corners of Trudy's mouth ticked upward, and Logan realized she didn't think his teammate's suggestion was the most asinine thing she'd ever heard, and that scared the crap out of him. Bolting from his seat, he paced back and forth in front of them, trying to wrap his head around what they wanted him to do. "I was a prisoner in an Afghani hellhole, listening to my buddies being whipped within an inch of their lives before those bastards decapitated them, and you want me

"

to stand there and let someone bullwhip me? You're both fucking crazy!"

"Logan, please, sit down and hear us out," Trudy instructed in that calm, soothing tone she often used when he was agitated.

He didn't respond immediately. After he'd recovered from his meltdown at the club and profusely apologized to Roxanne London, who'd waved him off as if it weren't a big deal, Logan went back to the Trident offices with Donovan and told Ian what had happened. Despite Logan's trepidation, his boss had been understanding and was actually surprised it hadn't happened sooner. Ian had agreed that an immediate consultation with Trudy was important and had gotten the psychologist on the phone to find out if she could squeeze him in.

So, here Logan was, with Donovan in tow, in Trudy's office overlooking the Tampa Riverwalk, wondering if they were both nuts. Maybe he was sleeping and dreaming about living in a parallel universe where he was the only sane person among them.

Running his hand through his hair, he glanced from one to the other as they waited for him to calm down and listen to their reasoning. Their stoic expressions had him throwing up his hands in defeat. Taking his seat again, he said, "Okay . . . explain how this is supposed to help me and not have me ending up in a padded cell."

The doctor looked at Donovan. "It's your suggestion, and I think with your background, you'll have a better chance of convincing him."

When Donovan nodded, Logan frowned. Despite having been in the military and combat, he didn't think there was anything the retired SEAL could say to persuade him to be whipped willingly. He was surprised when the man pushed off the desk and stood, grabbed the hem of his T-shirt, and pulled it over his head. Like all the men at Trident, he was in peak physical condition, but when he turned around, showing Logan his bare back, it was clear not everything was as perfect as it seemed. There were approximately a dozen white, crescent-shaped scars covering the man's back, and Logan wondered what they were from. Out of all his coworkers, Donovan was the quietest, only letting people see a small portion of what made him tick, so having him open up like this was unexpected.

Pivoting around again, Donovan returned to his spot, leaned on the desk, and pulled his shirt back on. "I was seventeen, and my bigoted father found out I was gay. Decided to beat it out of me—worst thrashing of my life. The scars are from his belt buckle. I'd been seeing a Dom at the time, so I had a taste of what the lifestyle was all about. Without getting into the rest of the shit that happened with my father, I ended up enlisting and was stationed at Pearl Harbor. I found a club, similar to The Covenant, where I could continue my training. Even though my introduction into the lifestyle was as a submissive, it was obvious to others I was a Dom. After talking with some of them, I realized they were right. I have an innate need to protect others, to help them, and was never very comfortable relying on other people, but having them come to me with their problems was something completely different. I like being needed . . . actually, I *need* to be needed. But in order to become a Dom—a good one—I still had to finish learning what it meant to be a submissive. A Dom should never do something to a submissive that they haven't experienced for themselves, so they know everything about the positive and negative responses that can happen."

Donovan straightened and took a few steps, sitting in another chair next to Trudy. He leaned forward and rested his arms on his thighs as he continued. "Anyway, I approached a Domme to help me, since I wasn't looking for a relationship with anyone at the time. Lani was a bisexual sadist, willing to take me on—first as a submissive and then as a Dom apprentice. After a while, I trusted her enough to tell her everything that'd happened. Her suggestion was to not only teach me how to be a Whip Master, but also to teach me how to release the emotional baggage I was holding onto as a result of the beating. It's called desensitization." He paused and raised his brow. "I know you haven't really been in the club, but do you know what a safeword is?"

Even though there was very little Logan knew about the lifestyle, it wasn't hard to walk in on conversations about it at the TS compound with Foster, McCabe, and all of the Alpha Team participating in it, along with any significant others. With a slight tilt of his head, he answered, "Yeah, I think. If the submissive says a safeword, then everything stops, right?"

The other man nodded. "Right. You've probably also heard the lifestyle mantra—safe, sane, and consensual. Nothing is done to a submissive that they haven't agreed to. The Dom ensures that all safety measures are taken and that the reason behind why the sub is scening is not self-damaging. There's a high level of trust in BDSM, and a sub needs be able to trust that their Dom will immediately stop if the safeword is said or know how to read the sub's body language to stop the scene, if necessary, without the safeword.

"There's more to it, and Polo will go into all of that with you in the class, but I wanted you to understand the basics, so you understand why I'm suggesting you try the whip. Lani showed me how to channel the painful memories and feelings I was keeping locked inside me and release them. Yeah, the whip hurts at first, but with training, you'll be able to associate that pain with pleasure, and that's where you'll find the release. I still have an occasional session with one of the Whip Masters at the club. When I do, I know I can stop it at any time—it gives me the power and control I didn't have with my father. *I'm* the one who says when enough is enough—no one else. As I began to desensitize, the whip, and my responses to it, were no longer a reminder of what I'd been through. It became a cathartic release. I now had the control, and I took that control and made the whip a positive tool instead of a negative one. It took a while, but once I could get through a session without breaking down or freaking out, Lani began to teach me how to transfer that power and control into helping other submissives. That's when I began to apprentice as a Dom."

Taking a gulp from the bottle of water that Trudy had given him earlier, Logan mentally sorted through what Donovan had told him. "So, what you're saying is if I learn how to control the . . . scene . . . that's what it's called, right?" When the others both nodded, he continued. "So, I learn how to control the scene and how to control my responses to it, I'll be able to purge my PTSD symptoms and episodes into a physical and emotional release."

Trudy paused from where she'd been making a few notes on her ever-present notepad. "Yes. It's not an absolute cure—most people are never cured of their PTSD—but I think it's an excellent idea. Desensitizing is a common treatment for post trauma—whether it's a physical, mental, or emotional response the person is suffering from. Actually, I'd been thinking about suggesting it to you, but up until today, I wasn't sure if you were ready to hear it. I'm not suggesting you walk into a room with just anyone and let them start whipping you—that would be disastrous even if I could find a trained person to agree to it, which I doubt I could. I think before you try anything, you should do some research on BDSM. Before you leave, I'll give you the links to some trusted websites on the subject. If you want to give it a try, the first few sessions would just be watching a Master practice, getting used to hearing the crack of the whip, and finding a way to associate it with something positive. Then, I want you to watch a few scenes with a Master and an experienced submissive. If and when you're ready to take the next step after that, I want two Whip Masters present—the second one will be observing you and your responses."

"That's what I did with Nick's first session," Jake added. "Roxy was there for it. I couldn't see his facial expressions, and with him never being exposed to that level of pain/pleasure before, I needed someone who could observe him to make sure I was sending him into subspace."

Logan stood and paced again, mulling over what they'd said. He had to be crazy to be considering it, but then again, he was crazy if he didn't do everything he could to save his job. He knew Ian had said that as long as he followed the rules that had been set forth when he was first hired, his job was safe, but if he ever thought he'd be a liability to either team, he'd hand in his resignation. There was no way he could live with someone being hurt or killed because he'd flipped out during a mission like he did in the club. "So, who do you suggest I do this with? You, Jake?"

The other man shook his head. "I'm the last person who should be whipping you for several reasons—the main one being we'll be working together. You're already going to be worried about everything that goes with this—you don't need to add our professional relationship on top of it. I also don't think it's a good idea for you to scene with any male Whip Master—if anything is going to trigger a flashback to Afghanistan, it's that. It was men—bastards that they were—who were doling out the torture. No. I think it's best if we set up something with Roxy and Charlotte. They're both top-notch Dommes, and Roxy has the added experience of being a physician." In addition to meeting Roxy back at the club a little while ago, Logan had met her and her wife, Kayla, at the barbecue to celebrate the fact Ian and Angie were expecting.

Charlotte, aka Mistress China, he'd also met two or three times before at the compound. The petite Asian-American was a force to be reckoned with if her Domme feathers were ruffled, but otherwise she was very nice. If he remembered correctly, she was a parole officer.

Inhaling deeply, Logan let it out slowly. "I don't know. I understand what you're saying, but I have to admit, it freaks me out. Let me think about it tonight, and I'll let you know tomorrow."

Trudy picked up her day planner and looked at her schedule. "I have a ten o'clock opening tomorrow. Do you want to come in then and we'll talk about it some more?"

"Yeah." He ran a hand through his hair, which was in desperate need of a trim. "That's fine."

After jotting down something on a piece of paper, she stood and handed it to him. "These are three excellent sites for you to explore. The first two have pages dedicated to desensitization."

Logan read the names of the websites. *BDSM 101. Fet Lifestyle. Beginner BDSM.* Between this and his new assignment, he suddenly had the feeling he'd tumbled down the rabbit hole. The only problem was he wasn't sure how to get out of it.

Taking a deep breath, Dakota shut the locker where she'd stored her things in the ladies' lounge of The Covenant. It'd been a long time since she'd been nervous about walking out onto a play floor—in fact, she hadn't been nervous at all with Davis. But then again, she hadn't been attracted to the man. Logan Reese, however, was someone altogether different.

The longer she'd sat next to her new partner in Sawyer's office that afternoon, the more she'd become aware of him.

She'd felt his gaze every time it landed on her, and it had taken everything in her not to glance over to see if it was as hot as it had seemed. She'd even replayed in her mind how he'd skill-fully disarmed those punks earlier, despite the fact she'd been annoyed at his alpha interference at the time. His body was honed to perfection and the way his muscles had moved with such fluidity hadn't been hard to miss.

Dakota had intended to get out of Sawyer's office as quickly as possible, to get her hormones back under control, but Reese had grabbed her elbow, and she'd almost sank to her knees as jolts of electricity at his touch scorched her skin. To top it all off, he'd then sweetly reintroduced himself, in a deep, sexy timber she'd felt between her legs. She'd seen the relief—and something else she couldn't name—in his eyes when she'd followed his lead, starting their brief relationship over. How the hell was she going to survive the rest of this detail without falling victim to his looks, charm, and natural Alpha tendencies?

Stepping over to a full-length mirror, she studied her reflection. Finding submissive fet-wear that also let her carry a weapon or two had been challenging. The snug, leather pencil skirt she was wearing completely hid the small caliber pistol strapped to her inner thigh, while a thin, stiletto blade was concealed inside her black and red corset, between her breasts. Her feet were bare, but with her training, she could still use them to do some damage with or without shoes.

At the top of the steps leading into the lounge from the second floor, the door opened, and footsteps resounded in the stairwell. Moments later, an attractive, curvy woman, with skin the color of mocha, strode in and nearly jumped five feet when she saw Dakota. Throwing her hand to her ample chest, she flashed a relieved smile. "Oh, my God! You scared the bejeezus out of me. I didn't expect anyone to be in here."

"Sorry, I didn't mean to startle you. I'm Dakota Smith,"

she said, giving the last name she'd been instructed to use for this assignment. While it was almost cliché, it was close enough to her real name to avoid confusion. "We have a class starting in a few minutes in the pit." Since she had no idea who the woman was, she wasn't going to announce the class was to train the new cops and agents going undercover in the clubs.

"Oh, Master Mitch didn't say anything about that yesterday." She held out her hand for Dakota to shake. "Hi, I'm Sasha Lewis. I'm a sub and work in the club's boutique. We just got in a new shipment of inventory on Saturday, and since we're closed today, I have to go through everything and get it all up on the display racks and shelves. I can't wait to see some of the new fet-wear that came in. By the way, I love that corset . . . it looks fantastic on you."

"Thanks." Sasha had a bubbly personality that was infectious, and Dakota liked her immediately, even though it was a little weird to be dressed in fet-wear while the other woman was in a comfortable pair of jeans and T-shirt. "It's nice to meet you. I don't mean to sound rude, but I have to get out to my Dom. Don't want to earn a punishment before the class even starts."

"Go. Run." The sub waved her hand toward the door leading out to the pit. "It was nice meeting you too. If you want a peek at the new inventory, knock on the boutique door before you leave. Have fun."

Pulling the door open, Dakota rushed out and ran right into a brick wall that let out a muffled *"oomph."* Hands grasped her shoulders and steadied her when she would have ended up on her ass. Her gaze had been downcast and roamed upward, taking in a pair of snug, black jeans covering an impressive bulge, a black, leather belt, and a black T-shirt that hugged its owner in all the right places. Before her eyes made it to the man's face, she'd known who it was, and she cursed her body's reaction to her new partner once again.

"Hey, are you okay?" Logan's concerned voice sent a shiver through her spine. "I came to get you because Marco's just about to get started."

His hands still cupped her shoulders as her gaze met his, and she didn't miss the heat flaring in his eyes. Goose bumps popped up all over her skin, and she took a step back, out of his reach. "Yeah. I'm fine. Thanks. Just talking to one of the club's submissives in the locker room."

Sticking his hands in his back pockets, he eyed her down to her toes and back up again. "You look nice. Really nice."

"Um. Thanks." Feeling herself grow wet at his appraisal, she stepped around him and walked toward where the other UC teams were gathered in the middle of the pit. Glancing to her left, she saw him fall into step next to her. "You . . . um . . . didn't get your leathers?" Not that he didn't look extremely sexy in his current attire.

"No. I . . . uh . . . didn't have time. Something came up that I had to take care of first. I'm going to head to the shop tomorrow, if you want to come with me. You know, make sure I pick out the right stuff. Aside from camos and jeans, I'm not a fashionista."

Dakota chuckled and relaxed a little. "I think you're the first guy I've ever heard use that word."

"What can I say? My younger sister is a full-fledged fashionista. Otherwise, I wouldn't know what the hell one was."

"All right, let's get started. We've got a lot of ground to cover." Marco DeAngelis was standing on the center stage of the pit in front of a large St. Andrew's cross. With his dark hair and good looks, Dakota was starting to think "being a hunk" was a requirement to be hired by the private security company.

Kneeling on a large, red pillow next to him was a gorgeous

blonde, dressed in a pink satin camisole and shorts. In perfect present position, her head was downcast while her hands rested palms up on her thighs with her knees shoulder width apart. Dakota had met the retired SEAL at several task force meetings and knew he was married, so that had to be his wife. His next words confirmed it as he stroked the blonde's hair, the expression of pure love on his face hard to miss. "My beautiful wife, Harper, has volunteered . . . sort of . . . to help me demonstrate a few things this afternoon, while our daughter is visiting her Aunt Jenn for a few hours. For those of you whom I haven't met, yet, I'm Marco DeAngelis. I'm a retired Navy SEAL and have been in the lifestyle for about fifteen or sixteen years now. I'd like to go around the room and have you quickly introduce yourselves, so I can put names to faces, please. Tell me if you're a newbie or how long you've been practicing."

While the self-introductions went around the room, no one mentioned they worked in law enforcement. While everyone in the pit knew their true purpose there, and the club was technically closed, there were a few employees doing things upstairs, including Sasha.

A few moments later, the Doms were sitting in chairs facing the stage, while their submissives were on pillows at their feet as DeAngelis began telling the inexperienced people there the basics of the lifestyle, stressing that everything was safe, sane, and consensual.

Since this was all stuff Dakota had known for years, she took the opportunity to study Logan. While he was listening to the lecture, every so often his gaze drifted to the corner of the stage where a portable rack, holding various toys and instruments used in BDSM, had been set up. Each time he did, his face paled a little—she wouldn't have noticed if she hadn't been watching him so closely—and he seemed distracted, which wasn't a good thing for a Dom to be on a play floor. Something was bothering him, and Dakota wished she knew what it was, but as long as it didn't interfere with the two of them being undercover together, then that was all that mattered. If she learned anything too personal about him, she was afraid her attraction to him would grow even more.

The two hours went by faster than she realized. As expected, aside from proper presentation, an intro to the different types of play that were and weren't allowed in most of the clubs, and all the other basics, there had been no full-scene demonstrations—those would start tomorrow DeAngelis told them. Before releasing them for the rest of the day, apparently a Shibari class was scheduled in the club that evening, he instructed each couple to talk about what they'd learned tonight and to check out three BDSM websites, then let him know if there were any questions before they started the class back up at 8:00 a.m.

When the class broke up, Logan stood and held out his hand to her. Hoping she wouldn't have the same reaction she'd had earlier to his touch, Dakota placed her hand in his and allowed him to help her up. And, *damn it*, the tingling started all over again.

Once she was on her feet again, she snatched her hand back. If he'd noticed anything was wrong, Logan didn't show it. "So, how does grabbing some dinner sound . . . you know, to get comfortable with each other? I have some questions that I'd rather ask you than Polo."

Polo? Huh? Oh, that's right . . . DeAngelis' Navy nickname. "Um . . ." Dakota took a deep breath and glanced around. It looked like the rest of the faux couples were talking about doing the same thing Logan had just suggested. *Well, if you and he are going to be believable undercover, then you better start getting used to him.* "Sure. Let me get changed, and I'll meet you upstairs." She almost burst out laughing when he raised an eyebrow at her. Damn, the man picked things up quickly. "I mean, is it all right with you, *Sir*, if I go get changed and meet you upstairs?"

He chuckled. "That's fine, little subbie."

Turning away, Dakota started for the ladies' lounge along with the other women. The whole way there, she felt Logan's eyes on her and resisted the urge to glance back at him. She hoped like hell they caught the Kink Killer soon because, if not, she didn't doubt she was going to wind up in her partner's bed for the first time in her career.

OMEGA TEAM
TRIDENT SECURITY

Twelve

Logan watched as Dakota disappeared into the ladies' lounge. The corset she was wearing had nearly knocked his socks off, and he wished she'd been wearing just panties and fishnet stockings with it.

A hand came down on his shoulder as Morrison chuckled at him. "You need a towel to gather up all that drool, Cowboy."

"Fuck you, Skipper." He gave his teammate a playful shove, and then strode toward the grand staircase leading up to the balcony floor with the other man following. "Besides, your new partner's pretty hot, too."

"Yeah, well, unfortunately, she plays for the other team. Told me point blank when I met her earlier. She's cool, though, and pretty funny, so the gig should be okay."

When they reached the top of the stairs, there were a lot more people than Logan had expected. Numerous couples were gathered at the bar, while a bartender served them drinks —mostly bottled water, but a few wines and beers were being consumed. Tiny Daultry and Mitch Sawyer, Ian and Devon's cousin, were talking to a tall man with a crew cut, wearing jeans and a black T-shirt. From his stance, it was clear he was, or had been, in one of the military branches.

Logan and Morrison stepped over to the small group, and Tiny grinned at them. "How was your first class?" While the former football player was the head of security for the club, it had surprised Logan to learn he didn't participate in the lifestyle.

"Interesting . . . let's leave it at that," Logan responded, dryly.

Mitch laughed. "And that's just the start. Wait until tomorrow—you'll be getting to the good stuff. Logan Reese, Kip Morrison, this is Stefan Lundquist. He's with the Coast Guard and is teaching the Shibari class tonight."

Before today, Logan had never heard of Shibari, which was the art of rope bondage commonly used in BDSM settings. As the three men exchanged greetings and handshakes, Tiny let out a low whistle. "Damn . . . who's the silver vixen?"

The two Omega teammates turned to see the gray-haired FBI agent they'd met earlier. Instead of using the stairwell behind the bar, she and another female federal agent had come up the grand staircase. She was one of those women who'd gone gray very early in life and still rocked it now in her early forties. Her hair was cut short and spiked. Add that to her shapely five-foot-ten-inch frame, she definitely drew appreciative looks from both genders.

Logan kept his voice low, so no one else could overhear, although someone had turned on the club's sound system and soothing jazz filtered out of the speakers, but not too loudly to drown out conversation. "That's Nikita Novik. A . . . friend . . . of Colt Parrish." The six-foot-eight mountain of a man's lower jaw was almost at his knees as he watched the tall drink of water sashay toward the heavy, wooden doors leading to the lobby, and Logan snickered. "Skipper, I think Tiny needs the towel more than I do, man."

The phone behind the bar rang, and the bartender picked it up. Seconds later, he called out, "Hey, Mitch. Ty's on the phone, wondering where you are."

"Tell him I'm on my way home, Dennis. Thanks." Turning back to the others, the club owner/manager added, "Today's Tori's birthday, so we're taking her out for dinner. See you guys later."

Now that was a relationship Logan didn't understand—two men and one woman and they were all in love with each other. He wasn't against it, but none of his past relationships with one woman had worked out, so he had no clue how they made it work with an added person in the mix. *To each his own.*

The door to the stairwell leading to the locker rooms swung open and out stepped Dakota and Skipper's new partner, Sheila Cummings. Logan eyed Dakota as the two women strode toward them. In a snug, Grunt Style, patriotic skull T-shirt and the jeans she'd been wearing that morning, she was just as sexy as when she'd been in her club wear. A twitch in his pants had him running baseball stats in his head to keep from getting hard—damn, if he was alone with her tonight, he'd probably do something stupid like hit on her.

Clearing his throat, he addressed his teammate and Sheila. "Dakota and I are going to Donovan's for some dinner and a beer and to discuss what we . . . um . . . well, get to know each other better. Care to join us?"

He thanked his lucky stars when the two glanced at each other, shrugged, and agreed to come along. Dakota seemed as relieved as he was that they'd have company.

Twenty minutes later, the foursome was settled into a booth at the back of the Irish pub owned by Jake Donovan's brother, Mike, who was currently training a new bartender. He'd given Logan and Kip a quick wave when they'd entered, telling them to take whatever table they wanted. While the place drew a hefty lunch crowd and was packed in the evenings from Wednesday through Sunday, Monday nights was sort of slow, like most restaurants. There was no one sitting near them, so they'd be able to discuss both the lifestyle and the case without being overheard.

After their food orders were taken, and a pitcher of beer had been emptied into four glasses, the idle chit-chat between them moved onto things they hadn't been able to discuss at the club. Sheila filled Logan in on her background—she was a lifestyle switch and had been with the Tampa PD for six years, the last two in the Special Ops Division. She glanced at the woman sitting across from her. "I'm glad to have another chick added to the squad. We need someone else who can pull off spandex tights and dress like a prostitute for the perverted 'john' stings."

Dakota laughed and shook her head. "I'm not on the squad yet. I'm still considered to be on loan from patrol. But from your mouth to the captain's ear . . ." She lifted her glass in a toast before taking a sip.

"You've got nothing to worry about, girl. From what I've heard, you're the only one Captain Bowman has already approved to take one of the two opening positions. He's just waiting for the higher ups to sign off on transfers into the unit —damn politicians and the budget are holding things up. And if it wasn't for that asshole, Fallon, cock blocking you all the time, you would've been on before I was. I know it's no consolation but be grateful you didn't have to work under him. We celebrated, without him, when he retired."

Logan had no idea who the women were talking about, other than the fact they were obviously the former and current supervisors of the Special Ops Division. He wondered what Sheila had meant about Fallon "cock block-ing" Dakota's transfer but didn't want to come out and ask. "So, tell us what we're looking for with this bastard. Since, from what we're told, KK is a Dom, what are we looking for?"

"KK?" Dakota snickered with an amused expression. "Okay, I guess that's better than saying that stupid moniker outright. Damn press." She got serious again. "Yes, the FBI behavioral analyst thinks he's a practicing Dom, which makes our jobs that much more difficult. If you've been in the lifestyle for a good amount of time, it's easy to spot the newbies or wannabes, unless a person is skilled in undercover work. Most people find it hard not to stare in a "holy shit" way when seeing certain things in a club for the first time. Also, eye contact or lack thereof is always an easy tell. Like DeAngelis said earlier, Dom's will never look away when they are speaking to subs unless there's a reason. Subs should keep their eyes downcast until the Dom orders them to look up, and then their eyes should be directed at the Dom. Looking away, while conversing one-on-one, is frowned upon, and that's usually an easy way to spot a new sub. When they're nervous, they'll look at everything and everyone but the Dom. This bastard has probably been able to pick out quite a few of the UC teams. He's probably known to the less exclusive clubs and maybe one or two of the more private ones. What the task force hasn't been able to figure out is where the hell he's keeping them while he's torturing them. According to the ME, he's letting them scream to the point they're popping blood vessels in their throats."

"Shit."

Logan agreed with Morrison. As former military, in this day and age, they'd both been exposed to the horrors of war and torture, Logan especially, but knowing what those poor women went through was a kick to the gut.

The two police officers filled their new partners in on the rest of the details from the case they hadn't had time to review, and it wasn't long before their dinners were served, and the conversation turned again at the waitress's presence. "So, Logan," Sheila said, "Kip told me he's a retired Army Ranger and LAPD sniper. Before TPD, I did two tours in the sandbox with the Army too. Where were you before Trident? You've got that military walk and talk."

He wasn't about to tell them where he was right before Trident, which was in a depressive pit, but he could tell them enough to satisfy their curiosity. Dakota was staring at him intently, clearly interested in whatever he was about to say. "Only branch that matters," he boasted. "The Marine Corps."

The two Army grunts scoffed at him, and Morrison shook his head. "Yeah, Cowboy was a high-priced bellhop."

Clearly confused, Dakota repeated, "High-priced bellhop? What does that mean?"

Sheila snickered. "I'm sure you've seen the Marines dress uniforms—they look like bellhops in them."

"Oh, jeez. I never thought about it that way, but I think you're right." The corners of her mouth ticked upward. "So, Cowboy, got any pictures of you looking like a bellhop?"

Even though he liked how she felt comfortable enough to tease him, he wasn't letting her get away with it. He was starting to understand why Ian, Marco, and the others always said they liked when their wives and girlfriends were bratty, because it gave them a reason to spank their asses. Right now, Logan's hand itched to pull Dakota across his lap and spank her before fucking her silly until she screamed his name in ecstasy. Of course, that was out of the question in the middle of Donovan's, and she'd probably either rip his balls off or shoot him if he tried. "Watch it, subbie," he said with a smirk, satisfied when her eyebrows shot up. "Or I'll tell Marco you volunteered for the spanking demonstration tomorrow. Of course, as your partner, it would be me lighting up your ass."

While she glared at him, Skipper and Sheila roared with laughter. Logan arched his brow at Dakota, daring her to challenge him. The tightening of her jaw told him he was going to pay for his words at some point in the next few days, and damn it, he was actually looking forward to it. She turned him on in a way no other woman had in years—if ever—and he began thinking of all the ways he could try to wind up in her bed after the case was over. Or maybe before then.

THE STENCH of blood filled his nostrils, flaring his need to inflict more pain, but alas, his latest piece of art was no longer breathing. A disappointment. Lily Stokes hadn't lasted long at all, and the Dom didn't think she deserved to be listed among his masterpieces. She was only partially completed. Without her screams of pain, his desire to finish what he'd started began to wane.

Taking a step back, he eyed her naked body, still being held to the St. Andrew's cross by the wrist and ankle restraints. He hadn't even had a chance to turn her around and decorate the front of her. Only her back, ass, arms, and legs were deep red with his mark—slashes from each strike of his bullwhip. Blood ran down her skin to the floor beneath her, while more was sprayed on the walls, ceilings, and the Dom himself. Dressed as he usually was when he was working on a new masterpiece, he wore only his leather pants and boots. His sculpted arms had bulged each time he sent the whip sailing through the air, and sweat coated his skin, mixing with the submissive's lifeblood.

He thought he'd chosen well, but for some reason, her heart had given out too soon. Should he continue and see if he could salvage what was left of her?

Running the leather strands of the whip through his loose fist, he contemplated her skin. There was still some room on the backs of her lower legs. Raising his arm, he reached back and then let the whip fly forward. A flick of his wrist at the last moment produced a satisfying crack, but that was the only sound he heard.

No scream.

No moan.

It was useless. Even his cock was softening, and it always stayed hard until he was done with his creations.

Frowning, he set the whip down on the bed she'd been tied to earlier and undid the restraints holding her up. She dropped like a sack of potatoes. Anger rose within him as he stared at her unblemished chest and abdomen. Rearing back, he kicked the bitch in the ribs several times, but even that didn't satisfy his lust. No, she didn't deserve to be one of his masterpieces at all.

After the sun went down, he'd load her body into his small boat and dump it in the Gulf of Mexico, just like he'd done to his first two victims. Back then, he hadn't known how much he wanted the world to see his art, and up until now, they'd been the only ones who wouldn't be on his list of confirmed kills until he departed this world, and they found the diaries and photo albums he was leaving to ensure his rightful place in history.

As he began to clean up and wrap the dead bitch up in a tarp, his mind shuffled through the other submissives who'd caught his eye recently. Which would be the one who'd redeem him? Two came to mind—Georgia Branneth from The Covenant, and that hot little cop, Dakota Smith. He was certain that wasn't the latter's real last name, but it was the only one he'd heard so far.

Making a female cop one of his masterpieces was a risk, but damn, she looked like she'd fight to the finish. He'd have to think about it, but first, he had to get rid of the wasted flesh that had sullied his track record. Then he'd plan who would be next.

Thirteen

Logan paced back and forth, his nerves on edge, and tried not to bolt from the club. "Man up, Cowboy. You can do this," he said aloud, thankful no one else was around to hear him talking to himself. "Just fucking chill."

The big, wooden, lobby doors swung open and in walked Charlotte Roth and Roxanne London—Mistresses China and Roxy. He'd been meeting them for the past week at 0600 hours, before either of them had to be at their respective offices. After talking things over again with Trudy, he'd decided to give the desensitization therapy a try, and she'd gone over everything with both women, as had Donovan.

Roxy was one of the pediatricians in the area who was on-call for when a child was brought into the ER after experiencing a traumatic event. She was board certified in Neurodevelopmental Psychology, which covered all ages from infancy to geriatrics. It made her qualified to perform desensitization therapy. She was also adept in reading the body language of submissives during scenes.

Their first session had been a bit of a surprise for Logan—

although he wasn't sure what he'd expected. Trudy had told him they weren't going to jump right into whipping him, but he hadn't anticipated what they'd had him do to feel more in control of the situation.

Charlotte and Roxy had set up three of the club's leather, wingback chairs into a "U" arrangement with Logan sitting between them. A small, empty side table had sat across from him. For the first half hour, they'd joked with him, listened as he told them what he could about his ordeal, and gave him word and image associations, so he had something else to think about instead of a damn whip. Then, he'd been instructed to close his eyes and find "a happy place." Yeah, they'd actually used those words, making him chuckle. He'd heard someone moving around as he thought of being with Dakota on a deserted island somewhere. He hadn't intended for her to be in his happy place—she'd just appeared.

Roxy had asked him to describe what he was feeling, and he told her about the warmth of the sun on his back, the sand between his toes, and the aroma of the suntan lotion Dakota was letting him spread over her body.

Well, actually, he'd left that last part out.

When he'd opened his eyes again, the table was no longer empty. A black, leather whip had been sitting in the middle of it, coiled like a cobra waiting to strike. As he'd stared at it, he was asked to describe what he saw and what it could be used for other than the obvious. That had made him think.

A rope to restrain someone.

Tie it to a tree limb and swing like Tarzan.

Shibari.

That last idea had made him think of Dakota with dozens of single-tailed whips wrapped around her naked body, bound for his pleasure . . . and hers. Yeah, he'd liked that image the best.

The next thing they'd had him do, after Charlotte had

picked up the whip's handle, letting the rest of the braided leather fall to the ground, had been to wrap his hand around hers, then direct their combined hands to run the leather up and down his arms and legs, and in between his fingers. Every few moments, the Domme had pulled her hand out a little further from under his until she was no longer holding the whip . . . it had been in Logan's hand alone. Once he'd felt comfortable holding it, Roxy had held up her cell phone. "I have a recording of a whip cracking. You'll hear nothing else."

The first crack had caused the blood to drain from his face, and bile had risen in his throat as he'd flinched. The recording was immediately turned off, and he'd been instructed to go to his happy place. The method to their madness was to give him something pleasurable to think about instead of the horror he'd gone through. He was learning to associate the loud *crack* with Dakota's beautiful body, instead of his buddies' tortured ones.

Each session had been run the same way, and he'd nearly jumped out of his skin when the recording began, having a few moments of panic and hyperventilation, but the two Dommes knew their business. They'd monitored his reactions and turned off the recording until he settled again.

The third day, Charlotte hadn't been able to make the session, after being called by the police about one of her parolees they were looking to rearrest on new charges, so it had just been Logan and Roxy. The doctor had shown him how to wield the whip, which gave him more and more control over the inanimate object and its destructive grip on him and his sanity. In fact, he'd been the only person all week to make the leather crack during the sessions up to that point. Roxy had demonstrated how to flick his wrist to make the leather sing as it arced through the air. At first, he'd only let the last two inches of the whip fly. He'd even flicked it against his arm, feeling the light sting. As the session moved along, he let more and more of the whip sail through the air, until he'd finally been holding the handle, letting the entire length snap with only the slightest movement of his wrist.

Today, however, was D-Day, so to speak, and he hoped like hell he didn't freak out again or puke all over the place. Today, he'd take off his shirt, and while one of the Dommes watched his reactions closely, the other would slash the whip across his back. He'd watched them practice yesterday and knew from his research they never broke the skin. They usually trained using a piece of paper taped to a wall or a St. Andrew's cross, but yesterday, they'd taken it one step further.

Before heading to the airport to return to California, Donovan had met them in the early morning hours. He'd removed his shirt, stood face first against the large, centerpiece cross, which had been pushed to the far end of the stage, and reached up, grasping the loops of the cross's Velcro restraints. While China lit up Donovan's back with the whip, Logan had sat in a chair, with Roxy at his side, her hand laying on his arm in comfort. She'd spoken to him in that soothing voice most doctors and shrinks seemed to have, keeping him in the present and in Tampa.

He'd been amazed at how quickly Donovan had relaxed into the sting of the tail which had left red stripes on his unbroken skin. One would think the muscular, six-foot-five man had been receiving a half-hour back massage instead. When it was over, the petite Domme, who was about a foot shorter than the Dom, had helped him to a chair they'd placed on the stage and given him a bottle of water to rehydrate, while she applied Arnica ointment to his back.

Instead of screaming in pain, Donovan appeared stoned for a bit until he'd recovered from what Logan had been told was subspace—basically the guy had been high on the endorphins swimming through his system.

"You sure you're ready for this, Cowboy?" Charlotte had loved his nickname and used it more often than his real name.

"I hope so." There was no mistaking the nervousness in his voice.

The auburn-haired Roxy stopped in front of him, her expression soft with understanding. "We don't have to do it today. You can practice with the whip some more if you're not ready to experience it."

"And waste a sleepless night trying to psych myself up for it? Nope, let's get this over with, so I can eat something without throwing up."

The women laughed at his words even though they knew he was only half joking. Logan followed them down the wide staircase to the pit and over to the stage. He lifted the chair Donovan had sat in the day before back up onto the raised platform as the two Dommes put down their purses and prepared everything else.

He'd been doing tons of research on the BDSM lifestyle, since being assigned to the case—some of it on the computer, but a lot of it had been during the long stakeout shifts he'd been working with Dakota. She had been great, answering all his questions. And, damn, just the thought of her had his dick stirring again . . . not something he'd expect to happen moments before he'd be getting whipped, but the female cop did something for him he couldn't explain. As much as he wanted her in his bed, he'd enjoyed getting to know her on a professional and personal level. The latter wasn't as personal as he hoped, but she'd opened up to him about her background and family a little bit, after he'd offered some of his own history, sans his last tour in the sandbox.

Next week, things would change between them again as they entered Heat together as a D/s couple—there would be intimate touching going on as part of their cover.

As Roxy and Charlotte climbed the two steps to the stage,

Logan's heart began to pound and he began to sweat, even though the temperature in the club was at a comfortable level . . . cool, even.

The two women had agreed Charlotte would man the whip while Roxy would observe his responses. He knew all he had to do was shout the word "red," and they'd immediately stop the scene and begin aftercare, but his legs still shook.

"Cowboy." He turned toward Charlotte when she said his name in a tender, yet firm voice. "What you're feeling is normal . . ."

Damn, I must have wimp written across my forehead.

". . . and it doesn't mean you're a wimp or anything. Far from it."

What the fuck? She can read my mind?

"Go to your happy place and start singing 'Ninety-Nine Bottles of Beer,' either out loud or in your head. Channel Clutch and the others. They're double-dog-daring you to do this, and you'll be damned if you lose a bet to them."

During their earlier sessions, he'd told them about his teammates, but not about how they'd been murdered. No. Instead, he'd told them what a great bunch of guys his friends had been, all the practical jokes they played on each other, and the mudslinging that always happened when they were busting each other's chops over one thing or another. He'd also mentioned how he'd sung that ridiculous song to screw with his captors.

Taking a deep breath, he nodded at the dark-haired woman, then did as she'd suggested. He didn't want to subject them to his horrible singing voice, so instead, he counted down those beer bottles in his head while sitting on the beach with Dakota. At least in his mind, she enjoyed his singing.

Ninety-nine bottles of beer on the wall, ninety-nine bottles of beer. Take one down, pass it around, ninety-eight bottles of beer on the wall.

Removing his T-shirt, he draped it over the arm of the chair then stepped toward the leather-covered St. Andrew's cross. Roxy positioned herself behind it, so she could see his face between the upper parts of the large letter "X." Goose bumps pebbled his skin. His jeans sat low on his hips, so his entire back was exposed.

Ninety-six bottles of beer on the wall, ninety-six bottles of beer...

He reached up and grabbed hold of the straps.

Ninety-five bottles of beer on the wall, ninety-five bottles of beer...

"I'm going to snap it a few times without striking you," Charlotte assured him. "First within view and then behind you. After that, I'll switch to a soft flogger to warm up your skin and bring the blood to the surface, just like I did with Jake yesterday." She moved to his side and held up the nine-tailed leather instrument for him to see, before letting it fall against his arm in a gentle caress. "That's exactly what it will feel like, no harder than that. And I won't hit you with this or the single tail without warning, okay?"

Logan swallowed a lump of fear blocking his throat. After surviving SERE training in the military, he could do this, he tried to convince himself. "Yeah, okay. I'm good."

Ninety-one bottles of beer...

She brought the two ends of the whip together and doubled over the length, holding it up in her hands for him to see. "I'm going to snap it. Watch the leather and listen to the sound it makes. It's an inanimate object. You have full control here—we just have to convince your internal fight or flight system of that fact."

When she yanked it taut, the two parts slapped together, the sound not as loud as it would be when the whip cracked at full-length. She repeated it several times, her gaze never leaving his face. "Good. Your muscles relaxed after the first few times.

We're ready to move on." She hung the whip around her neck. "I'm going to do some joint compression next. Since you're so much taller than me, I need you to kneel. I'd have you lay down, but the cleaning crew hasn't been here this morning, yet, and God knows what's on the floor."

Letting go of the restraints, Logan lowered himself to his knees. He bowed his head when Charlotte's strong, yet baby-soft, hands caressed his upper arms and shoulders. Using the heels of her palms, she pressed down, forcing the tension from his muscles and joints. Her hands never left his skin as they moved and pressed in an intermittent pattern. After about thirty of them, she then kneaded the surrounding flesh. If he wasn't anticipating what was coming next, he might have closed his eyes and fallen into a coma.

Giving his shoulders a final squeeze, Charlotte stepped back. "Stand and grab the restraints again. Keep your eyes on Roxy's. Try to stay here with us."

His gaze met the doctor's, and she gave him an encouraging smile. "No worries if you freak. I've already seen you do that, and we got through it just fine. And what happens here, stays here, Logan. Neither of us have talked to anyone else about this other than Ian, Jake, and Trudy, and that was with your permission." Her eyes shifted behind him, and she gave her fellow Domme a nod.

"All right, Cowboy." Charlotte sounded much further away than he'd expected. "I'm down on the play floor by the stairs— far enough away that I can't reach you at all. After each crack, I'm going to take a few steps closer. If you need me to slow down or stop, say yellow or red. Here comes the first one."

Even though he'd been warned and knew the whip couldn't hit him from that distance, he still startled when the loud *crack* split the air. His muscles seized briefly, his fists tightening on the restraints that he could release at any time.

"Breathe, Logan. You're holding your breath. Breathe."

He hadn't realized that's what he'd been doing until Roxy pointed it out. Inhaling deeply, he slowly let it out again.

Take one down, pass it around, seventy-four bottles of beer on the wall.

"One more. Inhale, exhale."

After doing as he was told, he forced his muscles to relax once more, and then nodded. "I'm ready. Again."

Although he'd been told she'd move closer in between the targetless strikes, the next *crack* sounded as far away as the first. This time, he remembered to keep breathing. Sweat covered his entire body, but his gaze remained on Roxy's face. Apparently, she didn't see anything in his expression or body language that would cause her to stop the scene, since she stayed quiet.

Realizing Charlotte was waiting for a word from him that she should continue, he said, "Again."

The sequence was repeated until Charlotte was standing on the stage once more. Logan's knees were quivering, and his pulse and breathing had increased as he fought the urge to run like a coward. His best friend's voice resounded in his head. *You can do this, Cowboy. Don't let the bastards win. And whatever you do, don't piss your fucking pants in front of the ladies.* Yeah, that was definitely something Clutch would say.

A soft thump sounded behind him and then Charlotte stepped to his side so he could see her again. She no longer had the whip in her hands—instead, she held up the six-tailed flogger. Running the tails up his arm, she gently caressed him. As she dragged it around his back, the leather stayed on his skin, over his shoulders to his other arm. She then lifted the handle and the tails fell less than an inch onto his arm again. Moving to his back, she did more of the same, from his shoulders to the flesh just above the waistband of his jeans and up again. Logan was surprised to feel his eyelids grow heavy as the tempo and force of the strikes intensified. They were far from painful—he'd had insect bites that had hurt worse.

Several minutes passed, and the skin on his back tingled with the increased blood flow. His body glowed with perspiration, but he was more relaxed than he'd expected to be at this moment. Charlotte's soothing voice floated to his ears. "All right, Cowboy. Stay in that zone. You're in your happy place. You have all the control, but don't move if you can prevent it. I'm going to crack the whip three times. If I think you're good, the fourth one will hit your right shoulder blade. I'll pause and make sure you're still okay. It'll hurt—Jake told you that—but reach past the pain and feel the heat. Ready?"

With Charlotte's tone of voice, Roxy's gentle gaze, the warm-up they'd given him, Clutch's urging to keep it together, and Dakota on the beach, wearing a white string bikini and thong, they were keeping him grounded, despite his anxiety and fear. "Ready."

The first loud *crack* sounded, and he stiffened but didn't move. Roxy inhaled deeply and Logan followed suit, letting it out slowly.

Crack.

Logan's jaw tightened. *Happy place. Happy place.* Dakota's hands went to the string around her neck.

Crack.

Jesus Christ, this is it.

Seconds ticked by. Logan heard the *crack* before he felt the strike. The tip of the whip licked his shoulder blade, right where the Domme had said it would. It felt like he'd gotten stung by hundreds of bees at the same time. His fist clenched as he rose up on the balls of his feet. "Shit!"

"Breathe, Logan," Roxy prompted. "In and out . . . that's good . . . again. Find your happy place. The heat of the sun is on your back. That's what you feel. It's warm and spreading across your skin, covering your entire back. Start with your hands and relax your muscles down your arms to your torso, then legs and feet. Breathe."

Swallowing hard, he opened his hands, willing each muscle in his body to relax one by one, until he was once again, flat on his feet. He inhaled through his nose and out his mouth, concentrating on Dakota's bikini dropping from her breasts. Damn, they were incredible—round, firm, and begging for his attention.

"Here we go, Cowboy. Left shoulder blade. Ready?" When he only nodded, Charlotte added, "Verbal response, love. Ready?"

"Ready."

A second or two later, the whip stroked his skin again. This time, in addition to feeling the sting of the bees, he heard them, but it sounded like their numbers had multiplied into the thousands. A hiss escaped his lips, and while he rolled forward on the balls of his feet, he immediately brought his heels back down. He didn't need Roxy's encouragement, breathing in and out, pushing the pain away as Dakota's hands went to the strings holding her thong to her hips.

As the scene progressed and the whip caressed his skin over and over, his mind floated—in fact, it felt like his entire body began to float. His cock was hard as a rock, and he wasn't sure if it was from the subspace he was achieving or because Dakota was now gloriously naked on the beach in front of him. Her sun-bronzed skin, high, perky tits, and waxed pussy were pure perfection. She held her hand out to him, beckoning him to come closer.

Cowboy.

He tried to step forward, but something was preventing him from doing so.

Cowboy.

Her tongue darted out to wet her—

"Cowboy. It's over. Step back, love."

It took Logan a moment to realize it hadn't been Dakota calling his name, but Charlotte. His body and mind tingled as he released the restraints, lowering his arms. The two Dommes stood on either side of him, holding him by his upper arms and the belt loops of his pants, as Roxy said, "Sit down, Logan. The chair is right behind you. Just bend your knees and sit."

Once he was in the chair, one of them covered him with a soft blanket, but in his mind, it was Dakota's long hair draped over his skin, teasing him. His eyelids closed, and he let her embrace and comfort him.

Fourteen

Dakota stared out the tinted window of the SUV she and Logan had been using to covertly observe the members of Heat coming and going each night for the past week. Stakeouts were the most boring part of undercover work, but although she wouldn't admit it to him, she'd been enjoying the shifts, sitting across the center console from him. After the first few training classes, and the club stakeouts that started two days later, she'd become more relaxed around him. They spent the hours in the parking garage across the street from the private club talking about all sorts of things—their careers, movies, books, and the lifestyle, among other topics. They also busted each other's chops, experienced spirited arguments, laughed over funny experiences, talked about the case, and even had moments of comfortable silence. The only subject Dakota had avoided was her family. She'd told him the bare minimum, hoping to satisfy his curiosity—her father was a retired cop, her mother had passed away, and she had one brother—end of story.

Although Logan had been talkative about his time with

the Marines and Trident, she had a feeling there was a lot he hadn't told her. Well, he'd mentioned he'd been in the elite Raiders and couldn't talk about most of his missions, just like the Navy SEALs and the Army's Delta Force, which she understood, but she got the feeling he was holding something else back. There'd been times his voice had strayed from its normal, relaxed tone to a tense one, before he cleared his throat and changed the subject.

"I'm hungry," he said, reaching for the cooler filled with drinks, sandwiches, and snacks they'd been stashing in the back seat after their first tour outside the club. "Want your turkey club, Koko?"

Drumming her fingers on the armrest, she nodded, not even bothering to correct him, yet again. She was actually getting used to the nickname he'd been calling her the past few days. He'd said it sounded more personal, something her Dom and lover would be calling her, for when they started going into the clubs. "Yeah, sure. As long as you're back there. Thanks."

"No prob." He had to lean toward her to rummage around and grab the sandwiches, and Dakota inhaled his scent as subtly as possible. Damn, he smelled delicious. To hell with the sandwich, she'd rather eat him.

Oh jeez, I did not just think that.

Yup, she had, and the thought made her damp between her legs and started her clit throbbing. Out of the corner of her eye, she saw his soft, brown hair and longed to thrust her fingers into the strands.

Get a grip, Dakota. He's your partner and off-limits.

Yeah, trying to convince her body of that fact was getting harder each day—hell, each hour.

Trying to get her lust under control, she forced her mind to think of something else. Unfortunately, what popped up was what her father had been bitching about earlier in the day. One of his buddies still on the department had told him she was on loan to SOD.

"What are you doing in SOD? It's not like patrol where you've got a partner sitting next to you to bail you out of trouble. You've got to think fast, otherwise you can blow a whole investigation, not to mention getting yourself killed."

"What's that frown for?" Logan asked.

She glanced at him to see he was holding the sandwich out for her to take. "Thanks . . . um, nothing really."

"Didn't look like nothing. Talk to me, Koko. It'll feel good to get whatever it is off your chest. It'll also kill some time. A lot of my intel missions had to be done in radio silence, so it's kind of nice having someone to talk to."

"What part of 'no tomatoes' did they not understand?" She picked them off and dropped them on the white butcher paper the sub had been wrapped in. When he didn't answer her rhetorical question, she shrugged. Before she could stop them, the words flew from her lips. "My father's an ass."

"In general, or about something specific?"

"A little of both, I guess." Why she was telling him this, she had no idea, but it felt right, having a strong shoulder to dump on. "I've been trying to prove to him for years that I'm good enough to be on TPD, but he wanted my brother to be the cop. Me? I was supposed to marry a guy who could take care of me, because I obviously can't take care of myself."

Swallowing a bite of his roast beef Logan snorted. "Not from where I sit. There's only two other women I've sparred with over the years who could throw me on my ass. You're number three, and I'm man enough to admit that. You can cover my six anytime."

As long as I can keep my eyes off your fine ass and on the task at hand.

"Thanks, that means a lot." She paused. "I just wish for once he'd say he's proud of me, you know? Things got worse after my mother passed away. Instead of her death bringing us closer, it pushed us further apart."

Reaching over, Logan gave her shoulder a comforting squeeze. "I'm sorry to hear that. Death screws different people up in different ways, whether it's from guilt or grief or whatever. I know from personal experience."

Taking his hand back, he stared out the windshield, and she immediately missed the intimate connection. "Friend or family member?"

"Friends—plural. Teammates. People I knew like the back of my hand and others I had only known a few hours before seeing them blown to bits or shot down. That cliché 'war is hell' is one of the biggest understatements out there."

"I'm sorry." He shrugged at her sympathy, and seconds of silence ticked by. They'd had enough of a downer conversation for the night, and she searched for a topic they hadn't discussed yet that would lighten the mood. "So, being from Virginia, does that mean you're a Baltimore Orioles fan or Washington Nationals fan?"

"Baseball, huh?" He smirked. "You know what they say when people start talking about baseball? What they're really talking about is sex." He waggled his eyebrows at her, and she almost choked on a bite of her sandwich.

"Think again, Cowboy. I really am talking about baseball —smart ass." She rolled her eyes which drew a throaty laugh from him, and just like that her hormones started raging again.

The rest of the shift was filled with mindless but fun chatter as they got to know each other better. With each hour that passed, she found herself becoming more and more attracted to her partner, which scared the heck out of her and turned her on at the same time. When the last of the employees of the club locked the doors for the night, Logan started the SUV and drove her back to the condo complex, parking in a spot closest to her unit. Dakota allowed him to climb out of his truck, walk around to her side, and open the passenger door for her, as any good submissive would do.

In the past, she'd found it difficult to let a man open doors, pull out a chair for her, situate himself between her and the road on a sidewalk, or perform any other act of chivalry, not wanting to appear the weaker sex. In the clubs and bedroom, it was fine, but out in the real world, she was always trying to prove to her father, co-workers, and anyone else that she was as tough as nails and didn't need their help. God forbid her fellow officers thought she couldn't handle being their backup. But with Logan doing those things, Dakota felt . . . well, pampered. He truly seemed to enjoy doing them— he was a natural Dom, not giving things like that a second thought. She found herself wondering about his parents. They sounded like a great couple from what he'd told her, and they'd obviously done a great job raising him and his sister, who Dakota had learned was an elementary school nurse.

As she took the hand he offered to get out of the truck, she felt that tingling and awareness she always did from his touches, which was never more than innocent, despite his occasional flirting. What the hell was it going to be like when they entered the club and there would be a lot more physical contact for their cover?

When they reached her temporary condo, Logan took the keys from her hand and unlocked the door, before handing them back to her. He'd been uncharacteristically quiet during last night's tour, but tonight he seemed back to normal. She was curious about what had caused the personality shift.

"So," he began, stuffing his hands into the back pockets of his jeans while staring intently at her. It seemed as if he was trying to resist touching her, and that just made her crave it even more. "Tomorrow night, we head into the club. Thankfully, I'm a lot less nervous about it. I-I just want to thank you for helping me understand the lifestyle better and not getting mad or laughing at all my questions. I appreciate it."

The whole time he was talking, Dakota's gaze had been on his lips—she was dying to know if they tasted as good as they looked. Were they firm or soft? Only one way to find out.

Throwing caution to the wind, she went up on her toes, grabbed the front of his T-shirt, and kissed him full on the mouth. She didn't know which one of them was more surprised. She was rarely the aggressor when it came to physical contact with a man, being a sexual submissive and all, but she didn't want to wait any longer to find out if what she was feeling was only one-sided.

After a moment's hesitation, Logan grabbed her hips and pulled her flush against him—his erection was impossible to miss. Pivoting, he sandwiched her between his body and the door, trapping her, not that she minded at all. One of his hands skimmed around to her ass and cupped it, while the other rose to the nape of her neck, his fingers delving into her hair and tilting her head to his liking. His mouth devoured her, his tongue slipping between her lips the second she parted them. A moan sounded, and Dakota had no idea if it had come from him or herself.

Her arms went around Logan's neck, and he bent his knees, lifted her, and urged her to wrap her legs around his hips. His rigid cock rubbed her clit through their clothes. Reaching down, she found the doorknob and turned it. If he hadn't had such a tight grip on her, they would have fallen when the door swung open, but somehow, he'd been ready for it. He stepped inside before kicking the door shut again. His mouth left hers for her neck as he pressed her against the foyer wall. "What time will your roommate be home?"

"She won't," Dakota answered, tilting her head to the side to give him better access to the sensitive spot behind her ear. "Told me earlier she's crashing at her boyfriend's house tonight. He's a pilot and just got back from two weeks of flying around Europe."

"Bedroom or do I have to slow down and go home to a cold shower?"

Her heart rate and breathing skyrocketed as his fingers plucked her nipple through her thin shirt and bra. Her mind raged a war with her body. It was crazy, getting involved with a partner, but this case wasn't going to last forever. When it was over, Dakota would, hopefully, be staying with the TPD Special Ops Division, and Logan would be running off, saving the world with his teammates at Trident. This was a fling for both of them, and damn if she wasn't going to enjoy it in the here and now. "Fuck that! Bedroom . . . now . . . Sir."

He chuckled against her skin causing a shiver to run down her spine, and she knew that was the last demand she'd be giving him tonight. "Point the way."

In less than a minute, he was easing her down onto the bed, his head dipping further to put her breast in his mouth, clothes and all. Grasping the hem of her T-shirt, he dragged it up her body and over her head, but that was as far as it went, trapping her arms above her. "Grab the slats in the headboard, baby. I think I'm going to like giving orders in the bedroom."

And she was going to enjoy following those orders. When she did as directed, her "Yes, Sir" came out on a moan as he bit down gently on her nipple. She wanted to beg him to remove the last scrap of fabric separating his mouth from her puck-ered peak, but the anticipation was making her hotter. All she needed to do was feel—leave the rest of the world on the other side of her front door, and just feel.

Instead of reaching behind her and undoing the clasp of the bra, Logan sent it on the same route as her shirt, leaving it wrapped around her upper arms. "Beautiful, baby. Damn, you're so beautiful. Not that I expected anything different."

She hadn't realized her eyes had closed until he'd said those words. Lifting her lids, she saw him staring at her chest, almost in reverent awe. His gaze roamed upward to meet her own. "Last chance to kick my ass to the curb, Koko. Otherwise, I'm not going to stop until you've screamed my name so loud that your neighbors call 9-1-1."

Gone was the guy who'd been thanking her for not laughing at his questions, and in his place was one smokin' hot, panty-melting, confident alpha male.

"That would have to be really fucking loud, since the condo next to us is empty."

"Hmm. That sounds like a challenge if I ever heard one." His thumbs flicked her nipples, and she felt it in her core. Shifting down on the bed, he removed her sneakers and socks before undoing the snap and zipper of her jeans. Pulling on the waistband, he slowly dragged them and her thong down her legs, his eyes on each inch of her skin as it was revealed. Her pussy flushed under his heated appraisal, readying itself for him. It was clear he was in no hurry, and Dakota knew it would be hours before they were both sated enough to sleep.

Standing, Logan pulled his own shirt off and tossed it to the floor with her clothes. When his hands dropped to the waist of his black cargo pants, Dakota licked her lips in anticipation—it had felt huge pressed against her, long and thick, and she was dying to see if her estimations were correct.

He paused, and it took a moment for her to glance up at his face to find he was smirking at her, knowingly. "Impatient, baby? Don't you know curiosity killed the cat?"

"But what a way to go."

He barked out a laugh, and then quickly shed the last of his clothes. And, yup, he definitely met her expectations. Damn, his cock was a thing of beauty, already fully erect and reaching toward his navel. Her tongue could almost taste the bit of pre-cum on the purplish tip of it.

Climbing up onto the bed, Logan settled between her legs, pushing up on the back of her thighs to spread her even wider, and she was grateful she'd had a waxing appointment the other day.

Tilting her head up, she stared as he ran his hands up to the top of her thighs and let a thumb brush against her pussy lips and clit. Again, he wasn't in any hurry, content to just stroke her for a few moments. She had to squelch the urge to close her legs and trap his hands between them. His other thumb dipped into her core a scant half inch, and she moaned. "More . . . oh please, more."

"Was that a demand? Or a request? I'm not supposed to reward demands, and I sure as hell didn't hear a 'Sir' in there."

He was getting into the Dom thing, and although his tone had been teasing, she also knew he was starting to understand exactly what she needed. She grinned. "It was a request, Sir."

"Well, then, let's see what I can do to honor that pretty request."

His middle finger parted her folds, and this time, he pushed it further inside before pulling out again. He slowly fucked her with it, gaining a little more ground with each pass, but not as much as she was ready to beg him for. Dakota wanted him to impale her with it. Her eyelids shut as she concentrated on the sensations his fingers were creating. When his tongue replaced his thumb on her clit, she nearly hit the ceiling. "Oh, God!"

"Like that, baby?" He didn't wait for her answer as he repeated the action. Flattening his tongue, he drove the little bud of nerves crazy, and Dakota couldn't stop the moaning and keening coming from her lips. He added a second finger to the first one fucking her and thrust deep. It took everything in her not to move her hips. Damn, the man was talented when it came to sex. It wasn't long before he had her climbing higher and higher. "No coming until I say so, baby. Let's see how long it takes for me to make you beg."

Not long at all, she thought. But she'd heard the challenge in his tone, and she was going to hold out as long as she could, because it would make the end result much more explosive.

Her hands gripped the wooden slats harder when his fingers found that sensitive tissue deep in her pussy, rubbing it, not hard enough to send her over, but enough that she had to bite her tongue to keep from pleading for release. He spread his two fingers inside her and added his tongue to the torture as the thumb of his other hand found her clit again. The triple assault was more than she could take, and damn it, she couldn't wait any longer. "Please, Sir. Oh, please, let me come. Shit! I need . . ."

"I know what you need, baby. Get ready to fly."

His fingers and tongue increased their assault, and when her climax hit her hard, Dakota did what he'd predicted—she screamed his name so loud, she wouldn't be surprised if someone called 9-1-1 on them. Her body shook with the force of her orgasm as Logan drew it out as long as possible. Perspiration coated her skin as she floated back down, gasping for breath. He lightly nipped her inner thigh. "You're gorgeous when you come, Koko, fucking gorgeous. I could watch you do that all night long and never tire of it."

She glowed under his praise. "Thank you, Sir."

It had been a long time since she'd felt so incredibly feminine around a man, but Logan brought that buried part of her to the surface. He was dangerous—not to her body or mind, but to her heart. When his fingers began stroking her again, she pushed all thoughts from her mind other than how good he was making her feel. She'd deal with the rest of it in the morning.

"Infidels, *you will pay for coming to our country. You'll never see your American whores again. We killed your friends, like the disgusting pigs deserved, as we will kill you."*

"Fuck you, assholes," Clutch barked, giving their captors two middle fingers from where his wrists were shackled to the wall above him, despite his weakness. "Sit on 'em and rotate."

His voice was as raspy as Logan's felt. The two of them, and an unconscious Stash, were the only ones left alive. The others had been brutally whipped before being decapitated. And now it appeared one more of them would be dragged out at gunpoint for their torturous death. With Stash out of it, there would be no entertainment for the ISIS bastards, so that meant they'd choose between Logan and Clutch. They'd made a game of this after Moonshine and Gunny had been killed, drawing out the selection process of who would end up on the chopping block next. Logan couldn't stand it anymore. He'd never be the same, and he couldn't let them pick Clutch next—it was time to end this. He'd still go down with a fight, but he'd be damned if he let his best friend die before him.

Rolling to his knees, Logan stood.

"Cowboy, what the fuck are you doing?"

He turned a deaf ear to Clutch's question, knowing his buddy already had a clue what the answer was. "Take me, you fucking bastards! I'll kill as many of you as I can before I meet my Almighty God. Yeah, you're not the only ones who believe in the afterlife, but unlike you, I don't rape and murder in His name." The five men began shouting in Arabic at him, as Clutch did the same in English, but Logan just raised his voice. "Our Father, who art in heaven . . ."

Logan clenched his fists and finished the Lord's prayer before starting on the Hail Mary. A burst of gunfire into the ceiling above his head had him ducking as dirt rained down on him.

"You will pay for your insolence, infidel, but not today," the leader sneered.

He then spoke in rapid Arabic and pointed at Clutch. Logan's eyes went wide, and his stomach dropped when he realized his plan had backfired. "Shit! No! Take me, you bastards! Take me!"

They ignored him as one used a key to unlock Clutch's cell on the other side of Stash's. His teammate was already on his feet, ready to put up the fight of his life, but they weren't going to play fair. Before the bastards got within range of his fists, one pulled out a Sig Sauer they'd confiscated from the Raiders and shot him in his right knee. Clutch couldn't hold back the roar of agony as his leg gave way and he dropped like a stone before they released his shackles. "Son of a bitch! Goddamn fucking bastards! That's the only way you motherfuckers have a bloody chance in hell!"

Logan was also screaming at them as Clutch tackled one man around his knees, before throwing as many punches as he could. Another Afghani lifted the rifle he was holding and slammed it down on the back of the Marine's head, stunning him. The captor Clutch had been beating to a pulp, got to his feet and kicked him in the gut several times before aiming at his bloodied knee. Unable to bear the pain, Clutch vomited on several of their feet, which earned him another kick to his abdomen.

Watching in horror, unable to do anything but scream at them to stop, which, of course, went unheeded, Logan's heart sank as they dragged his half-unconscious best friend from the cell. The leader sneered at Logan, spat something in Arabic, and then walked out the door, slamming it behind him.

A sob rose up in Logan's throat. "Cluuuuuttttttcccchhhhh!"

"Logan! Logan! Wake up!"

His eyes flew open, and he was suddenly back in the present. Sweat poured from his body as he gasped for air. The last of his nightmare vanished with the realization of where he was and who he was with. Cautiously, without touching him, Dakota knelt in front of him on the bed. "Are you okay?"

"I-I didn't hurt you, did I?" His gaze roamed over her naked body, searching for any sign he'd hit her or something as he forced his fists to release the sheets he was gripping tightly.

"No. You were just thrashing around and yelling." Climbing from the bed, she pulled on his T-shirt. "Let me get us something to drink."

Thankful for a moment alone, he realized there had been no fear, pity, or reproach in Dakota's tone of voice. Rolling off the bed, he stumbled to the attached bath and turned the handle on the sink. Cupping his hands together, he splashed the cool water on his face several times, before staring at his reflection in the mirror. Droplets fell from his chin, and he grabbed a nearby towel as Dakota appeared in the doorway. Instead of the bottle of water he'd expected her to bring him, she was carrying two glasses of what appeared to be scotch or whiskey. "Is one shot of Jack Daniels okay?"

He reached for the one she held out toward him. "Yeah. Only one."

"I noticed whenever we had dinner or drinks, two was your limit no matter what you were drinking or when."

Tossing back the smooth liquor, he savored the burn down his throat. "If I don't stop at two, I won't stop until I get to the point I want to fight someone, so yeah, two's my limit."

"Want to talk about it?" Dakota asked before downing her own shot.

Logan shook his head as his gaze fell to her painted toes and trailed upward. "Nope." He stepped toward her, grabbed the bottom of his shirt, and yanked it over her head. "Talking is the last thing I want to do right now."

Grinning, she placed her glass on the counter next to his. "How about a shower and a blowjob . . . Sir?"

And, damn, if the sight of her toned, naked body and the offer of a blowjob hadn't already made his cock harden, then that last word would have—and once again, he thanked the hard-on gods that everything was in working order. It occurred to him this is what he'd heard the Trident women talking about. While their Doms took care of them, cherished them, there were times when the reverse was necessary, and they loved to cater to their Doms' needs, no matter what they were.

Bringing his hand to his groin, he stroked himself. "I think that sounds amazing."

Stepping over to the shower, Dakota reached in and turned on the water, waiting for the right temperature before taking his free hand and pulling him into the stall and under the spray. The shower was larger than he'd expected, and the water pressure was perfect, pounding on his back in a ruthless but incredible massage. Without a word, Dakota picked up a loofah sponge and poured some body wash into it. A citrus scent filled the air, reminding him of the orange spray they used at The Covenant to clean off the equipment. He closed his eyes as she ran the sudsy sponge up his arm, over his chest, and back down the other arm. Taking her time, she cleaned him from head to toe before tossing the loofah aside and rinsing him off. Once he was soap-free, she gently urged him to lean against the tiled wall.

Swallowing hard, he watched her take a towel from the rack outside the shower, fold it over several times, then drop it on the wet floor. She sank to her knees atop the towel in front of him. "Let me please you, Sir."

As if he could say no. "Suck me, Koko. Make me forget all about the hell in my nightmares."

He tilted his cock toward her waiting mouth and groaned

as her heat engulfed him. She hadn't hesitated or drawn out her seduction, going all in, which he was grateful for. He needed what she offered him. Her head bobbed up and down as she worked him over. Her tongue teased and tantalized every inch of his length, swirling it around his girth. She sucked, licked, and raked her teeth against his hard flesh uninhibitedly. Cupping his balls, she gently rolled them in her hand. His fingers gripped her wet hair, setting the pace he wanted. "Damn, baby. That feels incredible. Don't stop. God, please don't stop."

Taking him deep, Dakota swallowed, and Logan's eyes crossed as his head thumped against the tile behind him. "Do that again. Shit! Baby, I'm going to come down your throat. If that's not what you want, tell me now."

Her mouth released him long enough to say, "I want all of it, Sir."

She was going to be the death of him. His knees began to quiver as a tingling started low in his spine. Dakota hollowed her cheeks and sucked hard. His hand tightened in her hair. "Faster, baby. Faster."

Picking up the pace, she took him deep over and over, and Logan climaxed, shouting the nickname he'd given her. "Koko! Yes! Fuck! *Arrrgghhhh!*"

His hips bucked as she swallowed every drop he poured into her. Black and white spots danced in front of his closed eyelids, and he thought he'd never stop coming into her mouth. Gasping for air, he released his hold on her head as she licked him clean.

Pulling away, her gaze rose to his. "Think you can go back to sleep now, Sir?"

Reaching down, he grabbed her under the armpits and helped her up. Crushing his mouth to hers, he kissed her hard and long before finally lifting his head again. "Sleep is the last thing I want now, baby. Let's see how many times I can make you come before my cock recovers."

He shut the water off and grabbed another towel to quickly dry her and then himself. He'd told her the truth. The last thing he wanted was to go back to sleep where his nightmares awaited him. If only he could stay awake and in her bed for the rest of his life, he'd be a very, very happy man.

FIFTEEN

"Make the next right," Georgia Branneth instructed from the passenger seat of Tiny's SUV, thankful the big teddy bear of a man was driving her home. From what he and Master Devon had been able to determine, the alternator had gone out in her Toyota. She'd been unable to start it when attempting to leave The Covenant tonight. The club owner had assured her he'd have the Trident Security mechanics fix it for her tomorrow, while Tiny volunteered to drive her home. She'd texted her friend as soon as it became apparent she'd need a ride to the high school, where Georgia taught English and Janet was the vice principal, so she'd see it first thing in the morning.

She loved how the Doms at The Covenant were so protective of the subs, even outside of the club walls. Especially with that sick serial killer running around targeting submissives. Even though Tiny didn't participate in the lifestyle, he was just as protective as the Doms, if not more so, of the female members. Standing six foot eight, the man was the size of a refrigerator, and anyone would have to be insane to mess with him. She also knew he sometimes worked as a bodyguard when the Trident bosses needed him to, and he'd been armed at all times since they'd learned about the killer's choice of victim.

A yawn escaped her as she pointed out her small house to her escort who chuckled. "Tired?"

"Well, it is after midnight, and I've been up since six a.m. The only reason I went to the club tonight was for Colleen's birthday." Trident's office manager had become a good friend of Georgia's over the past year or so, having come out of her shell since working for the Sexy Six-Pack, as Devon's wife, Kristen, had dubbed the original men who'd started the business.

Pulling into her driveway, Tiny smiled. "I'm sure she was happy you could celebrate with her." He put the vehicle in park and added, "Stay there, Miss Georgia. Let me take a quick walk around the house to make sure everything looks good."

Georgia knew better than to object, and if she were honest with herself, she appreciated the gesture. Once he exited the SUV, he closed the door and locked her inside. He then turned on the flashlight he'd grabbed from under the driver's seat. It was one of those heavy-duty Maglites that could fracture someone's skull if swung hard enough. Her brother, Greg, who was a police officer in Miami, had given her two of them. One was in the house, and the other was in her Camry.

As Tiny rounded the side of her house, Georgia's gaze followed the glow of the flashlight until it disappeared. The silence surrounding the vehicle made her shift uncomfortably. Tipping her head forward, she checked the side-view mirror. Not seeing anything of concern, she then glanced over her shoulder, scanning the area directly behind the truck. Normally, she wasn't a scaredy-cat, but for some reason, tonight, she was on edge. When she spotted the beam from Tiny's flashlight bobbing from the far side of the house, she released a tense breath she'd been holding.

Finishing his inspection of her property, the big man strode to the passenger side of the truck and opened her door for her. "Everything looks okay. I'll walk you to your door."

Holding out his hand, he helped her down from the elevated height. At five foot four, she was dwarfed by both the man and his vehicle. She dug into her purse, and by the time they reached the front door, she had her keys out and ready. Unlocking the door, she swung it open and turned to thank her escort to find him frowning. "You didn't set the alarm?"

Shit. Of course he'd notice that. She usually set it, but some days, she was in such a hurry or in a mental fog, she forgot. Her brother would kick her ass if he knew, since he'd insisted on having it installed in the first place. "I must have forgotten. I promise it won't happen again. Thanks, Tiny. I appreciate the ride."

Bending down, he gave her a brotherly peck on the cheek. "Glad I could help. Now, lock the door and set the alarm, so I know you're safe."

"Yes, Master Travis."

He grinned at the snarked title he never used. "Brat. Get going."

Once she'd done as she'd been told, she waved at him through the door-side window, and then watched as he returned to his truck and drove away. Sighing, she kicked off her shoes and left them and her purse next to the hallway table. Yawning again, she stretched on her way to her bedroom. Tomorrow, or today as it was, would be a long day, and she'd be looking forward to a nap as soon as she got home from work. Thankfully, the gymnastics team's season, which she was the coach for, didn't start up for another week.

Flipping the foyer light switch off and the hallway one on with a flick of her hand, she headed for the bathroom. The small, two-bedroom ranch was the perfect size for a single woman. The neighborhood was nice and quiet, and she had a decent-sized plot of land. She'd spent many a weekend culti-vating the landscape by herself, planting flowers and shrubs to give herself a small Eden in Florida.

Flushing the toilet, she washed and dried her hands, then used a makeup remover wipe to clean her face. She shut off the light, making her way to her bedroom. Her hand reached for the switch that would turn on the beside lamp, but when she flipped the switch nothing happened. *Damn it.*

It seemed, lately, all her light bulbs were reaching the end of their lives, and she'd used the last spare one yesterday for the lamp in the second bedroom she used as an office. For now, there was just enough moonlight coming through the edges of her closed curtains for her to see. Mentally putting light bulbs on a shopping list for tomorrow, she reached down for the hem of her shirt. But she never had a chance to remove it as an arm wrapped around her waist at the same time a damp cloth was slapped over her mouth and nose.

Panic coursed through her as she struggled and fought against her much bigger assailant. She tried to hold her breath while she kicked and clawed at him, only finding fabric every-where she scratched. Twisting in his arms, she caught sight of his face out the corner of her eye.

What? Him?

He was a Dom she knew but had never played with.

Why is he doing this? What does he want? I have to get away!

Georgia continued to struggle as seconds ticked into minutes. Her mind blurred as her movements weakened. As she collapsed into darkness, her last thought was her brother was going to kill her if she died.

THE DOM LET Georgia drop to the floor. For a small thing, she sure was feisty—just how he liked them. When she woke up in his dungeon later, he was looking forward to her spirit putting up a fight.

Tucking the rag doused with an isoflurane derivative—chloroform didn't work like in the movies—into his pocket, he then pulled out a tourniquet and a syringe filled with a combination of barbiturates commonly used for anesthesia. He'd gotten very good at estimating his victim's weight so he wouldn't give them an overdose.

Quickly wrapping the tourniquet around her left bicep, he found a large vein and injected the drugs into her system. That would keep her out long enough for him to carry her out the back door and lock it behind them, then leave her in the shadows at the side of the house while he retrieved his vehicle from where he'd parked it three blocks away in a used car lot. The trip to his dungeon would be about fifty minutes at this hour of the night, with traffic at a bare minimum. After he chained her to the bed there, he'd return home and get some sleep. The fun wouldn't begin until she'd woken up from the drugs and had a few hours to panic over her predicament.

Stepping over to the bedside lamp, he screwed the light bulb back in place until it lit the room. The Dom glanced around to make sure he wasn't leaving anything out of place and there were no signs he'd ever been in the house. Turning the lamp back off, he bent down and picked up the petite woman. Luck had been on his side tonight. Since the police and Doms had been stepping up their game, making sure the submissives in the area knew to take precautions and being escorted whenever possible, he'd needed to step up *his* game too.

The internet was the greatest invention ever for research. For the past few weeks, he'd been practicing picking locks with a set of tools he'd found online. There were countless instructional videos on YouTube, and while he was still practicing harder locks, he'd been able to pick the one on Georgia's back door within five minutes. He'd been watching her for about three weeks now, and saw she was sometimes lax with setting the alarm system in her house. From a side kitchen window, he'd been able to see the alarm panel near the back door had been dark. Being careful not to leave any scratch marks on the brass, deadbolt lock, he'd gained entry about a half hour before she got home. He hadn't expected Daultry to drive her home and walk around the house with a flashlight, but the asshole hadn't come inside with the sub. If he had, the Dom would have shot him with the 9mm handgun he had holstered at his lower back. The big oaf was lucky he sucked at being a bodyguard—it'd saved his life.

An hour later, his new masterpiece was naked, blindfolded, and restrained spread-eagle on the old hospital bed in the sparse, one-room building in the woods bordering Chassahowitzka National Wildlife Refuge. It had been used as a utility building a few decades ago, but then abandoned when a new one had been built a mile closer to the main road at another turnoff. The only other items in the concrete structure were a cabinet that held his tools and a St. Andrew's cross where his scenes took place, where his masterpieces came to life and then met their deaths at his hand. He was their Master and their executioner, and only he said when enough was enough. No one else. Him. The ultimate Dom.

Following Captain Bowman from TPD's Special Ops Division through the lobby of the FBI building, Ian and Devon flashed their government IDs to the armed guards manning the metal detectors. All three men were waved around the full-body scanner—the guards knew them by sight now and were aware of the weapons they were carrying—before approaching the bank of elevators. While they waited for a car to open, Ian tilted his head side to side, cracking his vertebrae. He'd gotten very little sleep last night and neither had Angie. They'd only gone to the club to celebrate Colleen's birthday, otherwise, they would have spent the Wednesday night at home. They'd only been home an hour or so, when Angie had made a beeline for the bathroom. They'd thought her nausea was a thing of the past as she entered her second trimester, but apparently, Little Bit hadn't liked something Angie had eaten, and she'd spent half the night in the bathroom. After her stomach was empty, the dry heaves had continued, and Ian had to make a 2:00 a.m. run to the store to get saltines and ginger ale for her.

When Ian had left their bed this morning, Angie was still sleeping, so he'd asked Kristen to check on her for him in a little while. The task force meeting was scheduled for 0900. After that, he'd be able to go back to the compound and catch a catnap for a bit.

The bell above the middle elevator car dinged, and when the door opened, Parrish came rushing out with two other agents on his heels. He spotted Ian, Devon, and Bowman immediately. "Good, you're here. We might have another missing submissive."

"Shit," Devon spat. "Who?'

Sympathy crossed the special agent's face, and Ian's stomach roiled like Angie's probably had last night. He knew what the man was going to say, but he didn't know the *who*. "It's a Covenant sub, isn't it?"

Parrish nodded as the blood drained from the faces of both Sawyer brothers. "We're not a hundred percent sure yet. Georgia Branneth didn't show up for work this morning. Her purse and keys are in the house, but there's no sign of her car."

"That's because it's at our compound," Devon informed

them. "It wouldn't start last night so Tiny drove her home. I told her I'd have Babs check it for her."

"Tampered?" Ian asked.

His brother shook his head. "I don't think so. Looked like the alternator was shot, but I can have Babs check now."

When he pulled out his phone, Bowman stopped him. "Hang on. If it was tampered with, it's evidence. Let's do it by the book. I'll get patrol over there and tow it back to the PD garage."

Devon nodded. "All right. I'll let her know they're coming and to make sure no one touches it."

"On the way to Branneth's house, give your man, Daultry, a call and have him respond there too. I want to know everything that happened after he left the club with her last night." With a hand gesture, Parrish got them all walking back toward the building's main entrance again.

Ian was glad the fed gave no indication Tiny was a suspect, because he'd put their friend and employee last on a list of over a million suspects before he even considered him to be their killer. If anything, Tiny was going to be devastated when he found out what happened. *If* Georgia had been kidnapped.

By the time they reached Georgia's small, ranch-style house, there were three patrol cars, two unmarked vehicles, an FBI Evidence Response Team Unit (ERTU) van, and, unfortunately, two news vans. Ian was certain more were on the way.

The uniformed officers had already begun to hang the yellow tape around the property, and their vehicles had blocked the road, so the press was stuck behind them, unable to get good shots due to the high shrubs blocking the view of the house. A patrol officer put his vehicle in drive and moved it a few feet to let Bowman, Parrish, and Ian's vehicles into the restricted area, before blocking the way again. Before climbing out of his SUV with its darkly, tinted windows, Ian took the

Tampa Rays baseball cap Devon had retrieved from the back-seat, and placed it low on his head, hiding his facial features from the news cameras. His brother donned another cap. The last thing they needed in their businesses was to be identified while investigating a crime scene.

Getting out of the vehicle, they strode purposely toward the front steps of the house—at least there they were out of camera range—and met with Bowman, Parrish, and the other feds. There was also a woman Ian didn't recognize standing next to SA Novik who made the introductions. "This is Ms. Branneth's friend and vice principal at the high school, Janet Benson. Ms. Benson, this is Special Agent in Charge Colt Parrish, Captain Al Bowman, and investigators Ian and Devon Sawyer."

Parrish gently shook the pale woman's hand. "I'm sorry we had to meet this way, Ms. Benson, and I know you've already told your story more than once already, but please start at the beginning."

Taking a shaky breath, Janet told them what little information she had. "All I know is she sent me a text at fourteen minutes after midnight to say she was getting a lift home from the club she goes to because her car wouldn't start and asked me to pick her up on my way to school today. I pulled up at ten to seven and honked the horn. When she didn't come out, I rang the doorbell and called her cell and got no answer. I thought maybe she got her car started and forgot to tell me, so I drove to the school. When she didn't show up before the first bell, I swung by my house to get the spare key she gave me last summer to water her plants while she went on vacation, then came back here. When I saw her purse with her keys and cell phone in the foyer, and her nowhere to be found, I called 9-1-1." By this point, tears were rolling down her cheeks. "I-I know the type of club she belongs to . . . but no one else at the school does. She was afraid someone would find out, and she'd lose her job, which is why she went to that private club . . . um . . . The . . . The Covenant, I think it's called. She never went to the public ones." Her gaze bounced from one person to the next. "You—you think that serial killer has her, don't you?"

None of them wanted to be the one to confirm that, but Parrish sucked it up and did his best to sugarcoat it. "We don't know, yet, Ms. Benson. Yes, she fits the profile, but so far, all the victims were taken from their driveways. It appears Ms. Branneth made it inside—"

"She *did* make it inside—I walked her to the door myself and made sure she locked it and set the alarm."

Ian turned to see his employee and friend marching toward the group. Tiny looked like he'd driven through hell to get there, his face filled with concern and guilt. Not because he had anything to do with Georgia's disappearance, but because he'd been the last one to see her—well, almost the last person to see her.

At Ian's request, Devon hadn't given Tiny any of the few details they'd had so far when he'd called to tell the man to meet them at Georgia's house because she was missing. Nor did Devon ask for any details of what had happened in the wee hours of the morning. They needed to hear what happened from his recollection without tainting it with anything that was said or implied to him. Usually, a missing person case like this would require at least twenty-four hours before being investigated, but since the submissive fit the profile, they were waiving the normal waiting period.

Before Tiny could say anything more, Parrish held up his hand to stop him before addressing his agents. "Novik and Davis, please take Ms. Benson back to the office and get a full statement from her, along with a list of friends and family. You know the drill. Ms. Benson, we'll do everything we can to find out what happened to Ms. Branneth. Any information you can give the agents to help us will be greatly appreciated."

As the two agents escorted their witness from the scene, a crime scene tech exited through the front door. "SAC Parrish. We found something around back."

He pointed to the side of the house, indicating they should walk around instead of through the building. At the back door, another female tech was dusting it for prints while another male tech marked off two footprints in the soil next to the patio. Parrish started with the latter. "A set or two different?"

The man glanced up from his work. "Two different. One's about a size fifteen and the other is a size twelve."

"The fifteen is probably mine. I walked around the house last night with my flashlight to make sure she'd be safe." Tiny's eyes watered, and he turned his head to the side for a moment to regain his composure. It bothered Ian to see the big man, who would never hurt a woman, get so emotional because one in his care had possibly been kidnapped by a serial killer. "I didn't see anything. I locked her in my truck while I walked around, and then escorted her to the door. It'd been locked, but I noticed she had an alarm that wasn't set. She said she sometimes forgets to set it. Damn it! I should have searched the house. Fuck! This is my fault!"

"Hey, Tiny," Devon said. "Man, look at me, damn it. This is not your fault. If you'd seen anything that made you think she was in danger, you never would have let her in the house alone. You know how easy it is to buy a jammer for security systems. He could've gotten in after she set the alarm and you left . . . all it takes is the right equipment." He was right—even some of the best systems out there weren't completely un-hackable. There were numerous ways to bypass a system if you did some research. "Hell, for that matter, we don't know if she left the house after you drove off. We don't know anything right now. You can't beat yourself up. If I was the one to drive her home, without something triggering my Spidey-sense, I would have done exactly what you did."

It was obvious the man wasn't convinced, but he nodded in Dev's direction anyway as Parrish pointed at the female technician. "Any prints on the door?"

She shook her head. "No . . . but it looks like someone was wearing gloves and smudged the ones that would normally be there. The lock's been picked. It's not obvious though. There're no scratches on the surface here . . ." She indicated the brass surface plate of the deadbolt around the keyhole. ". . . but with the magnifying camera I can see some inside the lock, otherwise, I would have missed them." Her last words were directed toward Tiny. She'd obviously overheard his guilt-ridden statements moments earlier and was trying to reassure him there was no way he could've spotted the damage to the lock. The only way she'd been able to see the scratch marks left by a lock pick set was by using a camera so small it could fit on the head of a ballpoint pen. "I'll contact our list of locksmiths to make sure no one came here on a lockout call."

Twenty minutes later, there had been no more obvious evidence found although the techs were vacuuming and swabbing for trace evidence throughout the interior of the house. Devon volunteered to accompany Tiny to the FBI office where he'd be interviewed fully, so Ian could return to the compound and check on Angie. The eldest Sawyer brother was not looking forward to telling everyone, especially Boomer, that Georgia was missing. Before Kat Michaelson had come out of the Witness Protection Program, in desperate need of her now husband's help—he hadn't known she was alive after "dying" twelve years earlier—Boomer had played a few times with the pretty divorcee at The Covenant, and they were still friends.

Stopping at the driver's door to his truck, he glanced back up at the little house. Bile rose in his throat. During all these months the sick bastard had been kidnapping and killing submissives, Ian had sworn he'd be damned if one of The Covenant's subs was taken. He'd made sure all the club members took every possible precaution. But it hadn't been enough. They had approximately three days before Georgia Branneth's tortured body was found, posed somewhere public in or around Tampa.

Opening the door, Ian climbed in and cranked the ignition, starting the engine. But instead of putting the vehicle in drive, he punched the dashboard, ignoring the pain shooting through his hand and arm. "Son of a fucking bitch. When we catch you, death will be too good for you."

OMEGA TEAM
TRIDENT SECURITY

Sixteen

"Come on, you wimp. You've got a few more in you."

Logan's chest, shoulder, and arm muscles shook as he bench-pressed the 220-pound bar. It was hard to concentrate on the weight when Dakota's spandex-covered crotch was right above his forehead as she spotted him. Her hands followed the up and down motion of his, ready to grab the bar if he reached his maximum rep. For the past few days, she'd joined him in the Trident gym with its top-of-the-line equipment, and he was enjoying working out with her, but damn, her toned body was a huge distraction at times like this.

Growling, he pushed upward against the weight and gravity. Sweat coated his body, and his muscles screamed for him to stop, but like Dakota had said, he had a few more in him. They had the place to themselves this morning after Angie and Kristen had finished their treadmill workouts while little JD had slept nearby in a playpen under the watchful eye of Beau. They'd welcomed Dakota into their territory, and Kristen had given him a knowing wink. He'd thought he'd been doing a good job of disguising his attraction to her, but apparently Devon's wife didn't miss a thing when it came to physical chemistry between two people.

And as far as Logan knew, that was all that was going on between him and Dakota. The only other person who knew the two of them had slept together for certain was Dakota's roommate who had seen him sneaking out around 2:00 a.m. the other night. After his first night in Dakota's bed, he hadn't wanted to actually sleep with her, afraid he might hurt her if or when a nightmare struck him again. She hadn't pushed, clearly figuring out his reluctance, and hadn't argued when he kissed her goodbye before taking his leave.

He was also glad she hadn't asked what had caused his freak out that night. Trudy had warned him he might have an increase in his PTSD nightmares with his sessions with the two female Dommes, but she expected it to be temporary as his body and mind adjusted to the new meaning behind the whip. He was due to undergo another whipping tomorrow morning. They'd decided on once a week, so his body could recover. In the meantime, he'd meet with one or the other Domme and train to be the one wielding the sadistic implement.

Taking a deep breath, he faltered on his last press when the scent of Dakota's arousal assailed him. Seeing him all pumped, hot, and sweaty was doing something for her, which in turn, did something for him. His cock twitched in his shorts as he roared, putting all his energy and strength into one final lift. Once he had it high above his head, Dakota grabbed the bar and helped him place it in its cradle. "Not bad, stud."

His eyebrows shot upward as he rolled to a sitting position on the bench. "Stud?"

She circled around and handed him a towel to wipe his face with, before straddling his thighs, standing above him.

"Yup. Stud. You have to know you have an incredible body and every woman with a pulse wags her tongue when you walk by."

Barking out a disbelieving laugh, he tossed the towel onto his shoulder and grasped her hips, pulling her toward him. He kissed the silky bare skin between her black sports bra and spandex shorts, eliciting a moan from her as she placed her hands on his shoulders for balance. They really shouldn't be doing this there where anyone could walk in on them, but he couldn't help himself. And it wasn't as if they were breaking any rules by sleeping together. In fact, he didn't think anyone would be surprised if they found out. She was an incredibly sexy woman, and he'd have to be dead not to want her. However, a part of him wanted more than that, but he had nothing to offer her. He was damaged goods and would never risk letting his guard down around her again. Sex? Great . . . amazing, in fact . . . but sleeping together again was out of the question.

"Don't move, baby. I've got you right where I want you," he murmured against her skin. She tasted salty from her own exercise, as his lips and tongue brushed over her upper abdomen. Throwing caution to the wind, he brought a hand up between her legs and stroked her through the thin material.

Dakota's hands tightened on his shoulders, but she held herself still, enjoying his ministrations. "Oh, God, Sir! That feels so good! *Mmmmm.*"

Lifting his head, he pulled down one side of her bra, exposing a gorgeous tit and its dusky rose peak. His mouth closed around the nipple, and he teased it with his tongue and teeth. Dakota moaned louder and her hips began to move in time with the fingers at her pussy.

Leaving that side of her bra tucked under her breast, he exposed the other one the same way, laving it with equal attention. He slowed then stopped when he heard male voices out in the parking lot. Pushing her back a step, he didn't bother fixing her sports bra as he tugged her by the hand toward the women's shower and changing room that had been added since women had been invading the Trident compound, grabbing his duffel bag on the way. His cock was harder than granite, and he couldn't wait to take her again. Locking the door behind them, he strode over to the shower stall and turned on the water. It was obvious a lot of thought had gone into the showers in both the men's and women's rooms, as they were large enough for three people and had benches built into them. Logan doubted he and Dakota were the first ones to share a shower and some nookie in here. "Strip, Koko. I hope you're not in the mood for slow, because this is going to be hard and fast." Slow sex was for the bedroom. Adventurous sex was a whole different ballgame.

"Whatever you want, Master Bellhop," she countered with a saucy grin, shoving her shorts to the floor.

His hand froze on the zipper of his duffel bag where he'd thrown in two boxes of condoms earlier after stopping at a convenience store. He arched an eyebrow at her as she shed her bra. "Little brat, you'll pay for that."

"I sure as hell hope so, Sir."

His gaze followed her as she sashayed into the shower, swaying her hips. If ever a woman wanted to be spanked, it was her. DeAngelis had gone through a demonstration, followed by a "hands-on" practice session, so to speak, in their training class. While he'd spanked Dakota several times in class, with everyone else around, she'd been clothed. This was the first time he'd be spanking her with the intent to give her what she was clearly telling him she needed.

Grabbing a condom from a box, he followed her into the shower, and tossed it on the tiled bench. "Hands against the wall and present that fine ass for me, Koko. My brat deserves a spanking before I fuck her silly."

"If you insist, Sir."

Once she was in position, the multi-shower heads pelting them both with water, he ran his hands over both ass cheeks, squeezing and rubbing like he'd been taught, to bring the blood to the surface. It would help prevent bruising in addition to being erotic as hell. One of these days, he was going to ask her about fucking her ass, but for today, her pussy would do just fine. He couldn't get enough of this woman. "Ready, Koko?"

"Oh, yes, Sir."

He was about to start but remembered one more important question. "What's your safeword, baby?"

"Red, Sir." Her tone was one of approval, and it triggered something deep inside him. He was surprised how good it felt, knowing he'd done something that she'd praise him for, as subtle as it was.

"For a count of twenty." Lifting his right hand, he smacked it against her flesh, and then held it there, letting the heat spread outward.

"One, Sir," followed a loud moan from her pretty, little mouth, making him impossibly hard.

Logan moved his hand so he could see her skin. He'd hit her hard enough for the area to turn a little pink, but that would change as he continued, each strike a little harder than the last. In class, he'd been learning how to read his submissive's body to know when she could handle more or if he needed to back off. He let the next smack land on her left ass cheek.

"Two, Sir."

When he reached ten, Dakota was panting and moaning. Her skin was a beautiful shade of red along her buttocks and sit spots, and he was having a hard time controlling himself. He wanted nothing more than to impale her on his cock, but another thing he'd learned in class was to follow through with what he'd started, whether it was for punishment or pleasure. His submissive was trusting him to know what she needed and to ensure she got it. He'd get his physical satisfaction soon enough, but it meant more to him to give her what she wanted, what she craved. But that didn't mean he couldn't tease her a little along the way.

His hand slid down between her legs, and he found her soaked, and not from the shower. Her body was reacting to his discipline and readying itself for when he would take her. He thrust two fingers in her tight channel, and she clenched her inner muscles around him. "Oh, God, yes! Please, Sir!"

"Not yet, Koko. You have ten more to go, and then I'm going to fuck you from behind, until you shatter around my cock. I love how you scream my name when you come." Pulling his fingers from her core, he brought them to his mouth, licking her sweet cream from them. "Delicious, baby. Ready for your next ten?"

"I'm green, Sir. Yes, I'm ready. Please!"

The sound of flesh impacting wet flesh bounced off the tiled walls as steam swirled around them. He had no idea if anyone had come into the gym and could hear them, but he doubted it was anything they hadn't heard before, especially with all the Doms and subs running around this place, and right now he didn't care. All that mattered was him giving Dakota what she needed before they both found their release.

"Nineteen, Sir!"

"Last one, Koko." Before giving her the final slap, he reached down and grabbed the condom package, putting it between his teeth and ripping the foil open. His other hand lifted and fell right over the crack of her ass which was now glowing a beautiful shade of red. Quickly donning the latex barrier, he lined his cock up with her pussy. "Fast and furious, baby. I'm not going to be able to hold back. Get ready."

"Please! Yes!"

He pushed forward, her heat enveloping and scorching him. With a swift thrust, he was buried to the hilt. Her gasps and moans filled the air, and her tight walls were already starting to quiver around him. It wouldn't take much to send her over the edge.

Reaching around, his fingers found her clit and stroked it as he pumped his hips harder and faster, his pelvis bouncing off her tender ass. Her muscles seized as the orgasm hit her. It felt like the tightest fist had him in its grasp as he neared his own climax. When her keening lessened, he clutched both her hips and plunged deep over and over. "Fuck, baby! So tight! So fucking good! *Ahhhhhhhh* . . . fuuuuucccccckkkkkk!"

His legs shook as he emptied his seed into the condom. Black and white spots danced in front of his closed eyelids, and he never wanted to leave her body. Damn, he was in trouble. He was falling for her—hard. But she hadn't given him any indication this was anything more than just sex between them. She'd told him the other night she'd never slept with any of her partners before, and he believed her. However, they both knew he was only a temporary partner. When they caught the Kink Killer, she would go back to her job and a new case, and he would be sent on Trident's next mission anywhere around the globe. Would that be the end of this . . . this relationship . . . or whatever it was? God, he hoped not— he wasn't ready to let her go yet and wasn't sure if he ever would be.

A thousand bees buzzed in Georgia's head as she floated back to consciousness. Damn, she had to get a new bed. When had her mattress gotten so freaking hard? And where was her pillow?

Blinking her eyelids, she tried to turn onto her side—she rarely slept on her back—but her limbs wouldn't cooperate. Licking her dry lips, she tried again, but when her arms and legs stopped short, her eyes flew open. She was naked and in unfamiliar surroundings. Yanking harder on the restraints at her wrists and ankles, panic set in. Her heart raced in fear.

Where the hell am I? What the fuck?

Her gaze darted around the room she found herself in, as she tried to figure out where she was, how the hell she got there, along with a who, why, and what. The first thing she realized was she was alone in a concrete structure. There were no windows and only one closed door. Aside from the hospital-type bed she was tied to, there were a few wood cabinets to her left and a large, leather-covered, wooden St. Andrew's cross to her right. The floor, ceiling and wall around it were stained in brownish splatter, and it wasn't hard to figure out it was dry blood.

Oh, God! No! No! No!

It couldn't be! She'd been careful—well, careful enough—hadn't she? There was no explanation she could think of other than she was in the lair of the Kink Killer.

Maybe it's a dream. Close your eyes, and when you open them again, you'll see it's nothing but a dream.

Georgia knew her hopeful subconscious was wrong, but she tried it anyway. When she opened her eyes again, bile rose to the back of her throat. Nope. It hadn't made a difference.

You're in so much fucking trouble. Think. There's got to be a way out of here . . . think!

Georgia was about to scream for help, but without knowing if her abductor was outside waiting for her to wake up, she couldn't risk drawing attention to that fact. Pausing to listen, the only thing she heard was the sound of rain, pouring from the sky. She tried to recall the last thing she'd been aware of before she'd found herself in this horrible nightmare.

I was at the club . . . for . . . for Colleen's birthday. I drove home . . . no, my car wouldn't start. Master Devon was going to have his mechanics look at it. Tiny! Tiny drove me home.

And she was almost positive he'd walked her to her door. After that, it was all a blur.

Had Tiny done this? Was he the Kink Killer? No. Absolutely not. Besides, he'd driven away after you locked the door, hadn't he? No, it wasn't Tiny. Someone else had been inside the house.

An image teased her mind, but she couldn't bring it to the surface.

Does it really fucking matter right now who it was? Figure out how to get out of here and then worry about the details.

Twisting her head to the left, she eyed the leather strap around her wrist. It was attached to a chain which snaked down behind the mattress. Pulling on it, she tried to twist her hand out to no avail. She couldn't even make her two hands reach to try and use her fingers to release the buckle of the restraint. Glancing down, she yanked on the leather and chains connected to her ankles. If she could get her feet free, she might be able to move further up on the bed and give the arm restraints more slack to work with, but it was no use.

Turning her attention to her right wrist, she tried to slide her hand out. While the leather was still snug, she felt it give a little more than the left one had. Twisting and pulling, she ignored the pain of her skin abrading, her mind focused on nothing else but getting the hell out of there before . . . before whoever had kidnapped her came back. She'd heard rumors of what the Kink Killer had done to his victims, and if she had to chew off her arm to keep from being his next victim, then that's what she'd do.

She hissed as the leather worked its way into her tender skin and blood began to ooze out. It hurt like hell, but the wetness was making it easier for her to move the restraint further down her wrist where the heel of her hand stopped it again. Having dislocated her thumb numerous times over her childhood years in gymnastics, popping it out of its socket was something she did when she wanted to gross people out. Of course, she hadn't done it in a few years, but it wasn't hard to do.

Scooting up as far as the chains at her feet would allow, she angled her hand to hit the top of the short headboard. She had just enough slack to slam her hand against it. Once. Twice. The *pop* and pain that followed were nothing she hadn't experienced before, and she quickly went back to work, trying to slide her hand through the loosening leather. Her skin ripped more as she maneuvered her hand back and forth, pulling evenly instead of yanking.

"Fuck! Come on. You can do it. Just a little . . . more . . . *ahhhhhh* . . . shit . . . shit!"

Her hand slid free, and Georgia gulped for air as sweat covered her naked body. Not knowing how much time she had left, she popped her thumb back into place and shifted to her left side. Ignoring the agony of her abused wrist, she unbuckled the second restraint. Once free, she sat up and released her legs. Standing, her knees almost giving out under her weight, she grabbed the side of the bed to keep from falling. Her mouth was dry as a desert, and she licked her lips as she stumbled toward the cabinets. Hoping her clothes were in one of them or at least a bottle of water, she was disappointed to find they held nothing of use to her except a screwdriver. She could use that as a weapon. The rest of the items were cleaning products, other tools and hardware that were useless to her, and more chains and restraints. Well, she'd been naked in front of dozens of people before in the club. Being embarrassed trumped being tortured and killed any day of the week.

Hurrying to the door, she was relieved to see a deadbolt latch on the inside. Flipping it, she prayed there wasn't another lock on the outside. When she pulled on the handle beside the lock, she almost shouted "yes" when the door opened toward her. She eased it slowly until she had enough space to check what was on the other side. She was surprised to see nothing but trees, rocks, shrubs, and weeds. A squirrel scurried past, and birds chirped and flew overhead. The rain had slowed to a sprinkle and everything smelled new and fresh. Stepping out, she ignored the mud and pebbles poking the bottom of her feet and looked right then left. Before she went anywhere, she needed a pit stop—her bladder was about to burst. Ducking around the building, which had probably been a utility building for some company or parks department before being abandoned, she squatted and took care of business before investigating her surroundings.

There was a dirt drive running past the small structure—that was her way out of here, but she couldn't risk her abductor coming back and finding her walking along the road. Her best bet was to stay far enough away from it to be concealed by the foliage, while close enough to follow it out to a main road. But should she head east or west? What would her brother tell her to do?

See if there are any tire tracks in one direction and not the other.

Good idea, Greg. Maybe you won't kill me when you find out what a stupid idiot I was.

Georgia gingerly put one foot in front of the other and hurried over to the drive. Tire tracks went in both directions, but there were deeper ones and more of them to the right —west.

Moving back to the cover of the trees and shrubs, she picked her way through the forest. The only sounds were from the surrounding wildlife, which made her jumpy, and she tried to figure out where she might be. There were several national and state parks within driving distance of Tampa, as well as plenty of undeveloped land. While it was warm, the dampness from the mud under her feet and the last of the ebbing rain—and probably a healthy dose of fear—was causing her teeth to chatter and goose bumps to cover her skin. She watched the terrain in front of her, carefully, not wanting to trip or step in a hole or, God-forbid, on a snake or some other creepy crawler.

While it seemed like hours since she'd left her makeshift prison, in reality, it'd probably only been fifteen or twenty minutes. Unfortunately, she hadn't come across any streams or lakes to slake her parched throat and mouth. She wondered what drugs she'd been given to knock her out for so long. GHB and rohypnol popped into her head, but she quickly dismissed the "date rape" drugs. While she'd never been exposed to them, as a high school teacher she'd taken classes on them. Since those usually caused memory blackouts, and she could remember most of last night, it was doubtful either of those drugs had been in her system. Aside from the dehydration, and throbbing wrist and bare feet, the only other physical complaint she had was a pounding headache.

Rhythmic thumps reached her ears, and it took a moment to realize they were the sounds of tires on a highway or main road. At least she was heading in the right direction for civilization. Stubbing her toe on a rock, she cursed herself for being distracted. Shaking off the pain, she forged ahead. Another noise filtered through her brain, and she froze. A vehicle was coming down the dirt road which was only about thirty feet to her left. Afraid it was her captor returning to the scene of the crime, she ducked down behind several trees and dense shrubs. Peeking through the leaves and branches, she could just make out a beat up, blue, four-door sedan passing by. Definitely not a police or parks department vehicle, and she couldn't see the driver.

Georgia's heart rate increased as she held her breath until the car was out of sight, and then she took off in the other direction. Hopefully, she'd find the highway before he realized she was gone and came after her. Her life depended on it.

Branches and leaves slapped against her nude body, scratching her skin as she pushed herself as fast as she could under the conditions. She angled away from the dirt drive, heading northwest, putting as much distance between whoever had been in the sedan and herself. Her feet were raw and covered in mud, but still she pressed on. The drone of engines on the highway ahead of her grew louder until the foliage opened up. The paved road was only two lanes as one car and then another flew by her, their drivers oblivious to the naked woman emerging from the trees.

Panting and sweating, Georgia climbed over the guardrail and frantically looked in both directions for a vehicle she could flag down. To her left was a straightaway, and she could just make out the turnoff that had to lead to the building where she'd been held. To her right, the road turned sharply. And, damn it, all of a sudden, there weren't any cars around. Going to the left was out of the question. If that had been her abductor in the blue car, then he'd be coming back that way soon. In fact, she was surprised he hadn't already.

Limping on her abused feet, she crossed the road and hurried toward the bend. The shoulder was all dirt and rocks, so she stayed on the side of the pavement, along the white line. The sound of a vehicle speeding along was a relief when she realized it was approaching her from around the bend. But her heart caught in her throat when she heard the rev of another engine, this one behind her. Glancing back, she panicked as the blue sedan peeled out of the dirt turnoff and onto the asphalt road, directly toward her. Gasping for air, Georgia began to sprint, her feet slapping against the pavement, knowing it was futile. As she looked back again at her pursuer, the screech of tires was the last thing she heard as pain shot through her body. She felt herself go airborne as her world went dark.

Seventeen

Fuck! Fuck! Fuck! How the fuck had the bitch escaped!
He'd been a little late getting back to her after getting stuck in traffic behind a major accident that had temporarily shut down the lanes of the highway, but she still should have been restrained even if she'd woken up from the drugs. When he'd entered the utility bunker and found the bed empty, he'd been shocked and then panicked that the cops and feds were lying in wait for him, but when no one appeared, he quickly packed up his whips and restraints. He always used gloves in there so as not to leave any fingerprints in case someone discovered his dungeon.

Now, after double checking there was nothing around that could lead the fucking cops and feds to him, he climbed back into the beat-up, nondescript vehicle he used for hunting and headed back to the main road. He almost missed seeing her running naked down the road to his right.

Rage boiled within him. She didn't deserve to be a masterpiece now, but that didn't mean he wasn't going to kill her.

Punching the accelerator with his foot, he yanked the steering wheel to the right. The tires spun a moment before gaining purpose. Dirt and gravel flew behind the car as the tires squealed when they caught the pavement. The bitch heard him coming and glanced back with sheer terror in her eyes.

Hmm . . . maybe she could still be a masterpiece.

As he closed the distance between them, another vehicle came around the bend, and the Dom watched it impact the submissive's body, tossing her like a rag doll into the air. The other driver slammed on his brakes far too late to keep from hitting her, but it appeared he was going to stick around, which meant the Dom had to cut his losses and get the fuck out of there. Flooring the accelerator, he sped past the broken body of Georgia Branneth, confident she wouldn't survive her injuries.

Damn it! Now he had to find a new dungeon to continue his art . . . and select a new victim. His cock twitched as Dakota Smith's face and delectable body popped into his mind. Risky or not, she would be his best masterpiece to date. He just had to figure out how to get her away from that wannabe Dom, Logan Reese.

Dakota rushed into the emergency room on Ian Sawyer's heels with Logan right behind her. The partners had just come out of the gym at the Trident compound and found the owner throwing a ball for Beau to catch. He'd offered the use of the state-of-the-art facility as another way for Logan and Kip to bond with their new partners by working out together and sparring against each other.

A brief chat between the trio had been interrupted by Sawyer's cell phone ringing, and the resulting conversation with SAC Parrish had him barking for Dakota and Logan to follow him to Tampa General Hospital. A naked woman, fitting the missing Georgia Branneth's description, had been struck by a vehicle on Route 39 off I-75, near the Chassahowitzka National Wildlife Refuge. She'd been flown via helicopter to the trauma center. Ian didn't know her condition, other than she was unconscious, but if this was the missing submissive, she might be the only person who could tell them who the Kink Killer was.

SAC Parrish and SA Novik were in the hallway, outside a treatment room, speaking with a short, gray-haired man wearing blue hospital scrubs. The lead federal agent's attention swung briefly to the newcomers, before returning to the other man. "So, what you're saying, Doctor Rayburn, is you have no idea if or when she's going to wake up and be able to talk to us."

The physician nodded his head. "She came in unconscious, and her Glasgow Coma Score is a seven, which means she has some responses to pain, none of them verbal. If that doesn't improve within twenty-four hours, she's got a little less than a 50/50 chance of survival. The CT scan showed a subdural hematoma, and she's heading to surgery now. On top of all that, she's got a fractured left femur and wrist, and maybe a few ribs, but obviously, the brain is what we're worried about most right now. Do we know if there's any next of kin?"

"I know she's got a brother on Miami PD," Sawyer responded gravely. "I can have Captain Bowman call a supervisor down there for the notification. I assume a verbal consent over the phone will be fine for the surgery until her brother or other family members can get here."

"Yes, although, with her injuries, it's not necessary. If you can't get ahold of a family member, we're covered under implied consent." In other words, if they didn't operate right away, she would most likely die from her injuries, and they could assume the patient would want everything done to prevent that. "Oh, before I forget, we took photos of her wrists and ankles, at the request of the police officer who had come in with her, before we sent her for the CT. We couldn't wait for him to get a camera from the station. It looks like she'd been restrained somehow. The abrasions on her ankles aren't too bad, but she did do quite a bit of damage to her wrists, especially the right one. A lot of the skin is missing from struggling against the restraints. The officer is in that report office over there." He pointed to a room a few doors down the hallway. "He's got the SD card with the photos."

As the doctor hurried into another treatment room after a nurse called for him, the door to the ambulance entrance swung open and in walked Tiny, Mitch Sawyer, and a woman Dakota didn't recognize. She stood about five foot four and had long black hair framing her exotic Asian features. Worry was etched on all their faces, but Tiny seemed to be taking it the worst. "How is she?"

Not one to mince words, Ian shook his head. "It's not good." After filling them in on what the ER doctor had said, he addressed his cousin. "Mitch, can you look up her brother's name in the member files? I remember he's a cop in Miami, and we need to contact him."

"Sure thing."

As the co-owner and manager pulled out his smart phone and got to work finding the information, the woman who'd come in with him placed a comforting hand on Tiny's arm. The fifteen-inch size difference between the two of them was almost comical, but the grief on the pale, Black man's face was heart wrenching. He was blaming himself, and the woman knew it. "Come on, big guy. While Mitch is doing that, let's go to the surgical waiting room." She glanced at Ian. "We'll be there for her at least until her family can get here. She mentioned last night her folks were on a cruise in the Caribbean somewhere. It's their anniversary."

"Shit—happy fucking anniversary. Thanks, Charlotte. When Bowman talks to her brother, I'll make sure he finds out what ship. I'll send CC to their next port of call in the company jet and get them back here as fast as we can."

Once again, Ian Sawyer surprised Dakota. She knew he was protective of the subs in The Covenant. But to send his company's jet and pilot to pick up the couple on some island in the Caribbean showed how he took his role as head Dom of the club seriously and didn't care about the cost.

Tiny and Charlotte headed down the hall toward a bank of elevators, and Parrish tilted his head in that direction. "Novik, go with them. Keep me updated on her condition. Talk to security—tell them she's in protective custody. I don't want this bastard trying to get to her in here when he finds out she's escaped—if he doesn't already know. I'll call the office and have Stonewall send more bodies this way. Oh, and grab that SD card or get a copy of it. Reese, Swift, you're with Sawyer and me. Let's head to the accident scene and figure out where the hell she was running from."

About forty minutes later, they were standing on the edge of the accident scene. A state police escort had sped their civilian vehicles up the fifty miles faster than they could have gone without the lights and sirens. The driver of the car who had hit Georgia was a man in his late-fifties—a real estate agent on his way to meet a client. The poor guy was sitting on the guardrail behind his damaged vehicle, distraught. Dakota could see tears running down his cheeks as he spoke to someone on his cell phone. From the report one of the first officers on scene gave the newcomers, the driver had come around the tight bend and barely had a chance to hit the brakes when he came upon the naked woman running toward him in the middle of his lane. It had all happened so fast, and he couldn't remember if there were any other vehicles or people in the vicinity at the time. A few minutes later, two female drivers came across the accident and stopped to help. They'd stayed and given their information to the police, before being released from the scene.

It was easy to figure out where Georgia Branneth's battered body had ended up. There were some discarded, stained bandages and latex gloves in the middle of the road from when the paramedics had worked to stabilize her and place her on a backboard for transport. A small pool of blood was another indication of how serious her injuries were. The local cops had immediately shut down the road in both directions upon arrival, and an accident investigation team was in the process of measuring tire marks and photographing everything for evidence. They'd determine how fast the vehicle had been going before the driver had hit the brakes and impacted the victim. So far, there was no press in sight, and hopefully it stayed that way for now before they got a whiff on the big story that one of the Kink Killer's victims may have escaped and survived. The questions were, what direction had the naked woman been coming from and where had she been held? Had she, in fact, been kidnapped by the same sick bastard who'd killed all those other women? If she had, how did she escape?

SAC Parrish had commandeered the scene and was doling out orders to the police chief, who had responded, and several of his officers who weren't already busy with the accident scene and detours around it. "All right, our victim came from somewhere nearby. It's possible she escaped from a vehicle, but I don't think that's the case. She was being held close by. Chief, I want you and your men to take the north side of the accident, check both sides of the road. Look for bare footprints or any indication of how she ended up on the road. We'll take this south side. Go at least a mile. If we don't find anything, we'll spread out into the woods. I have about a dozen agents responding. Call in whomever you can to help search, but make sure they don't disturb any evidence. This is the first real chance we've gotten to catch this bastard."

If the older chief had any problem with being ordered about by a fed in his own jurisdiction, he didn't show it. "Our fire department has a search and rescue team we can utilize. They know their stuff about tracking in these woods and won't fuck up a crime scene if they can help it. I can have them out here within fifteen minutes."

"Do it."

It took a while, but Logan found a set of prints, that had to belong to Georgia, coming out of the woods on the opposite side of the road from where she'd been hit, about an eighth of a mile to the south. When the police chief strode over, Ian pointed a little further down. "Chief, what's that dirt road for? Where's it lead?"

"Basically, it's a fire road . . . there's a bunch of them along this strip, every mile or two, in case of a brush fire, we can get the needed equipment further in. They go in about a mile or so."

A uniformed officer with a K9 partner approached, and Parrish nodded toward Logan and Dakota. "You two, follow the dog. Chief, send two more uniforms with them just in case. I want this fucking bastard alive but not at the cost of one of my team or yours. Sawyer, let's go see what's down that road. We'll walk it, so we don't obliterate any evidence." Several federal agents had pulled up to the scene, and the SAC waved them over. "Davis. Melendez. You're with me too."

Once two more male officers joined them, the K9 handler got the animal on Georgia's scent, and the others followed them into the foliage. Their weapons were drawn and at the ready as they had no idea what was waiting for them at the end of the trail. Dakota shifted the bulletproof vest Sawyer had loaned her to wear over her T-shirt. It was for a much larger male, but was better than nothing, and Logan had helped her adjust the Velcro straps so it was as tight as they could get it. The female versions were curved slightly to accommodate their breasts, but with the extra room this one afforded her, the girls weren't squished. Logan's vest had been in the back of his SUV which the two of them had followed Sawyer in. Dakota was glad she'd thrown on a pair of jeans with her sneakers after their workout and sex-filled shower at the gym —it would keep her legs from getting scratched up in the brush.

As the dog weaved back and forth, his nose following the microscopic particles carrying the scent of the victim, Dakota and the others kept their eyes peeled on their surroundings. The K9 was a passive tracking dog, which meant he could walk them right up to their suspect—that was ideal with missing children or Alzheimer's patients, but not something you wanted when tracking a violent serial killer.

The big-eared Belgian Malinois reminded Dakota of the dogs-in-training back at the Trident compound. Keeping her eyes front, she addressed Logan to her right. "How's FUBAR doing?"

He'd told her about the pup that was probably going to fail out of the aggressive training during one of their stakeout shifts—it was the one she'd seen roll over for a belly rub the day she'd met her partner.

"Kat says he's a hopeless romantic and isn't cut out for guard duty. Babs officially adopted him the other day, and Tori, who trained Russell's service dog, is going to help her get him trained as a therapy dog. That way she can bring him to the veteran hospital when she goes for her therapy and stuff."

"Awesome. Glad he's going to a good home."

"Yeah. Him and Jagger have their own couch in the garage now and have become best buds."

While they trudged through the woods, they could occasionally hear and see the others on the dirt road, heading in the same direction parallel to them. It seemed as if the victim had known it was there and used it as a guide but was smart enough to know she might run into her abductor if she'd gotten too close.

"Hey, look over there," one of the cops to Dakota's left prompted. "Looks like an old utility building. There's a few of them around from back in the 70s and 80s, but the ones in this area were pretty much abandoned when the park rangers had their new headquarters built about two miles north of here. They moved all the equipment that was stored in these over there."

The concrete structure blended well with its thick, surrounding flora. There was only a dark green door visible on the side they could see and no windows. Keeping her weapon in her right, dominant hand, Dakota pulled out the FBI portable radio she'd been given back out on the road. She brought it to her mouth and pressed the transmit button. "Parrish. Sawyer."

The former's voice followed a squelch. "Parrish. Go."

"I think we're just about parallel to you. There's an old utility building about two hundred yards ahead of us, and the K9 is heading right for it. No signs of being occupied at the moment."

"Copy. Proceed with caution. We'll meet you there."

The tension among the five in the woods had increased and talking dropped to a minimum as the K9 lead them to the structure. While the two patrol officers covered the only door they could see, the handler held his partner back as Logan and Dakota circled around to see if there were any windows or other entrances. They worked well together, covering each other as they rounded the corners in silence so as to not alert anyone inside of their presence.

By the time they completed the inspection, Parrish, Sawyer, and the other two feds had arrived. Logan used hand signals to indicate to the others that there was only the one way in and out. Logan and Dakota stacked up behind Sawyer, who was holding a Maglite in his non-gun hand, on one side of the door jamb, weapons at the ready. They waited as one of the cops, standing on the opposite side, grabbed the doorknob and gently tried to turn it. When it did so without hesitation, he nodded at the trio, and then mouthed a countdown from three to one. Yanking hard, he swung the door wide, and Sawyer pivoted inside with Logan and Dakota on his heels, sweeping the room with his flashlight and weapon in the same direction. No one was inside, but there was no mistaking the fact they'd found where the Kink Killer had slaughtered his victims. Dried blood coated the floor, ceiling, and one of the walls beside a large St. Andrew's cross. A hospital bed with leather restraints and chains attached also had blood on them . . . fresher blood. Somehow, Georgia Branneth had managed to escape the bonds and run for her life. Only, now, she had a different fight for that same life.

Parrish stepped inside the large room and used his own flashlight to illuminate it. There was a switch for an uncovered light bulb hanging from the middle of the ceiling, but until they got the crime scene techs in there to inspect and photo-graph everything, nothing was to be disturbed if it could be prevented. The SAC took one last glance around then turned back to the door, pulling out his phone. "Everyone out. Let's hope the techs can find something we can use to catch this bastard, once and for all."

Eighteen

Dakota couldn't sleep, and she tried to convince herself it wasn't because Logan hadn't been lying next to her. He'd brushed his lips against her forehead before leaving her bed around 2:00 a.m., and she'd tossed and turned until finally giving up on falling back to sleep around 5:30. She'd tossed off the covers and gotten dressed in workout clothes before heading toward the Trident compound to use the gym. It was closer to her temporary condo than the ones at her police precinct and the SOD headquarters, and probably a hell of a lot quieter at this time of the morning when most cops were getting a workout in before their shifts started.

Pulling up to the guardhouse at the first gate, she rolled down her window and smiled at the big man who came out to greet her. "Morning, Murray."

"Good morning, Dakota. You're up early."

"Not as early as you, apparently."

"Don't let my bright eyes and bushy tail fool you. I just got here about twenty minutes ago and after only five hours sleep. Not that I'm complaining, since my girlfriend got home from three weeks visiting family in Ireland yesterday." He waggled his eyebrows, and it was clear what the couple had been doing to celebrate. "Anyway, you here for a meeting or the gym?"

"Gym. I didn't get much sleep either, so I figured I'd burn off a few calories."

"Trust me, darling, you don't need to. And no, I'm not flirting with you—my woman and Cowboy would both kick my ass—just stating a fact. Let me get the gate for you." He reached inside the shack and hit the button that rolled the iron gate to the left, granting her access.

With a wave at the guard, she drove through and up the quarter mile to the first parking area which was for The Covenant. Instead of pulling up to the inner gate, she slowed when she saw Logan's SUV with another vehicle parked outside the club.

That's strange. What's he doing here so early? There's no task force meeting.

After a moment's hesitation, her curiosity got the better of her and she pulled her SUV in next to Logan's and climbed out. She'd just pop her head in and see if he was free to work out with her—that was all.

Yeah, right. You want to have a reason not to trust him, so you can be the one to break it off first, just like you always do.

Ignoring her inner bitch, she took the stairs to the second-floor entrance two at a time. Her handprint had been scanned into the compound's security system, so she had access to the club, gym, and Trident's main office, instead of having to be buzzed in by someone else. When the lock clicked, she pulled the door open and stepped into the lobby. No one was there, but she hadn't expected to see anyone at this time of the morning. Striding over to the double wooden doors, she found one slightly ajar and widened the opening so she could step through.

Again, no one was in sight, but Logan's deep rumbling

laughter floated up from the pit. Dakota was about to announce her presence when she heard him moan and say, "God, that feels incredible. Don't stop."

A female replied, "Actually, let's take this into one of the playrooms where there's a bed, love . . ."

Whatever the woman had said next after "love" was low and muffled, but Dakota had heard enough. Jealous rage coursed through her when Logan said, "Sounds good to me."

What the fuck?

On silent feet, she quickly made her way to the balcony and looked down.

That son of a bitch!

Logan was taking off his T-shirt, his arm, shoulder, and back muscles rippling fluidly, and following that dark-haired chick, who had shown up at the hospital with Tiny, toward The Covenant's playrooms. The woman had on skinny, black ankle pants, a fitted black blazer, showing off her curves, and black heels that had to be four inches high.

That two-timing son of a bitch!

Neither of them had said anything about being exclusive, but Dakota had sort of assumed they were.

Well, you know what happens when you assume, you idiot. It makes an ass out of "u" and "me."

Well, she'd be damned if that happened again. The couple disappeared down the hall to where they were no doubt going to fuck like rabbits. No wonder he didn't want to sleep all night in her bed—he had to rest up for his morning honey. Well, fuck that. He wasn't getting back into Dakota's bed, that was for sure.

Turning on her heel, she stormed out of the club, hopped into her SUV, and didn't bother acknowledging a confused Murray on her way past the guard shack, speeding toward the highway. She drove aimlessly, for how long she had no idea, trying hard not to cry—Logan was just like every other bastard out there, and she'd dated plenty of them. Her vision blurred and she yanked the steering wheel, hitting the brakes. As the vehicle skidded to a stop on the gravel shoulder, her tears fell.

So why am I crying for him when I've never cried over any other man?

"Hey, Cowboy," Charlotte greeted him as she descended the stairs into the pit. She was dressed for work, which he hadn't expected her to be, since she was supposed to whip him again today. She usually wore something more relaxed then took a shower and changed before heading to her job. "Roxy can't make it this morning. She sent me a text—one of her patients was admitted very late last night and she only got a few hours' sleep. We'll work on your technique today and scene tomorrow instead. I'm not comfortable enough yet without having another Whip Master present. You've done great so far, but it's still new. Okay?"

"I'm okay with postponing it a day, but I'm not sure about the practice." Tilting his head to the side, he winced. "Must have pulled a muscle or something because it's really tight right here." He'd been massaging the back of his neck for the past few minutes, trying to work out the kinks.

She rounded the back of the chair he was sitting in by the stage and pushed his hand out of the way, then prodded the area. "Yup, you've got a nice knot there. Did your sexual aerobics with the pretty cop get out of hand?" she quipped.

Logan laughed, then moaned when she kneaded the sore spot. "God, that feels incredible. Don't stop."

"Actually, let's take this into one of the playrooms where there's a bed, love." She patted his shoulder then strode toward one of the hallways where the playrooms were located. "It'll be better with some massage oil and easier for me to work the muscle if I'm straddling you."

Having spent a lot of time with the Domme since she'd joined in his therapy, he knew nothing would happen in the bed between them other than her giving him a massage. They'd become good friends, and while she teased and flirted with him at times, it was all in jest and a way to ease his anxiety about the whip. "Sounds good to me."

Standing, he followed her, pulling his T-shirt over his head. He was almost to the hallway when he heard one of the wooden doors upstairs slam against the wall. Pivoting, he glanced at the stairs, waiting for whoever had walked in to make an appearance. When no one did, he assumed it was Mitch or one of the other employees—no one else would be there this time of the morning.

"It'll probably be better if you take a break from practicing the whip today too." Charlotte was waiting for him in the doorway of Playroom #3. Most of the rooms were decorated with different themes, but this one had a basic setup with just a spanking bench, a St. Andrew's cross, and a round, King-sized bed. One wall had a variety of implements hanging from hooks while a row of cabinets sat catty-corner to it. Charlotte strode over to the latter and quickly found a bottle of massage oil before retrieving a towel from a warmer sitting on the countertop. "All right, Cowboy, lay down and let's get your vertebrae vertical again."

"Do you need to stop anywhere on the way?"

"Nope."

Logan sighed as the traffic light turned green, and he hit the accelerator. For the third time since he picked Dakota up at the condo, he asked, "Is something wrong?"

"Nope."

Yeah, he wasn't stupid or naïve. The woman had a bug up her ass about something, and it was clearly up to him to figure it out because she refused to tell him what was wrong. Everything had been fine when he'd left her bed around 2:00 a.m.— or at least he thought it had been. He was racking his brains trying to figure out what he'd done or said to piss her off, but he was coming up blank. "Look, obviously you're mad about something. Tell me, so we're not walking into Heat with you looking like you want to kill me."

"I'm a professional. No one in there will have the slightest idea there's anything wrong."

"Except for me. I haven't a clue what's wrong." Silence filled his SUV and he glanced over at her. "Koko—"

"Don't fucking call me that again."

What the fuck?

Yanking on the steering wheel, he pulled onto the shoulder of the road and slammed on his brakes with more force than necessary. Throwing the gearshift into park, he spun on her and intentionally dropped his voice in what he hoped was a convincing Dom tone. "All right. That's it. One of the things everyone has been stressing about this lifestyle is communication and honesty. So out with it, subbie."

She glared at him, her arms crossed over her chest. "Drive, Reese."

"Wrong answer, sweetheart. Try again before I haul you over here and tan your ass."

"Try it and you're a dead man."

No, he wasn't. Not anymore. Working at Trident had brought him back to the land of the living, giving him a purpose in life again, but Dakota had given him so much more. "Babe, I've been dead—that's no longer a threat that bothers me."

Her eyes narrowed in confusion, but before she could

question him, he glanced in the rear-view mirror and saw flashing lights. "Fuck. A cop just pulled up. Friend of yours?"

Hopefully, so they wouldn't have to deal with him for more than a minute. They had to get back on the road to Heat.

Ducking her head, Dakota took a peek in her side mirror and groaned. "Yup." She rolled down her window as the officer approached her side, his dominant hand resting on his gun.

"Is there a problem—Swift? Hey, what's up?" He eyed her and then whistled loudly. "Damn, sweetheart, I think you should wear short skirts and low cleavage at work—you'll have the criminals drooling and frozen in place—easy arrests."

Beside her, Logan, growled a warning, and she rolled her eyes. "Stop being an ass, Ric. Logan, this is Ric Hernandez, my longtime friend and partner. Ric, this is Logan Reese, my temp partner."

Yeah, she wasn't getting away with that "temp partner" shit. Despite her piss-poor attitude this morning, they had something special growing between them, and the last thing he wanted was to be a "temp" anything with her. "Actually, I'm more than that—I'm also her boyfriend."

He'd almost blurted out that he was her Dom too but didn't want to out her lifestyle if this idiot didn't know about it.

It was her turn to growl. "No, you're not."

"Yes, I am. Case closed until we have this out later." His stern expression dared her to challenge him again. He didn't take his eyes off her as he addressed her pain-in-the-ass friend who had placed his hands on the door frame, leaning on it. "You need anything, Hernandez, because we've got somewhere to be."

Grinning as his gaze ping-ponged back and forth between the two, the uniformed cop chuckled. "About time you're getting laid on a regular basis, Swift. Reese, we'll be having a discussion later to convince me you're good enough for her, but in the meantime, do me a favor and don't slam on the brakes like that and make me stop to see if there's a problem. Swift, I'll call you later."

Logan's opinion of the other man jumped up a few notches. It was clear Hernandez was just looking out for someone he cared about and nothing more.

Dakota's jaw dropped as she glared at Ric who just laughed, slapped his hand on the door frame, and then headed back to his vehicle. Putting the SUV in drive, Logan hit the button that dropped his window automatically, then waved as the cop climbed back into his patrol car before pulling back out into traffic. "I meant what I said, Koko, we're continuing this discussion later, and if you can't be open and honest with me, then my hand and your ass are going to get to know each other very, very well."

Nineteen

Dakota gnawed on the inside of her cheek as she tried to focus on the real reason they were at Heat and not on Logan's hand he insisted on keeping glued to her left hip as he stood on the opposite side of her, guiding her around the room. While the club was much nicer than most of the ones she'd been in over the years, it had nothing on the elegance of The Covenant. It was like sitting in Coach after experiencing First Class for a few trips. The warmth of his hand permeated the thin material of her floor-length skirt which exposed her legs up to her mid-thigh through a slit in the lacy material. A red and black corset gave her a little more coverage up top and allowed her to carry several weapons undetected.

The place was pretty packed tonight, which was a help and a hindrance at the same time. It gave them the cover to blend in, while also making the search for a killer, who might be selecting his next target, more difficult. There hadn't been any evidence at the utility shed where Georgia Branneth had been held that could give them the killer's identity, but with multiple samples of blood belonging to different people, it was a sure bet they'd come back as DNA matches to his victims. It might help them identify any victims they weren't aware of yet when compared to missing persons.

She was still pissed as hell at Logan, but now wasn't the time to show it. Scanning the crowd, she looked for anyone who seemed out of place or was too focused on a female submissive. It was like looking for the proverbial needle in a haystack. If only Georgia would wake up and tell them she'd recognized her kidnapper, because no one knew how this bastard would respond to losing her. Would he step up his game? Or would they get lucky, and he'd make a mistake . . . one that would cost him instead of someone else?

It was difficult to tell in this crowd who belonged and who didn't.

"Eight o'clock, black vest, silver buttons," Logan whispered in Dakota's ear, and she silently cursed the shiver she felt run down her spine to her core.

Turning into his arm, she glanced in the direction he'd indicated, which had originally been over her left shoulder. In this position, it appeared she was hugging her Dom while giving her a direct line of sight at the person he'd wanted her to check out. A male, about twenty-five years old, was standing alone while staring at a group of three female submissives. Tucked into his waistband was a bullwhip, which in itself wasn't unusual in this setting. What had sent Logan's hackles up, and then hers, was the way he was practically drooling over the scantily dressed women. While he was younger than the profile Dr. Suki Ralston had come up with for their killer, they still had to rule him out. Pivoting a little further, she pointed her chest at the man, which gave the agents in a van outside a good look at him through the camera hidden among the silver adornments on her corset. She didn't need to repeat who they were singling out since the microphones they were both wearing had picked up Logan's earlier description. They had a club staff member with them, identifying anyone they needed information on.

A male voice came through her earpiece she was wearing. "Got it. Hang on."

Seconds passed and Dakota stiffened as the target approached the group of women, clearly having made his selection—a dark-haired submissive wearing a royal blue corset, matching panties, and nothing else. "C'mon, Davis," Dakota murmured into her microphone. "Hurry up."

"Cool your engines, Swift. The manager just ID'd him as Joe Kowalski—a new Dom, but not our guy. He was in the county lock-up for three of the murders. Larceny with no violent priors."

"Shit. What the fuck is he doing with a whip if he's a newbie?"

"He carries it for show, apparently, nothing else."

Dakota rolled her eyes. It was assholes like that who helped give the lifestyle a bad name.

The rest of the evening was more of the same. They'd spot someone who sent their radar blasting, before their backup agents shot down any possibles. By the time their shift was over, eight men had been eliminated as their killer, including another one who'd been hanging out in a vehicle in the parking lot. That one had been a private investigator on a divorce case, waiting to get pictures of the cheating wife when she came out of the club with her new Dom.

Logan drove her to the condo in silence. Now that they were alone again, she couldn't stop her anger from boiling over once more. If he thought he could talk his way back into her bed tonight, he was sorely mistaken.

When he parked the SUV, she didn't wait for him to climb

out and come around to open her door. She was out and halfway to her unit before he'd turned the engine off. The driver's door slammed shut, and she heard him muttering under his breath as he followed her. Keys in hand, she unlocked the door and stepped inside the condo, but his hand and foot prevented her from closing it again. "Damn it, Koko. Enough of this bullshit. What the fuck is up your ass tonight?"

He pushed his way into the condo, then shut the door. Turning on her heel, she tossed the keys and her small purse on the couch. A glance in the direction of the bedrooms told her that her roommate wasn't home yet. Perfect, because otherwise the woman would have gotten an earful.

Spinning around, she pinned Logan with a glare that had made many a criminal worry about getting their ass kicked. "Fine! You want to know what my problem is? It's you and your wandering eyes and dick."

"What the fuck are you talking about?"

She crossed her arms over her chest and cocked her hip to the side. "Don't play dumb with me, asshole. I know all about your fling on the side. Or am I the fling, and she's your main squeeze?"

Logan's jaw dropped as he stared at her. His eyes narrowed as he shook his head. "Okay, I repeat, what the fuck are you talking about? I'm not seeing anyone but you."

"Liar! You fucking shit! I can't believe you're looking me in the eye and denying you're screwing someone else. That takes balls, Reese, fucking balls." He opened his mouth, but she cut him off with a slice of her hand through the air in front of her. "I saw you with that dark-haired chick from the hospital. The Asian one with Tiny. I saw you and her getting quite chummy this morning at The Covenant."

"What are you talking about? You were at the club this

morning? For what? And there's nothing going on between me and Charlotte."

"Bullshit! Oh, my God, Reese! Give it up! You were caught red-handed. Now get out. I'm going to bed—alone!"

She'd barely gone two steps in the direction of her room before he grabbed her arm and spun her back toward him. Without hesitating, she brought her knee up and dropped him like a stone. Yeah, he wasn't going to be using his cock and balls anytime soon, but she couldn't care less.

"Fuck!" On his knees, he cupped his aching groin, moaning in pain. Wincing, he tried to catch his breath. "Woman—shit—you're going to regret that . . . when I can move again. Are you . . . out of your fucking mind?"

"I must have been when I got involved with you . . . I must have been fucking insane." Tossing her hands in the air, she paced back and forth.

Logan struggled to his feet, shifting his hips as he stood. His eyes were watering. "Damn it, woman! Shut up and listen to me, will you!" Stopping in her tracks, she glared at him. He lowered his voice, although it was clear he was trying not to raise it again. "I am not having sex with anyone but you."

"So why were you and that woman taking things . . ." She made quote marks with her fingers. "'. . . into one of the playrooms where there's a bed, love.'"

"Jesus." Running a hand down his face, he eased onto the couch. "I'll explain that in a minute, but you'll probably knee me in the balls again if I don't tell you what led up to it. I am not, repeat, *not* sleeping with Mistress China." He ignored the shocked expression on her face at the mention of the Domme's title. "Nor am I sleeping with the other Whip Master, Mistress Roxy, who couldn't make our appointment this morning. You walked in at the wrong time and misinterpreted everything. They're helping me with desensitization therapy." He winced again. "Shit. I'll tell you everything if you get me some ice for my balls. My mother still has hopes I'll give her grandchildren someday, and if I freeze the little swimmers right now, I might be able to save some of them."

His attempt at humor didn't draw any laughter from her, but she did relent, striding into the kitchen, retrieving a bag of frozen peas. Tossing them to him, she sat in the recliner. "What do you mean, desensitization therapy?" She knew what it was but had no clue what he needed desensitized and why.

Placing the ice-cold bag on his crotch, Logan moaned. "God, I'm going to spank your ass after you realize I'm telling you the truth." Taking a deep breath, he let it out slowly. His gaze wasn't on her, but on the ceiling directly above him. "All right. Let's start at the beginning. I was . . . shit . . . I was a prisoner of war in Afghanistan, Koko. Me and my team. I can't tell you a lot of it—it's classified—but my teammates were tortured with a bullwhip before they were killed. Their deaths were just as brutal. There were only two of us left by the time another team of Raiders and some SEALs found us."

He paused and swallowed hard. Dakota was stunned. She was horrified by both his story and how she'd attacked him while knowing only a small part of it. "Logan, I'm so—"

His gaze flashed to hers. "Let me finish, please. You can apologize when I'm done." She nodded and let him continue. "You know I have PTSD issues and nightmares. Part of the stipulations of my employment with Trident is I have to see a government-approved psychologist, experienced with PTSD, on a regular basis. The one I'm seeing is also a doctor The Covenant uses, as she did her dissertation on the lifestyle. A little over two weeks ago, I freaked out at the club while it was closed. I walked in on Roxy and Jake Donovan practicing, and the crack of the whip . . . well, it was bad. I totally checked out. Thank God, I didn't hurt either of them, because I could have. I wasn't there . . . I was back in that hellhole . . . living it all over again and not sure if I'd survive a second time.

"Donovan had gone through some shit when he was younger and had used desensitization therapy with the whip to get through it, before becoming a Whip Master. He suggested I try it. He and Trudy, my therapist, thought it was best if I did it with the Dommes, since our torturers had been male. I've had two sessions where I've had my back whipped, and they're also teaching me how to wield it. I don't know if I'll ever be able to do it to another person—I may just stick with the paper targets, but it seems to be working. I'm not cured—probably never will be—but I think I'm dealing with everything a little better now that I have an outlet for my PTSD. Enough that I'm going to continue seeing them.

"What you heard this morning . . . Roxy couldn't meet us. I was supposed to be whipped again today, but Charlotte didn't think I was ready not to have a spotter present to read my reactions, so she suggested I practice instead. But I had a kink in my neck that was bunched into a knot. She offered to massage it out for me . . . that's what you overheard. Yes, we went into one of the playrooms, but nothing happened in there but her massaging my neck. I swear. Please tell me you believe me."

"T-that's what you meant earlier when you said you'd been a dead man." When he nodded, Dakota swallowed the thick lump in her throat. She felt like such an ass. Standing, she knelt in front of him and grasped his hands. "I believe you, Logan. I-I'm so sorry I didn't trust you." She didn't wipe away the tears that rolled down, but he pulled one of his hands from hers and did it for her. "It's hard for me. With my dad and the guys at work, I've always had to prove I belong there. Men I've dated . . . it's difficult being a female cop. When they find out what you do for a living, either they're too intimidated and run for the hills or the first thing out of their mouths is 'So, do you have your handcuffs on you tonight?' Yeah, I've heard that dozens of times, and it's still not funny. As for dating a cop, fireman, or medic . . . I can't do that either, because I'd have to admit my submissiveness . . . it's who I am . . . and then I'd have to deal with proving myself as a cop all over again. That's why I like the lifestyle. I can get what I need without all the other stuff that goes along with dating. Until I met you. I told you the truth when I said I'd never even had a one-night-stand with anyone on TPD. This is the first time I've ever wanted someone I worked with more than I wanted to prove my worth."

His thumb had been caressing her cheek the entire time she'd been talking. "Oh, Koko. You never have to prove your worth to me. I already know you're the best thing that's ever happened to me. I've never said this to another woman before . . . I swear on my teammates' graves . . . I love you, sweetheart. After we catch this bastard, I want to take you out on a date . . . a real date. One with flowers and candlelight and slow dancing. I want—"

"Say it again." Her heart had almost stalled when he'd said those three little words she never thought she'd hear from someone she wanted more than her next breath.

"What? I love you?" He tugged on her hand until she stood. Tossing the peas aside, he pulled her down on top of him, so she was straddling his thighs. He cupped her cheeks in his hands, making sure she was looking directly at him. "I'll say it every minute of every day, if you want me to, until you no longer question the fact that I love you. I. Love. You. Dakota Swift."

A sob rose in her throat, and she began to cry harder. "I love you too, Logan. I think I fell in love with you when you pulled your white knight routine when those punks were harassing me. I just couldn't admit it to myself."

"Oh, sweetheart. Come here." He drew her closer until his lips met hers. Taking possession of her mouth, he plunged his tongue inside as she surrendered to him . . . the only man she wanted to surrender to ever again. Logan Reese was the other part of her she'd never thought she'd find.

Logan kissed her with abandon. His cock was throbbing, but this time it wasn't from the pain of being kneed. It was from the fact he was now harder than he could ever remember being. He'd once heard that sex with your soul mate was more intense . . . more incredible than anything a guy could experience. At the time, he'd laughed it off, thinking it was a crock of shit that romance authors had come up with —not that he'd say that in front of Devon's wife, who'd made a career out of being a romance author. But right here and now, with the other half of his heart and soul straddling his lap, he knew he'd been so wrong. They were still fully dressed, a fact he was about to remedy, and just having her in his arms was already the most amazing feeling in the world. She loved him—Dakota Swift loved him. And he loved her more than anything or anyone else in the world.

His hands palmed her ass through the sweatpants she'd changed into before they left Heat, and then he stood, lifting her. Her legs wrapped around his hips as he strode toward her bedroom. He sucked on her tongue and reveled in her moans. Kicking the door shut behind him, he propped her against the wall, using his body to pin her in place as his mouth left hers and nuzzled her neck. "This is no longer sex, sweetheart. I'm going to make love to a woman for the first time in my life . . . I'm going to make love with you."

"Yessss." Squirming to get closer to him, Dakota tilted her head to the side, inviting him to nuzzle the sensitive tissue behind her ear. Her fingernails dug into his shoulders, spiking his adrenaline and lust.

Holding her tightly, he stumbled to the bed and followed

her down to the mattress. "Undress me, baby," he ordered as he began to remove her clothing. He'd come to love her submissiveness, and from now on, it was his, and his alone. She would never surrender to any other man again . . . only him. And he would cherish every second of her submission.

Once they were both completely naked, he rolled onto his back, taking her with him so she was straddling him once more. He cupped her breasts, pushing them together. "Play with those gorgeous nipples, Koko. Pluck and roll them for me."

She did as she was told, her head dropping back on her shoulders. Logan trailed his hands down her body, letting one drop to her waiting pussy, the other skimming around to her ass. He was going to have to get a set of anal plugs soon because he wanted to fuck her ass one of these days. Even though it was on her yellow limit list, she'd told him she'd never been taken there. He'd be the first, and hopefully last, man to claim that part of her . . . it belonged to him . . . she belonged to him.

He ran his fingers over her clit and her soaked labia, gathering up her cream and pushing it backward to where his other set of fingers used it to lubricate her puckered hole. She moaned loudly as he pleasured her. His thumb pressed gently into her, while he eased two fingers into her heated core, making her gasp.

"Oh, God! Logan!"

Growling, he lifted the hand behind her and smacked her left ass cheek hard, eliciting a yelp from her. "What did you just call me?" Even though the dynamics of their relationship had changed, he still gave her the dominance she craved.

"Sorry, Master."

"Good girl." Yeah, he definitely loved being her Dom. There was plenty more he needed to learn, and he'd continue his training even after this case was over—if it was ever over—

but this power exchange, knowing she trusted him and willingly gave him her submissiveness, was heady stuff. He would do everything in his power to maintain that trust and give her everything she asked for and needed.

Twisting to his side, he placed her on her back. "Hands above your head, Koko."

She lifted her arms and grabbed hold of the comforter. His mouth latched onto one breast as he fucked her faster with his fingers. Sucking, licking, and nibbling on her ripe nipple, he forced her to climb higher and higher. Her writhing, moaning, and begging increased. "Please! Oh God, please, Sir!"

"Please what, baby?" he whispered against her skin before licking her distended nipple like an ice cream cone. "Tell your Dom what you want . . . what you need."

"You, Sir! I need you!"

He pulled out of her pussy and rolled toward the nightstand, grabbing a condom from the new box he'd thrown in there last night. After donning the protection, he spread her legs and dipped his head down. Running the flat of his tongue over her plump lips, he took a quick taste of her spice. If he wasn't so damn hard and desperately needed to be inside her, he would have eaten her until she couldn't come for him anymore.

Kissing his way up her body, he settled his hips between her thighs. His mouth took possession of hers again, letting her taste herself on his tongue. Lining his cock up with her slit, he thrust up and in, swallowing her gasp. Her heat enveloped him as he buried his shaft to the root. Pulling almost completely out, he repeated the motions over and over. She was tight as a glove, and he knew the moment her orgasm began to take hold as her walls quivered. Logan shifted onto his knees, spreading her wider, changing the angle of his assault, and sending her over the edge. She screamed his name as she climaxed and clenched around him. The pressure was more than he could stand, and with two or three more thrusts, he followed her into the abyss.

A short time later, he had her cleaned and sated, cuddling against his side as he pulled the covers over them. Swirling her fingertips across his chest, she tilted her head up. "Stay with me tonight. Please. I don't want to wake up alone in the morning. I want to wake up with you inside me, making love to me."

He wanted that too, but his heart twisted. "I'm afraid to. What if I have another episode?"

"I can handle it, Logan. You won't hurt me. Do you think we can try it?"

Her eyes begged him to stay as much as her words did. He didn't want to risk hurting her, but she was experienced in dealing with EDPs—emotionally disturbed persons—from being on the job for many years. It wasn't as if she wouldn't know how to respond if he had another nightmare, and she'd already seen him have one. He tightened his arm around her. "Yeah, we can try."

She was about to say something else when his stomach growled, and she giggled. "Someone's hungry."

Her stomach picked that moment to make itself known too. Logan tickled her navel. "Sounds like we're both hungry."

"Well, we're sort of out of luck. There's really nothing to eat in the house except those defrosted peas."

He chuckled. "I'll pass on the peas—I had enough of them tonight—but I can run out to Pop & Sons and grab us something to eat really quick."

Frowning, Dakota checked the bedside clock. "It's after two in the morning."

"So? The diner's open twenty-four hours, and I need calories if I'm going to be waking you up with my cock deep in your sweet pussy in a few hours."

The corners of her mouth swung upward. "Hmmm . . . you might be right."

"Of course I am." Climbing out of the bed, he stood and grabbed his cargo pants from the floor. Thankfully, he'd changed into them from his leathers before leaving the club. It felt weird wearing them outside a lifestyle setting. "What do you want to eat?"

She stretched under the covers like a satisfied kitten. "A bacon cheeseburger deluxe with fried onions and a side of cheese fries. Yes, it's a coronary on a plate, but I allow myself one every once in a while."

"A girl after my own heart," he said while pulling on his T-shirt.

"Damn straight. Oh, grab me a sweet iced tea too, please?"

After snatching his holstered gun, wallet, phone, and keys from where they were scattered on the floor, he leaned down and kissed her lips. "You got it, baby. I'll be back in a jiffy."

"Grab my keys from the living room, so you can get back in. Gina should be home soon," she added before yawning and settling further into the bed, her eyes already closing. He shut the bedroom door so she wouldn't be disturbed when her roommate arrived.

As he locked the front door, Logan found himself whistling as he strode to his car. While he was nervous about staying the night, and possibly having another episode in his sleep, his mind kept flashing back to the moment they'd both said, "I love you," for the first time and his heart soared. Once they caught the killer, he was going to request a few days off and take Dakota up to Virginia to meet his family. His mother would be tickled pink to meet her and would probably start planning their wedding. Someday . . . maybe not right away, but someday, he'd love to put a ring on Dakota's finger. But for now, he'd settle for a collar that would show the BDSM community she was claimed by her Dom.

As he stopped at the end of the parking lot, leading to the street, Gina Harvey pulled in, driving her Mustang. She must have recognized his SUV because she waved at him. Flashing a hand back, he turned right and accelerated into the light traffic. He wanted to get the food and be back in Dakota's bed as fast as he could. Maybe he wouldn't let her wait until morning to wake her up the way she'd asked him to.

Twenty

Having ditched the old sedan he'd been driving when that bitch escaped, the Dom sat in his truck at the other end of the lot from where that asshole from Trident had parked his SUV. He'd seen them walking into Heat earlier and knew they'd be there until closing—undercover, trying to figure out who he was. Since he'd already learned where the submissive cop was staying after following her home from the Trident compound one day, it had been simple enough to wait for her to return after her shift was over. But then her partner had to stay and get laid. If the guy hadn't been a trained operative, the Dom would have taken him out of the equation, instead of waiting for an opportunity to get by him. Now it seemed like the wait had been worth it as Reese headed to his vehicle. The love 'em and leave 'em types never stuck around after getting some tail.

The Dom watched as the SUV left the lot at the same time another vehicle entered. He recognized this one too. It was perfect timing. Climbing out of his truck, he strode across the lot like he belonged there, carrying his duffel bag. He had a talent for blending in and usually never drew a second glance from people. He crossed in front of FBI Special Agent Harvey's path to her condo and gave her a friendly nod as she eyed him. The blonde wasn't bad looking, but she hadn't drawn his interest like the dark-haired cop had. Officer Swift would be a perfect addition to his collection of masterpieces.

Without saying a word, he continued past the fed. As she neared her ground-floor unit, he silently changed direction on his sneakered feet. Her keys were in her hand as she prepared to unlock the door. Reaching into the open zipper of his duffel, he pulled out the silenced handgun. Without the tiniest pang of regret, he put two bullets in the back of her head and grabbed the keys from where they fell beside her. Within seconds, he had the door unlocked. Turning, he hooked his hands under her armpits and dragged the body into the foyer as quietly as he could, leaving it to bleed out on the wall-to-wall carpet.

Reaching over the lifeless form, he locked the door again.

After listening for any signs the cop had heard him, he stepped over to the couch in the living room and set his duffel bag down before pulling out the items he'd need. Since he hadn't had a chance to find a new dungeon, he would do everything here. Instead of posing her in a public spot, he'd leave her here. He couldn't risk being seen carrying her body out to the car in a few hours. He also couldn't risk her screaming, which disappointed him, so he'd use a ball gag to muffle her. He tucked one in the waistband on his left side, then hung a coiled bullwhip from the ball. The gun and a pair of handcuffs went to the small of his back—he'd need both gloved hands to subdue her. The last thing he grabbed was a washcloth which he soaked with liquid from a small bottle. He wouldn't need the syringe this time as he'd be playing with her here.

Once he was certain he had everything he needed, he inched down the carpeted hallway. The bathroom door and one bedroom door were ajar, so his focus was on the closed bedroom. Was his canvas asleep? Was she naked after fucking her lover?

Grasping the knob, he turned it slowly, then pushed the door open a crack. There was just enough moonlight breaching the edges of the blinds to allow him to see into the dark room. A lone figure was under the covers, her back to the door as she snored softly. The Dom eased into the room, his heart rate spiking in anticipation of the struggle she was sure to put forth. Step by step, he drew closer—her fate was sealed.

Surrounded by darkness, Georgia searched for a sliver of light.

Why can't I see anything?

And what was that incessant beeping noise tickling the edge of her consciousness? It was driving her nuts.

Mom? Dad?

She thought she'd heard them earlier, their voices wavering as if they'd been crying, but hadn't been able to find them to comfort them. Her whole body hurt from the roots of her hair to the tips of her toes. She couldn't remember ever being in so much pain. A constant buzzing sounded in her brain, and she wanted to push her way through the fog swirling around her.

Where am I?

A shiver of fear coursed through her. She tried to move her arms and legs, her fight or flight instincts clamoring a warning, but she couldn't move.

Oh God! He has me again! No, no, no! How did he catch me again? I have to escape! I have to! Wait . . . whose voices are those? Not his. No, I know who he is, but neither of those voices are his. I have to warn them. We have to get out of here before he comes back! Help! We have to run! Somebody help me!

Her breathing and heart rate increased as she tried to figure out how to escape. She didn't want to be his next victim. There was so much more she wanted to do with her life. She wanted to travel, find a great guy, one far better than her ex-husband, and have kids . . . but most of all, she just wanted to live to a ripe old age and have no regrets when her time came. It wasn't his right to take all that from her, and she'd be damned if she didn't fight him for it.

Find a way . . . find a way to live!

An antiseptic smell penetrated her nose, combined with a hint of . . . *cologne?* It was familiar, but she couldn't place it. The rich sandalwood scent enveloped her, bringing with it a bit of hope. Whoever was wearing it was someone she could trust . . . someone she just knew would keep her safe. If only she could find the source. She needed a hero to ride up on his gallant, white steed and rescue her—but that only happened in fairy tales. And she was never one to sit back and wait for a savior—she would fight to her last breath to save herself—but of course she wouldn't refuse any help along the way. First thing she had to do though, was find a light . . . wait!

There it is . . . just beyond my reach. C'mon, damn it! Reach for it! It's the only way out! Do it!

DAKOTA WOKE WITH A START, the odor of a chemical reaching her nose a second before a damp cloth was slapped over her face. Her instinct and training kicked in immediately. Her limbs thrashed as she tried to kick and punch her male assailant, but she was wrapped up in the blankets and couldn't do any damage. With a sudden yank of her body, she rolled onto her stomach and continued until she trapped his arm beneath her, forcing his hand to pull free from her mouth. The move also sent the covers sliding partially off her nude body. She brought her knees up as far as she could then kicked out, flipping him onto the other side of the bed.

Scrambling, she reached for her weapon, but found it wasn't on the nightstand as it should have been. *Damn it!* It was on the floor with her clothes. She tried to roll off the bed, but the bastard was on her again, trying to get the cloth back over her face. Dakota forced her elbow backward with all her might and was rewarded with a satisfying *crack* and an *oomph* as she connected with his face, followed by cursing. "Fucking bitch!"

She was almost to her feet when his arms wrapped around her and yanked her back. The next thing she knew, she was flying, then her body slammed against the dresser on the other side of the bed. The impact sent a few items that had been on top of the heavy piece of furniture tumbling to the floor. Agony shot through her ribs and right arm as she dropped to the floor. From there, she got her first look at her attacker, and her eyes widened in recognition. "You?"

"Yes, me," he snarled as he stood on the bed above her and grasped the handle of a bullwhip, which was lying atop the messed up covers along with a ball gag and handcuffs. "It's always the quiet ones, standing in the background, you have to fear most."

With a flick of his wrist, he snapped the length at her. Dakota was wedged between the bed and dresser and there was no way to avoid being struck, so she threw up her hands in a natural instinct to protect her face. With a *crack*, the tip of the whip sliced her forearm, burning her skin, and she couldn't hold back the cry of pain. She struggled to get to her knees, but this time the whip lit up her back. "Shit!"

The bastard kept swinging from above, and Dakota's body felt like it was on fire every place he hit. She had to get out of the corner he'd backed her into before he whipped her to death. Another strike landed on her upper arm, and as soon as she felt her skin break, she twisted so she was staring up at him. His mouth was turned up in a cruel smile while insanity raged in his eyes. When he swung again, instead of using her hands to protect herself, she went on the offense, snapping her arms out and letting the thin strip of leather wrap around them. Her hands closed around the whip, and she yanked hard, pulling him off balance. Unfortunately, the momentum brought him down on top of her.

They struggled, each trying to gain the advantage. Dakota fought for her life, using her hands, elbows, knees, feet, and even her head to attack him. Grunts and heavy breathing filled the room. Her skin was slick with blood and sweat, and the pain was overwhelming. Her head buzzed with a combination of adrenaline and whatever chemical she'd breathed in when he'd first attacked. That, combined with the fact the killer had a good sixty pounds on her and wasn't wounded, put her at a disadvantage as he grabbed her wrists and pinned them to the wall with one hand. Making a fist with the other, he punched her in the face. She saw stars as her cheek and jaw exploded with pain, and she tried to hang onto consciousness—she was dead if she didn't.

Her vision was blurred as he got to his feet, the bullwhip in his hand once again. This time, he was too close to her to let the leather fly, but that didn't stop him from aiming the thick handle at her head. Weakening, all Dakota could do was try to protect her head from taking a beating that would knock her out. The killer stepped back, giving himself more room, and let the tip of the whip sail through the air at her again. *Crack!* It licked her side, and she bit back a shriek. No way was she going to give this bastard the satisfaction.

Where was Logan? How long had it been since he'd left? Would he return in time to save her or would he find her dead body? *No!* She refused to let that happen. But her time was running out as the assault continued. Her gaze scanned what was in reach that she could use as a weapon and spotted a can of aerosol hair spray that'd fallen to the floor. Snatching it, she knocked it against the side of the dresser, popping the top off it. Praying the tiny hole was pointed in the right direction, she pushed onto her knees, extended her arm as far as it would go, and pressed the nozzle, sending a spray into the killer's face. He screamed as his eyes slammed shut and twisted his head to avoid getting hit with more.

As Dakota struggled to her feet, the bedroom door crashed open. She watched in horror as the killer, still partially blinded, spun toward the sound, pulling a gun from his lower back and aiming it at Logan. She lunged at the bastard as gunfire filled the room.

OMEGA TEAM
TRIDENT SECURITY

Twenty-One

The sound of the hospital room door opening had Tiny waking in an instant, his hand reaching for the gun on his hip, but he relaxed when Special Agent Nikita Novik strode in, looking as gorgeous as the first time he'd seen her at The Covenant. However, instead of the casual clothes, today she was in a standard, professional, dark suit, which couldn't hide her luscious curves—or the fact she was packing heat in a shoulder holster under the jacket. "How's she doing?"

"No change," he replied, wiping the last of the sleep from his eyes. He'd been at Georgia's side for almost the entire time since she'd been out of surgery—only taking time off to go home and shower before returning. The Sawyer brothers had arranged for a large, private suite in the hospital for the submissive—complete with a couch, recliners, and refrigerator —so at least Tiny was comfortable. It helped they made considerable donations to the facility every year.

The doctors had relieved the pressure on Georgia's brain but couldn't say when or if she would wake up. Each day that passed, he grew more worried she would never recover. While there were FBI agents rotating shifts outside the room, Tiny had been granted permission to also stand guard. Aside from members of law enforcement and Trident Security, Georgia's brother and parents, and medical personal, no one else was allowed in to see her.

Mr. and Mrs. Branneth had arrived in Tampa late last night and, after visiting the hospital, had gone with their son to a nearby hotel where Colleen had booked them rooms for the duration of their stay. They'd probably be returning in a few hours.

"Excuse me for saying, but you look like hell."

He grunted as he flipped the handle of the recliner he'd been sleeping in, returning it to an upright position, noting it was still dark outside the window. "Probably because that's how I feel. What time is it?"

"Oh two hundred." Her gaze softened. "It's not your fault, Travis."

She'd asked him what his full name was, after he'd returned from giving his report at the FBI building, and was the only person, other than his mother, who'd called him Travis in recent years. He refused to examine her reasoning too closely—there were far too many other things on his mind at the moment. "Yeah, it is. I should have searched the interior of the house. I should have checked under the bed and opened every closet before—"

The agent held up her hand to stop his recap of everything he'd failed to do. "We have no idea if he was already in the house when she got home or if he gained access afterward." Stepping closer, she frowned at him as she crossed her arms over her chest. "And who knows, maybe he would have shot or stabbed you if you'd gone in and found him there. You're not invincible and have to stop kicking your own ass over this. Sometimes bad things happen to good people. I see it all the—"

Her words were cut off when the EKG monitor attached to Georgia began beeping faster and louder. Tiny leaped to his feet and rushed over. "Georgia, honey, it's Tiny. Can you hear me?" She couldn't verbally answer him with the tube down her throat, which was hooked up to a ventilator to help her breathe, but she'd definitely heard him as her head turned toward him. Her wrists fought the restraints tying her arms down, and he laid a reassuring hand on the one closest to him. "Georgia, sweetheart, you're okay. You're at the hospital, and you're safe. If you can hear me, open your eyes."

The door to the room swung open, and two nurses hurried in. While one of the nurses silenced the annoying monitor, the other pulled out a penlight and shined it in her patient's eyes. Georgia winced and tried unsuccessfully to get away from the bright light. She blinked a few times and tried to lift her hands toward the tube in her mouth. "Georgia, I'm your nurse, Teresa. You've been intubated to help you to breathe, so just try to relax. Can you blink if you understand me?"

She stilled, then to Tiny's relief, she blinked her eyes several times, even though her gaze was unfocused. The nurse patted her arm. "Excellent. Diane, can you call the surgeon and see if we can have a respiratory therapist remove the tube?" The other nurse nodded and left the room. "Georgia, we'll get it out as soon as we can. In the meantime, can you squeeze my hand?"

While the nurse continued her command-and-response examination, Tiny stepped back and pulled out his phone, quickly shooting off a group text to Ian, Devon, and Mitch. As he was typing, a soft, ivory hand touched his dark arm, and he lifted his gaze to Nikita's. "I'm glad your friend's going to be okay, Travis."

The corners of his mouth ticked upward. "Thanks. So am I. Now I just hope she can tell us who the hell did this to her, so I can go kill the motherfucker. Excuse my language, but there's no other way I can think of describing him."

"I agree with the MF, but as for the other part . . ." She grinned. "Well, actually, I didn't hear anything after 'So am I.' You know, just in case I'm asked about it if the guy turns up dead."

Well, damn, he was beginning to like Special Agent Nikita Novik more and more. He was about to do something stupid, like ask her out in the middle of her case, but his phone rang. Ian and his bloody timing struck again.

Logan parked in a space close to Dakota's unit and grabbed the sack of food and two fountain sodas before exiting his SUV. The food run had taken a little longer than expected because he'd stopped at a fender-bender to make sure everyone was okay after seeing a young woman holding an infant. The cops hadn't been on scene yet, so he stayed with her and the idiot driving the car that rear-ended her until they arrived. The poor woman had been driving around, trying to get the baby asleep—ironically, the kid snoozed through all the excitement.

He hoped Dakota's roommate had gone to bed because he hadn't thought to stop and ask if she wanted anything from the diner. As far as Doms went, he was a work in progress. His mind had been elsewhere, otherwise he would've offered to treat the other woman to a late-night meal as well. He blamed it on the fact he was still trying to wrap his head around being in love with an amazing woman who loved him back. If Dakota was asleep, he was looking forward to waking her up, one kiss at a time. He'd start with her toes and work his way up her luscious body.

Nearing the condo, the hair on the back of his neck stood

up, and he slowed, scanning his surroundings. When he didn't see anyone else, he took another few steps to the door, his senses on full alert. Something on the concrete in front of the welcome mat caught his eye. The smeared dark substance registered just as the acrid aroma of blood reached his nose. It was fresh, leading straight to the door, and hadn't been there when he'd left.

Placing the food and drinks off to the side, Logan slid his weapon from the holster at the small of his back. He didn't need to check if it was loaded, but did finger the safety, making sure it was in the right position so the gun was ready to fire as he tried to turn the doorknob. It was locked so he retrieved Dakota's keys from his pocket.

Unlocking the door, he tossed the keys to the soft grass next to where the food was, then pulled out his cell phone. When the 9-1-1 operator answered, Logan kept his voice low. "This is Logan Reese from Trident Security. Task force officers need assistance . . ." He rattled off the address. "Possible officer down. Contact SOD and the FBI. Tell responding officers not to shoot the guy wearing tan cargo pants and a black T-shirt— that's me and I'm armed."

Through the phone, he heard the information being dispatched. "All units, all units, clear all radio traffic. Possible officer down. Available units respond to . . ."

Knowing help was on the way, Logan stuck the phone in his pocket without disconnecting the call. This way the dispatcher could monitor what was going on even if it would be muffled.

Turning the knob, he eased the door open, but it didn't go very far—something was blocking it. His gaze fell to the floor of the foyer. Gina Harvey's lifeless eyes stared back at him, blood soaked into the carpet around her head. She was beyond his help, and he put it out of his mind for the moment, concentrating on getting to Dakota. Pushing harder on the door, he was able to make enough room to squeeze through. He paused long enough to hear the sounds of a struggle coming from one of the bedrooms. It took everything in him to use caution as he approached. Getting himself killed wouldn't help him save the woman he loved.

Leading with his weapon, he hurried down the empty hall with a quick check of the dark bathroom and the bedroom Gina had been using. As he reached the door to Dakota's room, a loud *crack* sounded from behind it. The blood drained from Logan's face as he froze. His mind started to leave the here and now, returning to his Afghani prison, but a scream of fury and pain slammed him back to the present. Dakota needed him, and he wasn't going to fail her.

Gripping his weapon in both hands, he lifted his foot and kicked the door in, spinning into the room and finding his target. As a man on the other side of the bed spun toward him, Logan's brain didn't even register that he was familiar. All he saw was the bastard's hand coming up with a black handgun, aiming it in his direction. With muscle memory, Logan's body reacted, everything appearing to happen in slow motion. A split second was all it took to aim and shoot, but as his weapon fired two shots in rapid succession, horror coursed through him as Dakota lunged for her attacker whose weapon also went off. That bullet went wide, hitting the wall two feet to Logan's right, as the killer and Dakota both fell to the floor.

Fear unlike anything he'd ever experienced, not even in that hellhole on the other side of the world, came over Logan. Rushing forward, he kept his weapon pointed at the killer, but the man didn't move. One of Logan's bullets had struck him in the upper arm, however, the other had been straight and true, hitting the bastard between the eyes and killing him instantly.

Kicking the gun from the lifeless hand, he turned his attention to Dakota. She was unconscious, and his gut roiled as he saw all the blood and damage to her nude body, but the worst was the bullet hole above her left breast.

Sirens signaled the arrival of emergency vehicles pulling into the condo complex as he dropped to his knees beside her with a kernel of hope as he saw her chest rise with an inhalation. Yanking off his T-shirt, he pressed it into the wound to staunch the flow of blood. "C'mon, baby, stay with me. Don't let me lose you too."

When he heard voices and police radios squawking from the vicinity of the front door, he yelled at the top of his lungs, "Officer down, officer down! Get a damn bus!"

HAVING ROLLED out of bed after receiving Tiny's text, and then speaking to him on the phone, Ian and Devon burst into the private hospital suite, anxious to see that The Covenant submissive was indeed awake and on the road to recovery. They also hoped she'd be able to give them information about her kidnapper. In addition to Tiny, Mitch, Agent Novik, SAC Parrish, and Georgia's parents and brother, her surgeon, nurse, and a respiratory therapist were present. Even though it was one of the biggest rooms in the hospital, with that many people, it was a tight fit. They were all waiting on pins and needles for the man in blue scrubs to remove the patient's breathing tube. Georgia was clearly uncomfortable and wanted the thing out as soon as possible. After using a syringe to deflate the small balloon around the plastic cannula, that was holding it in place, the therapist gently pulled the entire thing from her throat.

Standing at the end of the bed, Mr. Branneth touched his daughter's foot through her blanket, his other arm was wrapped around his wife's shoulders. Happy and relieved tears stained the older woman's cheeks. They'd have plenty of time to comfort and pamper her with love after Ian and the others had the information they hoped she could provide. Ian was sure they'd be talking about a lot of other things too. As a cop, it hadn't taken rocket science for her brother to figure out she'd been kidnapped by the serial killer targeting submissives —something he hadn't known about his sister. Neither had her parents. The Covenant Doms would do what they could to help her explain everything to them, if she needed it. Finding out your sister or daughter was into BDSM wasn't something most people wanted to hear if they didn't under-stand the lifestyle. But stopping the bastard before he could take someone else was their top priority at the moment.

Georgia winced and coughed as the tube slid from her mouth. The nurse held a small plastic cup with water to her lips. "Just take a sip to wet your tongue and throat."

Doing as she was told, Georgia coughed a few more times as she tried to get her voice working again. "What—what happened?" she rasped harshly, her gaze going from one person to the next.

As the nurse moved away, Parrish stepped into the space she'd occupied near the patient's head. "Georgia, I'm Special Agent in Charge Colt Parrish. Can you tell us what you remember?"

She frowned. "I-I don't know—" Her words were cut off as her eyes widened in fear. It was evident something had popped into her mind. Something that scared the fucking hell out of her.

Ian reached for her hand that the respiratory therapist had freed moments earlier, and squeezed, then tried to keep the urgency from his voice. "It's okay, little one. You're safe among your family and friends. I swear no one will hurt you. Tell us what happened. Do you know who took you?"

God, please let her know!

Her wide-eyed gaze met his gentle one. "D-Dennis." She swallowed hard. "Master Dennis."

Fuck!

Stunned, Ian was about to ask if she was sure, when his cell phone chirped in his hand, at the same time Devon and Parrish's did. Glancing at the screen, the blood drained from his face.

Fuck! Fuck! Fuck!

TRIDENT SECURITY
OMEGA TEAM

Twenty-Two

His hands on top of his head, Logan paced back and forth in the hallway outside the emergency room they were treating Dakota in. He was still shirtless, covered in her blood, and probably looked like a mad man. She was still alive, that's all he knew, having held her hand for the entire ambulance ride, letting go only when forced to as they wheeled her into the trauma room. Back at the condo, he'd barely had a moment to yank the covers off the bed and cover her naked body before her fellow officers burst into the room. Only once the paramedics arrived had he backed away to give them some room, then handed his weapon to the first TPD supervisor on scene. They'd need it for the investigation, but he knew what they'd find—it was his bullet that had hit Dakota.

"Cowboy!" Ian stepped in front of his path. How he'd gotten there so fast was beyond Logan's thinking right then. In fact, Devon, Mitch, Tiny, Agent Novik, and SAC Parrish were there already. "What happened?"

Tears filled his eyes. "I shot her! I fucking shot her, Ian!"

"Shit," the man spat in a low voice before grabbing

Logan's upper arm and dragging him into an empty treatment room, away from the growing crowd of police officers. "Someone get him a shirt and towel he can clean up with."

Logan shook his head vehemently. He didn't want to clean the blood off himself. It was hers, and he'd been the one to spill it. "I shot her, man."

"Okay, you said that—I'm sure it wasn't on purpose. Now tell us what happened."

He hadn't realized Parrish, Novik, and Captain Bowman, who'd just arrived, had followed them into the room and shut the door. They silently gave him a moment, letting him roam the small room as best he could. Taking a deep breath, he let it out slowly. "It was Dennis Hardwick, your bartender."

"We know," Devon answered, stopping Logan in his tracks. "Georgia Branneth woke up a little while ago and told us right before we got the notifications of an officer down."

Officer down. His officer. His partner. His woman.

Swallowing hard, he sat on the edge of the unoccupied gurney. A knock at the door had the female fed stepping to the side and opening it. Someone handed her a scrub shirt and towel, before the door shut once more. Logan took both when she offered them to him, but he tossed the towel aside and just pulled the shirt on. "We—Dakota and I—are sort of seeing each other." If anyone was surprised about that small bomb, they didn't show it. "We were hungry after the shift, so I ran out to a diner not far from her condo. Gina—Agent Harvey was driving into the lot as I was pulling out. I was gone about twenty—twenty-five minutes, tops. I stopped at a fender bender, otherwise I would've been back sooner. Shit!" He thrust his fingers through his already unruly hair in frustration. He'd just realized if he'd returned sooner, he probably wouldn't have been able to save the federal agent but may have saved Dakota a lot of pain and fear . . . and not shot her.

"Easy. Don't Monday morning quarterback," Parrish said. "What happened when you got back to the condo?"

He knew they just needed the short version here—a detailed investigation into the shooting would come later in the day. "There was blood on the ground in front of their condo that hadn't been there when I left. I ditched the food and used Dakota's key to unlock the door. Agent Harvey's body was partially blocking it in the foyer. She'd been shot in the head." His gaze met Parrish's. "I'm sorry."

The man gave him a stoic nod, clearly having been alerted to her line-of-duty death already.

"I drew my weapon . . . heard him attacking Dakota in her bedroom . . . kicked the door in. He turned toward me, weapon up, we both fired."

"So, he shot her, or you did?" the SAC asked, trying to make sure he understood everything correctly.

"I did! Damn it!" He stood and started pacing again. "I fired twice. One hit him between the eyes, the other was a through-and-through on his upper arm. It must have deflected and hit her when she lunged at him—probably to save me. She'd hit his arm, sending his shot wide. Next thing I knew, they were both on the ground."

"Who called the cops?"

"I did. The second I saw Gina's body." He stepped toward the door Novik was blocking—he was done for now, and only one thing mattered. "I've got to check on Dakota. I have to see her."

The female agent glanced at her superior who nodded. "Let him go. We'll get the full report in a little while." His gaze returned to Logan. "But it has to be done today, Reese."

Novik sidestepped and opened the door for him. In the short amount of time he'd been giving the abridged version of what had happened, the number of people in the emergency room had increased dramatically. There were uniformed and plain-clothes officers and agents all over the place. Logan's own teammates, McCabe, Foster, and Morrison, along with the Alpha Team, had arrived and were talking to Mitch and Tiny. Foster and McCabe hurried over when they saw him emerge from the room with the Sawyer brothers.

"You okay?" McCabe asked, eyeing the blood on Logan's hands and arms.

He shook his head. "No. Not until—"

"Where's my daughter?"

Logan pivoted to see a pale, older man, dressed in sweat-pants and a T-shirt, being escorted by two police captains in full uniform. Although he'd been younger in a newspaper photo, after he'd delivered a baby on the side of the road about ten years ago, Logan knew this was Gavin Swift, Dakota's father. Logan had been curious one day and Googled Dakota. He found her name mentioned several times for various police department calls and awards—like the time she'd interrupted a domestic violence incident, saving a woman's life and arresting her husband, all before backup arrived. Her father had also popped up a few times.

Stepping in the man's path, Logan growled. "If you say anything to her other than you're glad she's alive and you're proud of her, I'll kick your fucking ass."

The man's eyes went wide. "Who the hell are you?"

"Dakota's boyfriend."

He scoffed. "She doesn't have a boyfriend."

"You obviously haven't even asked if she has one lately. You've been too busy making her feel like she'll never measure up to your fucking expectations."

His ashen face turned red. "What? Get the hell out of my way!"

If Ian and Dakota's friend and former partner, Ric Hernandez, hadn't picked that moment to get between them, Logan wasn't sure he could've held back from decking the man. Ian pushed his employee back a few steps. "Easy, Cowboy. We're all worried. Now's not the time to get into this."

Glaring at her father, who was giving it back in spades, he finally moved out of the man's way. He'd made his point. There was no way he'd allow *anyone* to put his woman down ever again.

After the elder Swift joined a few older officers down the hall, another man stepped forward, looking like he'd also just rolled out of bed, and shook Ric's hand before addressing Logan. "I'm Dakota's brother, Gerry." He tilted his head in his father's direction. "Thanks for standing up for her to the old man. He's been tough on us all our lives, but, to be honest, I think it's his way of saying he loves us—he just doesn't know any other way to express it. Do we know how she is? All they were able to tell us was she was shot by the Kink Killer and she's alive."

Unable to admit to Dakota's brother that he'd been the one to shoot her, Logan replied, "She also got beat up a bit. Her blood pressure was low on the way over here, and she's still unconscious, but the medics said she was holding her own. Just waiting to hear what the doctors have to say."

The door to the trauma room swung open, and the ER physician stepped out. He was immediately surrounded by the brass, Dakota's family, Ric, and Logan, while the others held back, giving them room. "She's stable. We're sending her up to the OR in a few minutes. The bullet is lodged just under her left shoulder and doesn't appear to be life-threatening, but it put a small fracture in the collarbone. She's still unconscious but responding to painful stimuli. I think that's the result of the assault—she took a few blows to the head. Everything else appears to be superficial. We'll clean up the wounds from the whip while she's still in the OR. While she may have a few scars from them, I think most will heal completely."

"She's my daughter. Can I see her?" The man's voice broke, and it wasn't until that moment that Logan realized her father was terrified he'd almost lost her. But that still didn't mean he could make her feel as if she'd let him down.

The doctor nodded. "For a minute, and then you'll have to wait until she's out of surgery."

Gavin Swift moved toward the entrance to the trauma room, then paused, glancing over his shoulder at his son and Logan, his expression somber. "Gerry, grab whatever-his-name-is and come with me. She'll need to know you're both here for her too."

Dakota winced as she tried to get comfortable in the hospital bed. She couldn't wait to get the hell out of there. Three days of being constantly monitored and prodded was worse than getting whipped and shot in the first place—well, almost. At least the nurses had removed the damn urine catheter last night.

She still had the on-demand morphine drip hooked up to her IV, but she didn't want to push the button, even though the wounds from the whip burned white-hot. The drugs made her woozy, and she wanted to stay alert for when Logan woke up. He'd been glued to the recliner in her room since she'd come out of surgery, only disappearing to use the bathroom or take a quick shower down the hall. The nurses had taken pity on him and allowed him to use it after one of his teammates had brought him a change of clothes.

She studied him from her bed. His dirty-blond hair could use a trim, and whiskers covered his jaw and lip. She kind of liked the scruffiness—she'd always been a sucker for the bad-boy look as long as the persona didn't go with it.

Yesterday, he'd filled her in on everything that'd happened.

She was still shocked, as everyone else was, that the Kink Killer had been working at The Covenant under their noses all this time. He'd been hired as a bartender about a year after the club had opened but hadn't been in the lifestyle before that. His training to be a Dom began a few months after he'd started working there.

"They found a shit-load of evidence at his apartment," Logan *informed her while he held her hand, as if he couldn't bring himself to release her for a mere second. "Apparently, three women on the missing persons' list had been his first two kills and a recent one—Lily Stokes. According to a journal he kept, he'd dumped their bodies out in the gulf and regretted it after the first two. He found he got a greater thrill when the other bodies were discovered. As for Stokes, she died faster than he'd expected. He was pissed about it, so that's why she wasn't posed in public like the others."*

"Do they know what started it all? Usually there's a trigger."

He shook his head. "Not that they've found yet. Dr. Suki Ralston and Parrish are pouring over everything they can find on him, but they still don't know what set him off. Suki said they may never know. It's almost like the lifestyle—some people don't know why they need it, they just do. Same goes for sociopaths.

"Hardwick called his victims his masterpieces. Believed he was immortalizing them or something. You could have been one of them."

Logan swallowed hard as he stared at their joined hands, and she cut him off before the next words flew out of his mouth. "If you apologize for shooting me one more time, Cowboy, I'm going to hit you over the head with the bedpan." She'd been hearing "I'm sorry" from him for the past three days—ever since she'd awakened after the surgery. "I never would've gotten hit if I hadn't been scared out of my mind that he was going to shoot you. It happened. I'm still alive because of you, while he's not. I love you and don't blame you, so cut the bullshit and stop feeling guilty."

"Yes, ma'am," he replied with a grin. "And I love you too."

"Now that you can repeat as many times as you want," she said with a saucy smile.

He leaned over and gently kissed her lips. "I love you, I love you, I love you. But you still deserve some punishment for kneeing me in the balls."

"Jeez . . . you mean shooting me doesn't make us even?"

"Hey, you're awake."

Her gaze met Logan's drowsy one. "So are you. I don't know how you can sleep in that chair."

"I've slept in worse places." He stood and stretched the kinks out of his back and neck. "How do you feel?"

"Like I've been tenderized." She was glad to see her lame joke made him smile as he stepped over and took her hand. Dr. Trudy Dunbar had been in to see her that morning at Ian's request. It was a given Dakota was going to have some PTSD issues for at least a while over her experience, and the psychologist had agreed to take her on as a client after she was released from the hospital. Maybe she and Logan could have side-by-side desensitization therapy—or not.

She and Logan wouldn't be the only ones with lingering issues over the case. Brody Evans was apparently giving himself hell for not finding something in Hardwick's background that would point to him being a serial killer, but there hadn't been as far as anyone could tell. He'd had a normal childhood with doting parents and two sisters, all of whom were horrified at the man he'd become. Dakota felt sorry for them—since the killer's name had been released, his family had needed to go into hiding from the press and threats from people who thought they should have known their loved one was a sociopath.

A knock on her door had them both looking up to see her

father enter the room, and Dakota tensed as she had for the past few days, every time he came to see her. She was waiting for him to say, "See, I told you so," knowing it was coming sooner or later.

Her father nodded at Logan before turning his attention to her. "Hi. How're you feeling?"

"Okay. Just ready to get out of here."

A small grin spread across his face, and Dakota realized he looked much older since she'd gotten shot. "You've got the same energy your mother had. She could never sit still for long either." He held up a brown paper bag as he stepped closer to her bed. "Got you some muffins. I wasn't sure what flavor you liked, so I got a few different ones. I know how much hospital food sucks."

It wasn't surprising he didn't know her preferences, but she was caught off guard by the fact he'd brought her anything in the first place. "Um. Thanks."

He placed the bag on the bedside tray, then stuffed his hands in his pockets and rocked back and forth on his feet. Silence filled the room as the three of them stared at each other, but then her father's gaze fell to the floor. "Listen. I . . . um . . . I know I'm not good at expressing myself—never was. I still have no clue what your mother saw in me. I . . . uh . . . I just want you to know that I'm . . ." His water-filled eyes lifted and met her dry ones. ". . . I'm proud of you, Dakota. I'm sorry I never told you that before. You're a damn fine cop, and I couldn't be prouder if I tried."

Dakota's jaw dropped as Logan gave her hand a reassuring squeeze. "Dad . . ." Tears welled up in her eyes and a lump formed in her throat. "I thought you hated me being a cop . . . didn't think I should be one."

"Are you kidding? No, I guess you're not. I don't think that at all, sweetheart. I love that you followed in my footsteps . . . I wish Gerry had too. But I was also afraid for you. In this day and age, with the blue line all having targets on their back, I worry. When they knocked on my door the other night, and I opened it to see the two captains standing there, I almost had a heart attack. I thought you were dead, and I wouldn't let them say anything at first because I was so afraid I'd lost you." Tears rolled down his weathered cheeks. "I haven't been the greatest of fathers—I know that—but that doesn't mean I don't love you. I'm so sorry, Dakota. I'm so, so sorry I failed you as a father."

She began to sob as she reached out with her free hand, beckoning him closer. He took it, then cupped her cheek, wiping her tears away while ignoring his own. "I'm so sorry, baby. I don't know how, but I swear I'll find a way to make it up to you. I love you."

That just made her cry harder and her heart clench. "It—it's okay, Dad. I love you too."

With another squeeze of her hand, Logan stood and silently left the room, giving the father and daughter some time alone. When the door closed, the elder Swift gestured toward it. "By the way, he's a keeper. But don't tell him that."

A half sob/half laugh burst from her lips. "I won't."

Epilogue

With one arm in a sling, and her free hand clasped with Logan's, Dakota walked beside him in reverence of the vast size of Arlington National Cemetery. Photos and videos didn't do it justice. A light breeze on the sunny day brought with it the scent of freshly mowed grass and the mournful notes of "Taps." Logan raised their joined hands and pointed far up on a hill to their right, where a funeral was taking place and a lone bugler was standing off to the side, welcoming another deceased veteran to hallowed ground. As a police officer, it was the one song that never failed to bring a tear to her eye, having heard it at far too many law enforcement funerals over the years.

They'd arrived early so he could take her to watch the changing of the guards at the Tomb of the Unknown Soldier, which had been breathtaking, before heading back past the parking garage toward where his teammates were buried. Tomorrow, she was going to meet his parents and sister for the first time, and she was nervous as hell since the last time a lover had introduced her to his family had been many years ago. Tara Reese had recently gotten engaged to her longtime boyfriend, and on Saturday, there would be a large engagement party for the happy couple. But today, Logan had wanted to introduce her to someone special—but he'd refused to tell her who, insisting it was a surprise.

As they followed the road past rows of white stones, Logan stopped sooner than she expected. "Is this it?"

He shook his head. "No. Just wanted to stop and pay my respects to this kid for a moment."

Dakota read the stone. *Brian Chadwick. Cpl. US Army.* "My God, he was only twenty when he was killed in Afghanistan. A baby."

"Not old enough to drink, but old enough to lay down his life for his country." He tugged on her hand. "Come on, beautiful. Don't want to be late."

He'd been calling her "beautiful" since he'd noticed her frowning at her reflection in the hospital. Slash wounds and bruises had covered her head, torso, and arms, in addition to the bullet wound. The black and blue had faded to purple and yellow before disappearing altogether, while the marks from the whip were taking a little longer to heal. She'd hoped they'd be completely unnoticeable for when she met Logan's family, but a little makeup might be needed to hide the last of them.

A little further down, on the opposite side of the roadway, she noticed a couple in their thirties standing amongst the white markers, but it was the little boy, about seven years old, with them, who caught her attention. He was facing one of the graves, his legs shoulder width apart, his head bowed in respect, and his hands clasped at his lower back—a near-perfect parade rest posturing. She glanced up to see Logan smiling as he also realized what the boy was doing. When they approached, no one said a word as Logan let go of her hand and positioned himself to the boy's left, mimicking his stance.

"Attention!" Logan ordered, and he and the boy brought their left feet to meet their right, shoulders back, hands cupped loosely at their sides, chins up, and eyes front. "Present arms!"

Dakota watched in awe as they both lifted their right arms, bringing their flattened hands up, fingers together, angled toward their temples. A few seconds passed as they saluted the graves, before Logan gave the command, "Order arms!" and they both returned to the "attention" stance. "Parade rest!" Once they were in their original positions, Logan chuckled before giving the final commands. "At ease and fall out."

"Logan!" The little boy leaped into the man's arms and was rewarded with a big hug.

"How're you doing, Charlie? You grew a few inches!" Setting the boy on his feet again, Logan grinned at him. "And you've been practicing a lot."

"Daddy's been teaching me. Was it good?"

"It was perfect."

The boy's mother smiled as she and her spouse stepped closer. "Logan, this is my husband, Paul."

Logan shook the other man's hand. "Nice to finally meet you." He waved Dakota over. "This is my girlfriend, Dakota Swift—she's a Tampa police officer. Dakota, this is Paul and Dawn Roberts. Paul is also on-the-job in Alexandria, just outside of D.C. And this is my little buddy, Charlie." He tousled the kid's hair.

After shaking hands with the boy's parents, Dakota took hold of his as well. "It's nice to meet you, Charlie."

"It's nice to meet you too." He turned his attention back to the retired Marine. "Are you one now, Logan? Are you?"

To Dakota's amazement, Logan blushed and shrugged

before glancing her way. "I think you better ask Dakota that question, buddy. She's not only my girlfriend, but she was also my partner for a while."

Her eyes narrowed in confusion. "What are you both talking about?"

"Is Logan a hero yet?" his idol-worshiper asked.

There was obviously some story behind this, and she'd get it from Logan later, but for now she answered the boy's question, knowing her man was uncomfortable calling himself a hero. "Yes, he is, Charlie." She gestured toward her injured shoulder. "I was shot, and Logan saved my life." Of course, she left out the part about the bullet coming from Logan's weapon. "He also made sure a really bad guy would never hurt anyone again."

Charlie threw his arms around Logan's waist. "I knew it! I knew you were a hero like your friends and my dad!"

After patting him on the back a few times, Logan took a step backward. "You sure did, buddy."

"'Kota? Do you know Logan's friends?" He pointed to the graves.

The boy's smile and joy was infectious. "No, Charlie. I never had a chance to meet them, but I've heard a lot about them."

"They're heroes too." Starting at the grave they'd originally saluted, he patted each stone belonging to Logan's teammates. "This is Clutch and Gunny and Flipper and Kandy and Pluto and Preacher and Scooby and Hammer."

At Logan's stunned expression, Paul laughed. "He's had them all memorized since you emailed what each of their nicknames were. Every time we come to visit his grandfather's grave, he stops here and makes sure he has them all correct."

Swallowing what had to be an emotional lump in his throat, Logan held up his hand. "That's awesome. High-five, Charlie!"

"High-five! Oh, and Logan's nickname is Cowboy!" he announced, just in case they hadn't already known.

The glee and wonder Dakota saw in her lover's eyes warmed her from head to toe. With each day that passed, he was enjoying life more. He'd never forget his teammates and what they'd all gone through, and a part of him would always feel some guilt that he'd come home when they hadn't, but he was learning to live with it. He would continue to honor their memories by being the best man he could be and would do it with her at his side. She'd never expected to fall in love with him, but it definitely had happened. She almost couldn't remember the woman she'd been before she'd met him. They'd both grown . . . for the better. Her relationship with her father was on the mend, although she was certain it would be a rocky road ahead for both of them.

As for her job, she'd been shocked when Ian Sawyer had offered her a position with Trident. After discussing it with Logan, she'd turned the job down. Her career was with Tampa P.D., and after she was cleared for full duty again, she was permanently assigned to the Special Ops Division.

But Sawyer's offer hadn't been the only surprise in the past week. The second one had come when Logan had asked her to move in with him. While things were still new between them, she hadn't hesitated to say yes. He'd gone from being her partner, to being her friend, lover, and Dom, and she couldn't be happier. She wanted to be in his bed every night and wake up to his arms wrapped around her every morning. He'd told her that someday he was going to get down on one knee and ask her to marry him . . . when the time was right. For now, they were both content to let their love grow between them.

"'Kota! Stand next to Logan. It's time."

Charlie's command brought her back to the present to find everyone was lined up in front of Clutch and Gunny's graves. "Time for what?" she asked as she joined them to Logan's left.

"It's time to salute them again, and then we're going to lunch."

As the small group honored Logan's teammates, the somber notes of "Taps" floated through the air once more. Another hero was being laid to rest, but this time, instead of shedding a tear, Dakota's heart felt lighter. One day, Logan would be laid to rest here, of that she was certain, but until then, she was going to cherish him and every day they had together. And maybe, someday, they'd have a little girl or boy who would look at Logan with the same adoration as Charlie was looking at him now . . . after all, he was a true American hero.

If you're following the best reading order of the Trident Security series and its spinoffs, up next is
Salvaging His Soul: Trident Security Book 11.
Now available.

As many of my readers know, I don't normally include a play-list in my books (I usually have the TV on in the background). However, I'd be remiss if I didn't include the song that was the inspiration for the Arlington scenes. "Last Band of Brothers," by Keni Thomas, is a song that rarely fails to bring a tear to my eye. If you listen to the words, you'll understand why. When I was first writing Logan visiting his teammates' graves, I had no idea little Charlie was going to walk up to him. But like most of my characters, he emerged from the depths of my mind, surprising me, and became an amazing part of the story. This book is dedicated to all those who have served this great country I'm honored to live in. To those who never came home, and those who came home different than when they left, I thank you. Your sacrifices will never be forgotten.

***Denotes titles/series that are available on select digital sites only. Paperbacks and audiobooks are available on most book sites.

THE TRIDENT SECURITY SERIES

Leather & Lace

His Angel

Waiting For Him

Not Negotiable: A Novella

Topping The Alpha

Watching From the Shadows

Whiskey Tribute: A Novella

Tickle His Fancy

No Way in Hell: A Steel Corp/Trident Security Crossover (co-authored with J.B. Havens)

Absolving His Sins

Option Number Three: A Novella

Salvaging His Soul

Trident Security Field Manual

Torn In Half: A Novella

***HEELS, RHYMES, & NURSERY CRIMES SERIES**

(WITH 13 OTHER AUTHORS)

Jack Be Nimble: A Trident Security-Related Short Story

***THE DEIMOS SERIES**

Handling Haven: Special Forces: Operation Alpha

Cheating the Devil: Special Forces: Operation Alpha

THE TRIDENT SECURITY OMEGA TEAM SERIES

Mountain of Evil

A Dead Man's Pulse

Forty Days & One Knight

THE DOMS OF THE COVENANT SERIES

Double Down & Dirty

Entertaining Distraction

Knot a Chance

THE BLACKHAWK SECURITY SERIES

Tuff Enough

Blood Bound

MASTER KEY SERIES

Master Key Resort

Master Cordell

HAZARD FALLS SERIES

Don't Fight It

Don't Shoot the Messenger

THE MALONE BROTHERS SERIES

Take the Money and Run

The Devil's Spare Change

LARGO RIDGE SERIES

Cold Feet

ANTELOPE ROCK SERIES

(CO-AUTHORED WITH J.B. HAVENS)

Wannabe in Wyoming

Wistful in Wyoming

AWARD-WINNING STANDALONE BOOKS

The Road to Solace

Scattered Moments in Time: A Collection of Short Stories & More

*****THE BID ON LOVE SERIES**

(WITH 7 OTHER AUTHORS!)

Going, Going, Gone: Book 2

*****THE COLLECTIVE: SEASON TWO**

(WITH 7 OTHER AUTHORS!)

Angst: Book 7

SPECIAL COLLECTIONS

Trident Security Series: Volume I

Trident Security Series: Volume II

Trident Security Series: Volume III

Trident Security Series: Volume IV

Trident Security Series: Volume V

USA Today Bestselling Author and Award-Winning Author Samantha Cole is a retired policewoman and former paramedic. Using her life experiences and training, she strives to find the perfect mix of suspense and romance for her readers to enjoy.

Awards:

Wannabe in Wyoming (co-authored by J.B. Havens) won the bronze medal in the 2021 Readers' Favorite Awards in the General Romance category.

Scattered Moments in Time, won the gold medal in the 2020 Readers' Favorite Awards in the Fiction Anthology category.

The Road to Solace (formerly *The Friar*), won the silver medal in the 2017 Readers' Favorite Awards in the Contemporary Romance category.

Samantha has over thirty-five books published throughout several different series as well as a few standalone novels. A full list can be found on her website.

Sexy Six-Pack's Sirens Group on Facebook
Website: www.samanthacoleauthor.com
Newsletter: www.geni.us/SCNews

facebook.com/SamanthaColeAuthor

instagram.com/samanthacoleauthor

bookbub.com/profile/samantha-a-cole

goodreads.com/SamanthaCole

tiktok.com/@samanthacoleauthor